Known to Evil

Also by Walter Mosley

OTHER FICTION

The Tempest Tales

Diablerie

Killing Johnny Fry

The Man in My Basement

Fear of the Dark

Fortunate Son

The Wave

Fear Itself

Futureland

LEONID McGILL MYSTERIES

The Long Fall

Fearless Jones

Walkin' the Dog

Blue Light

EASY RAWLINS MYSTERIES

Blonde Faith

Cinnamon Kiss

Little Scarlet

Six Easy Pieces

Bad Boy Brawly Brown

A Little Yellow Dog

Black Betty

Gone Fishin'

White Butterfly

A Red Death

Devil in a Blue Dress

Always Outnumbered,
    Always Outgunned

RL's Dream

47

The Right Mistake

NONFICTION

This Year You Write Your Novel

What Next: A Memoir Toward
    World Peace

Life Out of Context

Workin' on the Chain Gang

Known to Evil

WALTER MOSLEY

RIVERHEAD BOOKS

a member of Penguin Group (USA) Inc.

New York   2010

RIVERHEAD BOOKS
Published by the Penguin Group
Penguin Group (USA) Inc., 375 Hudson Street, New York, New
York 10014, USA · Penguin Group (Canada), 90 Eglinton
Avenue East, Suite 700, Toronto, Ontario M4P 2Y3, Canada
(a division of Pearson Penguin Canada Inc.) · Penguin Books
Ltd, 80 Strand, London WC2R 0RL, England · Penguin
Ireland, 25 St Stephen's Green, Dublin 2, Ireland (a division of
Penguin Books Ltd) · Penguin Group (Australia), 250 Camber-
well Road, Camberwell, Victoria 3124, Australia (a division of
Pearson Australia Group Pty Ltd) · Penguin Books India Pvt Ltd,
11 Community Centre, Panchsheel Park, New Delhi–110 017,
India · Penguin Group (NZ), 67 Apollo Drive, Rosedale, North
Shore 0632, New Zealand (a division of Pearson New Zealand
Ltd) · Penguin Books (South Africa) (Pty) Ltd, 24 Sturdee
Avenue, Rosebank, Johannesburg 2196, South Africa

Penguin Books Ltd, Registered Offices: 80 Strand, London
WC2R 0RL, England

Library of Congress Cataloging-in-Publication Data

Mosley, Walter.
    Known to evil / Walter Mosley.
        p.   cm.
    ISBN 978-1-59448-752-1
    1. Private investigators—New York (State)—New York—
Fiction.   2. Political corruption—New York (State)—
New York—Fiction.   3. New York (N.Y.)—Fiction.
4. Domestic fiction.   I. Title.
PS3563.O88456K58   2010   2009042643
813'.54—dc22

Printed in the United States of America
1   3   5   7   9   10   8   6   4   2

BOOK DESIGN BY NICOLE LAROCHE

In memory of Ella Mosley

I miss you, Mom.

Known to Evil

D on't you like the food?" Katrina, my wife of twenty-three years, asked.

"It's delicious," I said. "Whatever you make is always great."

In the corner there sat a walnut cabinet that used to contain our first stereo record player. Now it held Katrina's cherished Blue Danube china collection, which she inherited from her favorite aunt, Bergit. On top of the chest was an old quart pickle jar—the makeshift vase for an arrangement of tiny wildflowers of every color from scarlet to cornflower blue to white.

"But you're frowning," my beautiful Scandinavian wife said. "What were you thinking about?"

I looked up from the filet mignon and Gorgonzola blue cheese salad to gaze at the flowers. My thoughts were not the kind of dinner conversation one had with one's wife and family.

I have a boyfriend now, Aura Ullman had told me that morning. *I wanted to tell you. I didn't want to feel like I'm hiding anything from you.*

"Where'd you get those flowers, Mom?" Shelly asked.

His name is George, Aura told me, the sad empathy in the words making its way to her face.

I had no reason to be jealous. Aura and I had been lovers over the eight months Katrina abandoned me for the investment banker Andre Zool. I loved Aura but gave her up because when

Katrina came back, after Andre was indicted for fraud, I felt that she, Katrina, was my sentence for the wrong I had done in a long life of crime.

"I saw them at the deli and thought they might brighten up our dinner," Katrina told her daughter.

Shelly had been trying to forgive her mother for leaving me. She was a sophomore at CCNY and another man's daughter, though she didn't know it. Two of my children were fathered out of wedlock; only the eldest, sour and taciturn Dimitri, who always sat as far away from me as possible, was of my blood.

Do you love him? I hadn't meant to ask Aura that. I didn't want to know the answer or to show vulnerability.

He's very good company . . . and I get lonely.

"Well?" Katrina asked.

Something about those flowers and the echo of Aura's voice in my mind made me want to curse, or maybe to slam my fist down on the plate.

"Hey, everybody," Twill said. He was standing in the doorway to the dining room; dark and slender, handsome and flawless except for a small crescent scar on his chin.

"You're late," Katrina scolded my favorite.

"You know it, Moms," the seventeen-year-old man replied. "I'm lucky to get home at all with everything I got to do. My PO got me workin' this after-school job at the supermarket. Says it'll keep me outta trouble."

"He's not a parole officer. He's a juvenile offender social worker," I said.

Just seeing Twill brought levity into the room.

"It's not a he," Twill said as he slid into the chair next to me. "Ms. Melinda Tarris says that she wants me workin' three afternoons a week."

"And she's right, too," I added. "You need something to occupy your mind and keep you out of trouble."

"It's not people like me that get in trouble, Pops," Twill sang. "I talk so much and know so many people that I can't get away with nuthin' somebody don't see it. It's the quiet ones that get in the most trouble. Ain't that right, Bulldog?"

"Can't you be quiet sometimes?" dour Dimitri said.

Twill's pet name for his older brother was an apt one. Like me Dimitri was short and big-boned, powerful even though he rarely exercised. His skin was not quite as dark brown as mine but you could see me in every part of him. I wondered why he was so angry at his brother's chiding. Even though Dimitri never liked me much he loved his siblings. And he had a special bond with Twill, who was so outgoing all he had to do was sit down in a room for five minutes and a party was likely to break out.

"Leonid."

"Yes, Katrina?"

"Are you all right?"

Even though we'd drifted apart like the continents had—long ago—Katrina could still read my moods. We had a kind of subterranean connection that allowed my wife to see, at least partly, into my state of mind. It wasn't just Aura's decision to move on that bothered me. It was my life at that table, Dimitri's uncharacteristic anger at his brother, and even those delicate flowers sitting where I had never seen a bouquet before.

There was a feeling at the back of my mind, something that was burgeoning into consciousness like a vibrating moth pressing out from its cocoon.

The phone rang and Katrina started. When I looked into her gray-blue eyes some kind of wordless knowledge seemed to pass between us.

"I'll get it," Shelly shouted. She hurried from the room into the hall, where the cordless unit sat on its ledge.

Katrina smiled at me. Even this made me wonder. She'd been back home for nearly a year. In that time her smile had been tentative, contrite. She wanted me to know that she was there for the long run, that she was sorry for her transgressions and wanted to make our life together work. But that evening her smile was confident. Even the way she sat was regal and self-assured.

"Dad, it's for you."

2

Standing up from my chair and moving into the hallway, I felt as if I were displaced, another man, or maybe the same man in a similar but vastly different world: the working-poor lottery winner who suddenly one day realizes that riches have turned his blood to vinegar.

"Hello?" I said into the receiver.

I was expecting an acquaintance or maybe a credit-card company asking about a suspect charge. No one who I did business with had my home number. The kind of business I was in couldn't be addressed by an innocent.

"Leonid," a man's voice said, "this is Sam Strange."

"Why are you calling me at my home?" I asked, because though Strange was the legman for Alphonse Rinaldo, one of the secret pillars of New York's political and economic systems, I couldn't allow even him to infringe on my domestic life, such as it was.

"The Big Man called and said it was an emergency," Strange said.

Sam worked for the seemingly self-appointed Special Assistant to the City of New York. I say seemingly, because even though Alphonse Rinaldo was definitely attached to City Hall, no one knew his job description or the extent of his power.

I had done a few questionable jobs for the man before I decided to go straight. And while I was no longer engaging in criminal activities I couldn't afford to turn him down without a hearing.

"What is it you want?" I asked.

"There's a young woman named Tara Lear that he wants you to make contact with."

Sam rarely, if ever, spoke Rinaldo's name. He had an internal censor like those of old-time printers who replaced "God" with "G-d" in books.

"Why?"

"He just wants you to speak to her and to make sure everything's all right. He told me to tell you that he would consider this a great favor."

Being able to do a favor for Special Assistant Rinaldo was like winning six lotteries rolled into one. My blood might turn into high-octane rocket fuel if I wasn't careful.

Not for the first time I wondered if I would ever get out from under my iniquitous past.

"Leonid," Sam Strange said.

"When am I supposed to find this young woman?"

"Now . . . tonight. And you don't have to find her, I can tell you exactly where she is."

"If you know where she is why don't you just tell him and he can go talk to her himself?"

"This is the way he wants it."

"Why don't you go?" I asked.

"He wants you, Leonid."

I heard Twill say something in the dining room but couldn't make out the words. His mother and Shelly laughed.

"Leonid," Sam Strange said again.

"Right now?"

"Immediately."

"You know I'm trying to be aboveboard nowadays, Sam."

"He's just asking you to go and speak to this Lear woman. To make sure that she's all right. There's nothing illegal about that."

"And I'm supposed to tell her that Mr. Rinaldo is concerned about her but can't come himself?"

"Do not mention his name or refer to him in any way. The meeting should be casual. She shouldn't have any idea that you're a detective or that you're working for someone looking after her welfare."

"Why not?"

"You know the drill," Strange said, trying to enforce his personal sense of hierarchy on me. "Orders come down and we do as we're told."

"No," I said. "That's you. You do what you're told. Me—I got ground rules."

"And what are they?"

"First," I said, "I will not put this Tara's physical or mental well-being into jeopardy. Second, I will only report on her state of mind and security. I will not convey information that might make her vulnerable to you or your boss. And, finally, I will not be a party to making her do anything against her will or whim."

"That's not how it works and you know it," Sam said.

"Then go on down to the next name on the list and don't ever call this number again."

"There is no other name."

"If you want me you got to play by my rules."

"I'll have to report this conversation."

"Of course you do."

"He won't like it."

"I'll make a note of that."

He gave me an address on West Sixtieth and an apartment number.

"I'll be staying at the Oxford Arms Club on Eighty-fourth until this situation is resolved," he said. "You can call me there anytime, day or night."

I hung up. There was no reason to continue the conversation, or to wish him well, for that matter. I never liked the green-eyed agent of the city's Special Assistant.

Alphonse had two conduits to the outside world. Sam was the errand boy. Christian Latour, who sat in the chamber outside Alphonse's office, was the Big Man's gatekeeper and crystal ball combined. I liked Christian, even though he had no use for me.

I stood there in the hall, trying to connect the past fifteen minutes. Dimitri's uncharacteristic barking at his brother and their mother's newfound confidence, the crude vase and its lovely flowers, and, of course, the memory of Aura in her heartfelt concern and almost callous betrayal.

I WENT TO THE closet in our bedroom, looking to find one of my three identical dark-blue suits. The first thing I noticed was that the clothes had been rearranged. I didn't know exactly what had been where before, but things were neater and imposed-upon with some kind of strict order. My suits were nowhere in sight.

"What are you doing?" Katrina asked from the doorway.

"Looking for my blue suit."

"I sent two of your blue suits to the cleaners. You haven't had them cleaned in a month."

"What am I supposed to wear?" I said, turning to face her.

Sometimes when Katrina smiled I remembered falling in love with her. It lasted long enough to get married and make Dimitri. After that things went sour. We never had sex and rarely even kissed anymore.

"You have the ochre one," she said.

"Where's the one I wore home tonight?"

"In the hamper. The lapels were all spotted. Wear the ochre one."

"I hate that suit."

"Then why did you buy it?"

"You bought it for me."

"You tried it on. You paid the bill."

I yanked the suit out of the closet.

"Where are you going?" she asked.

"It's a job. I have to go interview somebody for a client."

"I thought you didn't take business calls on our home phone."

"Yeah," I said, taking off my sweatpants.

"Leonid."

"What, Katrina?"

"We have to talk."

I continued undressing.

"The last time you said that I didn't see you for eight months," I said.

"We have to talk about us."

"Can it wait till later or will you be gone when I get home?"

"It's nothing like that," she said. "I've noticed how distant you've been and I want to, to connect with you."

"Yeah. Sure. Let me go take care of this thing and either we'll talk when I get back, or tomorrow at the latest. Okay?"

She smiled and kissed my cheek tenderly. She had to lean over a bit because I'm two inches shorter than she.

I PUT ON THE dark-yellow suit and a white dress shirt. Since I was going out for such an important client I even cinched a burgundy tie around my neck. The man in the mirror looked to me like a bald, black-headed, fat grub that had spent the afternoon drying in the sun.

I was shorter than most men, and if you didn't see me naked you might have thought I was portly. But my size was from bone structure and muscles developed over nearly four decades working out at Gordo's Boxing Gym.

"HEY, DAD," TWILL CALLED as I was going out the front door of our eleventh-floor prewar apartment.

"Yeah, son?" I said on a sigh.

"Mardi Bitterman's back in town. Her and her sister."

Mardi was a year older than Twill. She and her sister had been molested by their father and I had to intervene when Twill got it in his head to murder the man.

"I thought they had moved to their mother's family in Ireland."

"Turns out that they weren't related," Twill said. "Her father bought Mardi from some pervert. Her sister, too. I don't know the whole story but they had to come home."

"Okay. So what do you want from me?" I was impatient, even with Twill. Maybe the fact that his relationship to me was the same as Mardi to her father cut at me a little.

"Mardi's taking care of her sister and she needs a job. She's eighteen and on her own, you know."

"So?"

"You're always sayin' how much you want a receptionist. I figured this would be a good time for you to have one. You know, Mardi's real organized like. She'd tear that shit up."

Twill was a born criminal but he had a good heart.

"I guess we could try it out," I said.

"Cool. I told her to be at your office in the morning."

"Without asking?"

"Sure, Pops. I knew you'd say yes."

3

I grabbed a cab at Ninety-first and Broadway and told him to take me to an address on Sixtieth near Central Park West. The driver's last name was Singh. I couldn't see his face through the scratched-up plastic barrier.

It didn't make much sense, me taking Katrina back. After twenty years of unfaithfulness on both sides of the bed you would have thought I'd've had enough. I should have turned her away after her banker had run down to Argentina. But she'd asked me to forgive her. How could I seek redemption for all my sins if I couldn't forgive her comparatively minor indiscretions?

And now Katrina wanted to talk—about us. Maybe it was over—now that I had waited too long.

"You sure this is where you want to go?" Mr. Singh asked me.

I looked up to see at least half a dozen police cars, their red lights flashing up and down the block—like Mardi Gras in hell.

If it was any other client I would have turned around.

One police unit showing up at a crime scene was a domestic disturbance; three was a robbery gone bad; but six or more cop cars on the scene meant multiple murder, with the perpetrators still at large.

A goodly number of people were standing along the opposite side of the street looking up and pointing, asking what had happened and giving their opinions on what must have gone down.

"Two of 'em," one older man was saying. He wore slippers, pajamas, and a battered gray parka to keep out the mid-November chill. "Marla Traceman says that it was a black man and a white woman."

I walked up to the front door of the building where there stood a tall policeman with a stomach like a sagging sack of grain, barring anyone from coming into the twelve-story brick structure.

"Move along," the hazel-eyed white man told me. He was maybe fifty, a few years my junior.

"What happened here?" I asked.

His reply was to raise his graying eyebrows a quarter inch. Men who lived their lives by intimidating others often developed such subtleties with age.

"Stackman or Bonilla?" I asked. "Or maybe it's Burnham this far north."

The question was designed to short-circuit a needless confrontation. I knew most of the homicide detectives in Manhattan.

"Who're you?" the six-foot cop asked.

I pay a lot of attention to how tall people are. That's because even though I'm a natural light heavyweight I don't quite make five-six.

"Leonid McGill."

"Oh." The cop's face was doughy and so his sneer seemed to catch in that position like a Claymation character.

"Who's the detective?"

"Lieutenant Bonilla."

"Lieutenant? Guess she got a promotion."

"This is a crime scene."

"Apartment 6H?"

The sneer wasn't going anywhere soon. He brought a phone to his jaw, pressed a button, and muttered a few words.

"Excuse me," a man said from behind me. "I have to get by."

I took half a step to the right and turned. There stood another fifty-year-old white man—maybe five-nine. This one was wearing a camel coat, pink shirt, and too-tight dark-brown leather pants. At his side stood a thin blond child. Possibly twenty, she could have been seventeen. All she had on was a red dress made from paper. The hem barely covered her groin and only her youth held up the neckline.

It was no more than forty-five that night.

The man made the mistake of trying to push past the officer. He was met with a stiff, one-handed shove that nearly knocked him down.

"Hey!" Camel's hair said. "I live here."

"This is a crime scene," the cop replied. His tone promised all kinds of pain. "Go and take your daughter to a coffee shop, or a hotel."

"Who the hell do you think you are?" the outraged john shouted.

The girl grabbed his arm and whispered something in his ear.

"But I live here."

She murmured something else.

"No. No, I want to be with you."

She touched his cheek.

"Mr. McGill?"

A black woman in her late twenties, wearing a neat black uniform, had come out from behind her sadistic senior. She had some kind of rank but wasn't yet a sergeant. We stood eye-to-eye.

"Yes?"

"Lieutenant Bonilla asked me to come and get you."

There was something in the woman's gaze that was . . . curious.

"Thank you."

She turned. I followed.

"Where the hell is he going?" the angry resident hollered. "How can he go in and you keep us out here in the street?"

"Listen, mister," the big-bellied cop said. "You'll have to—"

The glass door shut behind us and I couldn't hear any more of what transpired. But even though I was cut off from the dialogue I knew its beginning—and its end.

The man had met the woman in some quasi-legal club, probably in an outer borough. They'd done a few lines of coke and come to an agreement on a price; he probably had to pay part or all of that sum before she got into the car service that brought them to the crime-scene apartment building. But she'd leave soon because the hard-on in the john's pants was also pressing on his good judgment. Pretty soon the cop on the door would lose his temper and use the phone to call for backup. The girl would fade into the night and the man would go to jail for interfering with a police investigation.

In the following weeks he'd go back to the club where he'd met her, wanting either the money he'd laid out already or the sex that money had paid for. If his luck changed he wouldn't find her.

THE YOUNG OFFICER BROUGHT me to an elevator and pushed a button for the sixth floor. My heart sank a little then. Irrationally I'd hoped that the crime had nothing to do with my mission.

I wondered if Sam Strange, or even Rinaldo himself, was setting me up for something far more sinister than a talk.

"So you're the infamous Leonid Trotter McGill," the woman cop said. She had a heart-shaped face and a smile that her father loved.

"You've heard about me?"

"They say you've got your finger in every dishonest business in the city."

"And still," I said, "I struggle to make the rent each month. How do I do it?"

Her smile broadened to admit men other than blood relatives.

"They also say that you beat a man twice your size to death just a few months ago."

I saw no reason to call into question a growing mythology.

We were passing the fifth floor.

"How old are you?" she asked.

"Old enough to know better," I said, and the door to the small chamber slid open onto a dingy, claustrophobically narrow hallway.

THERE WERE AT LEAST a dozen uniformed cops and plainclothes detectives standing in and outside of apartment 6H. The woman who brought us there led me past two unwilling uniforms at the door, down a small pink entrance hall, and into a modest living room replete with fifties furniture in baby blue, chrome, and faded red.

"Leonid McGill," newly promoted homicide detective Bethann Bonilla said. It was neither a greeting nor an accusation; just a statement like an infant might make, mouthing a phrase and learning about it at the same time.

Before responding I took in the murder scene.

Equidistant between the baby-blue couch, kitchenette, and window lay the corpse of a blond woman in a brown robe that had opened, probably at the time of her death. The window looked out on the buildings across the street. The dead woman was certainly young at the time of her demise, she might have been pretty. It was hard to tell because half of her face had been shot off.

She lay on her back with one thigh crossed over her pubis as if in a last attempt at modesty. Her breasts sagged sadly. It's always upsetting to see the details of youth on a dead body.

In a corner, behind the blue couch, was what is now commonly called an African-American male in a coal-gray suit. This man was lying on his side. He had been a tall and lanky brown man with a face that was serious but not intimidating. There was the handle of a butcher's knife protruding from the left side of his upper torso. The haft stood out at an odd angle, as if someone had wedged the blade into the man's chest. There wasn't much blood under the wound.

"Congratulations," I said to the detective, who stood only half a head taller than I.

"What?"

"You're a lieutenant now, I hear."

"I work hard," she said as if I were insinuating her position was somehow unearned.

"Yes," I said. "I've experienced that work firsthand."

Four months or so before, Bonilla had been working on a series of murders. For a while she liked me for the crimes. It's a hard business, but even in the worst places you meet people you like.

"Why are you here?" she asked.

Bonilla wore clothes that made her look, for lack of a better word, bulky. A discerning eye could tell that she had a slender figure but in her line of work that didn't get a girl very far. The pants suit she wore was dark green and the shoulder pads made her look like a high school football wannabe.

"I got a call," I said.

"From who?"

"She said her name was Laura Brown." Lying is the private detective's stock-in-trade. I jumped into the role with both feet. "She told me that she needed to find a missing person rather quickly. I told her my day rate and she said she'd double it if I came here tonight."

There were plainclothes detectives standing on either side of me. I pretended that they were straphangers and I was taking the A train at rush hour.

"What was the name of the person she wanted to find?"

"She didn't say and I didn't ask. I figured we'd get down to details when I arrived."

The detective's Spanish eyes bored into me. I noticed that she'd trimmed her black mane but decided that this was not the moment to talk about hairstyles.

"And what are you doing here?" she asked again.

"I just told you."

"Don't get me wrong, Mr. McGill, but you don't seem like the kind of guy who would come into a room where your profit had been cut short."

"I didn't know when I was downstairs what had happened. My client might have been alive. For all I knew the crime was unrelated to my business. I still don't know. What's the victim's name?"

The lieutenant smiled.

I hunched my shoulders.

"What else did this Laura Brown tell you?"

"Not a thing. She said that someone had recommended me but she didn't give a name. That's not unusual. People don't like me thinking about them, I've found. I can't understand why."

"Did she mention anyone?"

"No."

Bonilla squinted and, in doing so, came to a decision.

"We figure the guy for being the shooter," she said, "but there's no gun in evidence. *She* certainly didn't stab him."

"Anyone hear shots?"

Bonilla shook her head slightly.

"Wow," I said. I meant it. A hit man with a silencer getting killed with a kitchen utensil seconds after he makes his bones.

At that moment I really hated Alphonse Rinaldo.

4

When I was maybe five, my father, an autodidact Communist, took me down to Chinatown. He was always trying to teach me lessons about life. That day he bought me a woven finger-trap. I pressed my fingers in from either side of the bamboo tube at his request.

"Now pull them out," he said.

I remember smiling and yanking my hands apart, only to have the fingers tugged at by the stubborn toy. Try as I might the cylinder held like glue to my fingers. My father waited till I was near tears before telling me the secret: you had to press both fingers *toward* each other, increasing the size of the tube, before you were able to get free of it.

The humiliating experience left me in a sour mood.

"What have you learned from this?" my father asked after buying me a ten-cent packet of toffee peanuts from a street vendor in Little Italy.

"Nuthin'," I said.

Tolstoy McGill was tall and very dark-skinned. I inherited his coloring. He laughed and said, "That's too bad because I just taught you one of the most important lessons that any man from Joe Street Sweeper to President Kennedy needs to learn."

Like all black children, I loved President Kennedy, and so my father had my interest in spite of the mortification I felt.

"What?" I asked.

"It's always easier getting into trouble than it is getting out."

I WAS REMINDED OF my father's lesson while wondering how to get away from Detective Bonilla and her investigation.

"Maybe you should come down to the precinct with me," she suggested.

"No," I said, feeling the bamboo walls closing in.

"Material witness," she said. Those were her magic words.

"So is this Laura Brown?"

"Doesn't matter," Bethann said. "She told you her name was Laura Brown."

"I've given you everything I have."

Bonilla was one of the new breed of cops who didn't see the world in black and white, so to speak. My actions in the last case she worked, the one that, no doubt, earned her the promotion, were inexplicable. On the one hand, I had beaten a much larger, much stronger man to death; on the other hand, I had saved the life of a young woman by putting myself into jeopardy.

"Come in here," she said, leading me into the bedroom.

The other cops stared at us but little Bethann was made from stern stuff. She wasn't intimidated by the men she worked with.

THE BEDROOM WAS SLOPPY the way some young women are. There were clothes everywhere. Pastel-colored thong panties and stockings and shoes were scattered across the floor. The bed itself was unmade. Open makeup containers were spread across the vanity.

"There's a standing order to bring you in if there's ever a chance to do so," Bethann said to me when we were out of earshot of the rest of New York's finest.

"If you say so."

"Why is that?"

"Haven't they told you?"

"I'm asking you."

I looked at the thirty-something officer, wondering about the possibilities for, and ramifications of, truth.

"THE TRUTH," MY IDEOLOGUE father once told me, "changes according to what point of view is beholding it."

"What does that mean?" I must have been about twelve because not too long after that Tolstoy was gone forever. My mother soon followed him the only way she could—in a casket.

"A dictator sees the truth as a matter of will," he said. "Anything he says or dreams is the absolute truth and soon the people are forced to go along with him. For the so-called democrat, the truth is the will of the people. Whatever the majority says is the law and that law becomes truth for the people.

"But for men like us," my father said, "the only truth is the truth of the tree."

"What tree?" I asked.

"All trees," Tolstoy McGill proclaimed. "Because the truth of the tree is its roots in the ground, and the wind blowing, and the rain falling. The sun is a tree's truth, and even if he's cut down his seed will scatter and those roots will once again take hold."

"DO YOU BELIEVE THAT a man can change, Lieutenant?" I asked Bethann Bonilla.

"What does that have to do with my question?"

"That order to arrest me refers to another man," I said. "The man I used to be. I can't deny my history and I won't admit to a thing. All I can tell you is that you will never catch me doing the things your department thinks I'm doing. I'm not that man anymore."

The detective felt my confession more than she understood it. She wondered about me—it wouldn't be the last time.

"Do you know anything about what happened here tonight?" she asked.

"Is the dead girl Laura Brown?"

After a moment's hesitation the policewoman said, "No. I don't think so."

"And what is her name?"

"You'll find out in the morning news anyway, I guess. It's Wanda Soa. At least we're pretty sure. A few neighbors gave us descriptions. One outstanding detail is a tiger tattoo on her left ankle."

"I don't know a thing about it, then. She might have been using the name Brown. She might have called me. The caller ID said unknown. You're welcome to check my home phone records. But I've already told you all that I know."

Often—in books and movies and TV shows—private detectives mouth off to the police. They claim civil rights or just run on bravado. But in the real world you have to lie so seamlessly that even you are unsure of the truth.

My father didn't teach me that. He was an idealist who probably died fighting the good fight. I'm just a survivor from the train wreck of the modern world.

"You can go home, Leonid," Bonilla said. "But you haven't heard the last of this."

"Don't I know it. I'm still trying to figure out the finger-trap my father bought me when I was five."

5

On the street again, I was loath to go home. I didn't know what Katrina wanted to talk about but another loss right then would have thrown me off balance in the middle of a tightrope act with no net.

So I went down to a bar called the Naked Ear on East Houston. It was once a literary bar where striving young writers came to read their poetry and prose to each other. Then for a long time it was a haven where NOLITA (that's the real estate acronym for North of Little Italy) stock traders met to flirt and brag. Since the current reversals on Wall Street the bar was floundering, looking for a new identity.

I was told by the owner that they didn't change the name because the word "naked" seemed to bring in curious newcomers every day.

I didn't care what they called themselves or who sat at the mahogany bar. I only went to the Ear for two reasons. One was to think, and drink, when I was in trouble; the other was to pay my respects to Gert Longman.

I HOOKED UP WITH Gert back when I was more crooked than not. She identified criminal losers who had not yet been caught at their scams and perversions. I framed these lowlifes for crimes that other crooks needed to get out from under—all for a fee, of course.

As is so often the case with deep passion, I didn't understand the kind of woman Gert was. Because she did work for me, I figured that she was bent, too.

She had a great smile and a fine derrière.

When we became lovers I neglected to tell her that I was married, not because I was ashamed but because I didn't think it mattered. How was I to know that she had dreams of two-point-five children and a picket fence?

We broke up but still worked together from time to time. I offered to leave Katrina, but Gert told me that it was over, completely.

And then one day the daughter of a man I'd caused to go to prison had someone kill Gert, just to see me cry.

I toasted her loss with three cognacs at least once a month. I never liked going to cemeteries.

LUCY, THE SKINNY BRUNETTE bartender, smiled when I mounted a stool in front of her.

"Hello, Mr. McGill."

"You remember my name."

"That's a bartender's job, isn't it?" Lucy had very nice teeth.

"It used to be that Republicans believed in less government, and people all over the world saw America as the land of opportunity. Things change."

"I guess I'm a throwback, then. Three Hennesseys straight up?"

"You're a relic."

While the thirtyish bartender went to fetch the brandy I turned my mind toward yet another reason I came to that bar: whenever I find myself in serious trouble, I take a time-out and try to fill in the shady areas with reason.

It wasn't the murder that bothered me. I didn't know the dead woman and I hadn't had anything to do with her, or her apparent killer's, death. Alphonse Rinaldo most certainly didn't know that she was dead. He might have been worried about her but he didn't kill her. And even if I gave the police the name and office address of my client they would have never even seen his face. They would get a call from the chief of police to lay off that avenue of inquiry and that would be that.

I didn't know, for a fact, who the dead woman was, but that didn't bother me either. I had done my job.

No, I hadn't done anything wrong as far as the deaths or my responsibility to the NYPD was concerned. Legally I was covered.

"Here you go, Mr. McGill," Lucy said.

She placed three amber-filled and extremely fragile cylinders of glass before me. I picked up one and tilted it at the sky beyond the ceiling.

A siren passed by outside.

"Was it a good friend?"

"You *are* old school," I said to Lucy.

"I don't know," she said. "I think anybody could see that you're going through a ritual with these drinks. You don't come here to meet people or to pick up girls. I pay attention, because you're the sweetest drunk I've ever had in here."

"You're gonna make me blush, child."

"I'm not that young."

"Maybe not," I said. "But I sure am that old."

Lucy gave me a very nice, almost speculative, smile and strolled off to a couple sitting a few stools away.

LEGALLY I WAS COVERED but the job wasn't over and it had turned from seeing that the subject, Tara Lear, was all right to maybe dodging guns with silencers on them and spending long nights under the bright lights of police curiosity.

This was a job that I couldn't walk away from. I could turn down loan sharks and godfather wannabes if they asked for my services. They could get angry and come after me if they wanted to try. I might have to do some fancy footwork but I could hold my own even against real-life mafiosi.

But Alphonse Rinaldo was no street hood or thug. He was the real thing, the thing itself.

At the end of my first drink I was pretty sure that Sam Strange was being up front with me. He was less likely to cross his boss than I was. He liked his job, and the protection of Rinaldo's office.

By the end of my second brandy I was confident that even the Big Man hadn't expected the crime I stumbled across. If there was impending danger Rinaldo would have told me, not for my safety but for his own interests. Why would he drag his name, albeit unspoken, into the crime scene at all?

No, it wasn't a setup. The situation had simply escalated faster than Alphonse had anticipated.

I'd taken the first sip of the third brandy when my cell phone made the sound of a far-off migrating flock of geese.

"Yes, Katrina?"

"You hadn't called," she said.

After so many years together a whole chapter of life can be reduced to three or four words. We could have discussed her new habit of waiting up for me since coming back and passing the half-century mark. She was no longer looking for a new man, she said. But even if she was—while she was there she was going to act like my wife.

"I'm on the job," I told her. "It got more complicated than I thought it would."

"Oh."

If we were new lovers, or even just five years into the marriage, that conversation would have spanned half an hour.

"Be careful," she said.

"Good night."

"I guess it's just you and me," Lucy said as I disengaged the call.

I looked around and saw that the bar was empty.

"Business is bad, huh?"

"It's a lull."

"Before the storm?"

Lucy was looking right at me. It had been a long time but I still remembered that look.

A bear growled restlessly.

"Hello?" I said into the cell phone.

Lucy was walking away. She was skinny but she had nice hips.

"Have you spoken to the woman in question?" Sam Strange asked.

"No."

"And?"

"There was a complication."

"What kind of complication?"

"Murder."

"Tara?"

"Maybe."

"This is no time to be coy, Mr. McGill. He's called me three times for an update."

I was watching Lucy clean up at the bar sink, remembering the lyric *Where did our love go?*

"The dead girl was named Wanda Soa, I'm told. Somebody shot her in the face. The probable killer was six feet away, stabbed in the chest. No gun was found."

"Do the police know?"

"Indeed they do."

"Did they, did they speak to you?"

"At length."

"And why haven't you called in to report?"

Giving no answer worked better than words on that question.

"I'll report to him and get back to you if there's anything else," Sam Strange said.

He hung up and I turned off my phone, preferring the slightly addled silence that three shots of good liquor provided.

"Walk me home," Lucy said. She wasn't giving me a choice.

6

Lucy took my arm half a block from the bar and we walked in silence. I made no comment when we passed Gert's building. Four blocks later, on a quiet, not to say desolate, block, she stopped.

"This is me," she said, nodding her head toward the door.

Extricating herself from the crook of my arm, she took out a single, imposing-looking key. This she used on the lock.

"You're very quiet," she said, building on the unspoken intimacy between us.

"Just thinking."

"Yes?"

"When I was a younger man I would have thrown a fine young thing like you over my shoulder and carried you up those stairs."

"I don't know about that. I live on the fifth floor."

I shrugged. It was the same dismissal I had for those who had threatened me with violence over the decades.

"If you can carry me to my door you can do whatever else you want."

I was already breathing hard. Lucy yelped and giggled when I slung her over my shoulder and started walking, two steps at a time. When I got to the third floor I felt her rise up to look at me.

When I was half a flight from her floor she said, "You're really going to do it."

THE APARTMENT WAS SMALL and neat, nothing like Wanda Soa's place. There was a window that looked out on a brick wall, and vintage furniture with dark-green coverings.

"I don't have any liquor in the house," she said.

Her coffee table was an old wooden trunk.

"Bartenders shouldn't drink," I said.

She smiled and asked, "What are you going to do with me now?"

She sat down on the short sofa and gestured for me to sit next to her.

"When I first meet a woman I like to talk a little bit."

She nodded, leaned over, and then kissed me like she meant it. We went at that for a very long time, at least an hour and a half. Our hands explored a little bit but mostly we just massaged each other's tonsils with our tongues. Now and then she reached down to squeeze my erection. Once or twice I ran my fingers between her thighs. But for the most part it was the kissing that mattered.

That was the first time that I'd been frisky so soon after seeing a death. I realized that I needed someone to hold me and kiss me, to tease me with a little squeeze now and then.

"Let's go to bed," she whispered after sticking her tongue in my ear.

We kissed for a few minutes more.

"I'm married," I said, a timid bookkeeper on holiday in Atlantic City.

"So? I am, too."

"Where's your husband?"

"Not here."

The kissing got passionate there for a bit and then I leaned away.

"I don't want to do this," I said. "Not right now."

In a brazen gesture she laid a hand on my pants where the erection strained.

"It sure feels like you want to."

I stared into her eyes and she increased the pressure.

I barely moved.

"You know, I never bring men home from work."

"Uh-huh."

"I like you."

"I like you, too. I just need a little while to get over a couple'a things. Can you give me that?"

The question made her smile. She lifted the hand from my pants and caressed the side of my neck.

"I like it when a big strong man asks so sweetly," she said. "But I need some more of those lips before you can go."

I DIDN'T GET HOME until two-thirty in the morning, my virtue still pretty much intact.

By then Katrina should have been in bed, lulled by the chatter on one of her favorite TV channels. At that hour there would probably be some kind of health or exercise infomercial playing, but Katrina wouldn't know; she just needed the background noise to comfort her natural restlessness.

My wife was not in bed, however. She was sitting at the dining room table in her pink pajamas and turquoise robe.

"Where have you been?" she asked when I walked into the room. There was no friendliness in her voice.

"I told you. The job got more involved than I thought."

"I tried calling you twelve times."

"I was being sly, honey," I said. "I had to turn the cell off."

I was trying to figure out what was wrong. Katrina hadn't been jealous of me in twenty years. Both of us were having multiple affairs in the heyday of our marriage. The term "jealousy" wasn't one of our ten thousand words.

She fell against the backrest of her chair and began to cry.

"What's wrong?" I asked, wondering about the smell of Lucy's perfume on my clothes.

"Dimitri," she said, "and, and Twill. They went out and haven't come back. I tried to call but both their phones are off, too."

Every now and then young Twilliam took pity on his shy, morose brother and introduced him to a particular kind of girl or woman he came upon in his barely legal activities. I'd seen a few e-mails between them when Twill had come across someone he thought D might like. It's supposed to be the other way around—the older brother is supposed to teach his younger sibling the ropes, but that wasn't the case in our home. Twill was the reincarnation of an old soul that had spent one lifetime after another in prison or on the run.

Lately my youngest, and favorite, son had been running an online fence. He never saw or spoke to anyone, just had his e-wallet fat with transfers from a dozen different buyers and providers.

I was looking into how to short-circuit his illegal enterprise but thus far the weak link eluded me.

I couldn't see how that particular endeavor would get both kids in trouble.

"It's okay, baby," I said to my wife.

She sniffed and I wondered if she got a whiff of my make-out session.

"I'm worried, Leonid."

"You know Twill. He probably met some girl wants a college man for a night or two. That's the one thing would keep Dimitri away from here."

"You think so?"

"I'm sure of it. They'll call in the morning. Probably call me, 'cause they're so afraid of you."

I could see the tension release in her shoulders and face.

"Why're you so worried?" I asked.

"I don't know. Maybe I just feel guilty."

"Guilty about what?"

"Not taking care of our children."

"Children? Dimitri's twenty-two, and you know Twill was never a child."

Katrina smiled then, letting go the last of her fear.

"Go on to bed, honey," I said. "Go to bed and we'll hear from the boys in the morning."

7

There are three important furnishings in my den (which some-times serves as a second office). One is a big black desk where I read and, now and then, brood over my life. Across from the desk, hanging in the center of an otherwise empty white wall, is a small oil painting, *Alienated Man*, done by the genius Paul Klee. I'd been given the painting, quite recently, by a young woman who taught me, better than my Communist father ever could, that wealth was mostly just a trick of the mind.

Under the window sits a daybed that can also be used as a couch. I sat there for a while, looking over a dark swath that I knew was the mighty Hudson River.

Sitting in darkness, I experienced a re-revelation: I didn't want the life I was living; I never had. Home-schooled on Hegel, Marx, and Bakunin until the age of twelve, I—from then on a ward of the state—had gone, continuously, downhill.

I spent no more than three minutes feeling sorry for my lot. One hundred eighty seconds isn't bad in the wee hours when no one can see you, or hear.

I thought for a while about the women who populated my night: Katrina, who believed that adult love was either beauty and wealth or else an act of will; Lucy, who was more willing than I had ever been; Wanda Soa was dead; and a woman named Tara wasn't there—or maybe she was Wanda and dead two times. That should be enough for any man. But I wasn't interested in them. All I cared about was Aura Ullman with her Aryan eyes and Ethiopian skin, her natural and deep understanding of what it meant to live under a lawless star.

I DIDN'T REMEMBER LYING down on the daybed, much less falling asleep. But I was up before the sun. The boys hadn't come in—I would have heard Dimitri's racket if they had.

I was still clad in the dull-yellow suit.

I disrobed, hanging the ugly clothes on a standing rack near the door. Then I put on a checkered robe that was older than Dimitri and went down to take a cold-water shower.

I start out each case with a cold shower. I find that it modulates my depressive mood and makes up for the sleep I miss almost every night. It hurts down to the bone, but I rarely yell. I just shiver like a wet dog and clench my teeth hard enough to bite through a circus strongman's thumb. After that, nothing seems so bad or insurmountable.

As Gordo used to tell me, "Life is pain . . . unless you beat it to the punch."

WE LIVE ON WEST Ninety-first Street. My office is a few miles south, on Thirty-ninth between Sixth and Seventh avenues. I walk to work more days than not—to get out of the house before the false domesticity drowns me. I find that thinking comes easily while moving through the city streets where I had come to manhood.

The November sun was just threatening to rise when I, once again wearing that yellow suit, turned south on Broadway. The homeless night people were still out, going through the detritus of the night before: searching paper bags and collecting bottles, hording unfinished cigarettes and the odd coin.

"Hey, brothah," a hale black man dressed all in gray rags said in greeting on Sixty-third and Amsterdam. The street had tempered his body—and cooked his brain.

I nodded in passing.

"You know they comin', right?" he said.

"Who's that?" I asked, slowing.

"Gubment men with their guns an' fake black skins. You know they take white men and use needle dyes to make 'em look like us and then they loose 'em all up and down here wit' guns an' say we doin' it to ourselves."

"Yeah," I said. "Sometimes they don't even need the needles and dyes."

The street messiah smiled at me. His teeth were all there and healthy, yellowed ivory in color and strong. I passed him a twenty-dollar bill and moved along, on my own misguided way.

MY FATHER'S LESSONS, as long as he stayed around, were good ones. He was a sophisticated man, even though he'd been born in an Alabama sharecropper's shack. Self-taught as he was, he had an outsider's take on knowledge.

"People in the Party will tell you to ignore Sigmund Freud," he once told me, a ten-year-old boy. "They say that he's just a bourgeois apologist. Problem is, they're right about a whole lot of what he has to say. All that sex and nuclear-family crap is mostly nonsense. But when he talks about the unconscious, you have to listen to him. Just walk down the street and you can see that most people don't know what they're doing or why. That's the impact of the Economic Infrastructure, but it's still in the living human brain. The ledger informs us but it doesn't make us what we are—not physically.

"So when you decide to do something, anything, you have to wonder what frame of mind brought you to that decision. More times than not it will be a part of your mind that you hadn't considered."

I HATED MY FATHER for many years after he'd abandoned me and killed my mother by walking out on her.

I hated my father for leaving, but his lessons never left me.

Why would I walk downtown so that I'd arrive at the Tesla Building at exactly seven in the morning? I knew that was when Aura got there, that's why. My mind set me up for a supposedly chance meeting with the woman I loved and denied.

And so when I was across the street from the lovely aqua and green Art Deco entrance to the Tesla, I shouldn't have been surprised to see Aura walking arm in arm with a white stranger. He was wearing a dark-blue pinstriped suit which didn't seem to fit him all that well, and carrying an oxblood briefcase. They stopped before the door and kissed.

It was a languorous kiss. The kind of osculation one has after a long night of satisfying intercourse. My unconscious brain told my living heart that I had been running full out for a quarter mile. A cold sweat sprouted across my forehead and down my neck.

The lovers separated, took a step or two, and then, helpless, started kissing again.

I knew I was bound for trouble when I found myself in the middle of the street, heading straight for the pair. My fists were balled and my state of mind was what it was when the bell would ring in my club-fighting days.

I was ready to tear off that sucker's head.

I couldn't stop moving, so I changed direction. I veered off to the left, storming down the street, lucky that no innocent got in my way.

8

I was on Thirty-fourth a little west of Eighth Avenue before I knew it. Gordo's Gym had always been my refuge. I stood in front of the downstairs door breathing hard, unable to move now that I had come to a stop.

I'm fifty-four years old. At this advanced age I shouldn't go crazy like some teenager. My own lack of control, even more than that kiss, humiliated me. If I were another kind of man I might have fallen into a heap crying—after downing a fifth of bourbon.

It was at that exact moment that I realized the depth of my love for Aura. Before then I might have confused my feelings for attraction or deep friendship. But I knew, there on Thirty-fourth Street, that real love had emerged out of my subconscious—and I had waited too long to recognize it.

The all-purpose bear growled in my breast pocket. I suspected that it was Sam Strange. I had regained enough control to know that I couldn't talk to Rinaldo's legman right then. I would have cursed him and, in doing so, damned myself. So I let the call ring itself out and pushed the door open.

Halfway to the fourth floor a lion roared. That was Twill's assigned ring.

"You just about gave your mother an ulcer last night," were my first words. I was relieved to have someone I cared for to talk to.

"Sorry, Pops," Twill said. "Me an' Bulldog run into these two girls from Belarus and things got kinda hot and heavy."

"Belarus?"

"Yeah. That's part a' Russia. I told my girl I was nineteen. Sorry if we worried Moms."

"Have you called her?"

"No."

"Why not?"

"Because they knew this artist guy out in Southampton and we came out here to spend a couple'a days."

"Southampton? What about school?"

"You wanna talk to D?" was his reply.

"Dad?" Dimitri said on the line.

"Listen, son," I said, "your brother is on probation. It's against the law for him to leave the borough of Manhattan. What's gonna happen when the school reports him truant?"

"You could call 'em an' say that he's sick. Tell 'em he got the flu or something. I mean, that would really help us out. And, and, and you could call his social worker, too . . . and explain why he's not at work."

I couldn't remember the last time my blood-son had used more than a few words when speaking to me. All the rage and shame I felt sunk down under Dimitri's uncharacteristic behavior.

"You're asking me to lie for you and your brother?"

"It wouldn't be the first time you lied."

"What's going on with you, D?"

"I'm just asking you for this, all right?"

What could I say? Dimitri hadn't so much as shown a smile in my direction in five years.

"When are you two coming back home?"

"Just a few days. I swear."

"Are you in trouble? Do you need me to come out there and help?"

"No. It's nuthin' like that. It's just this girl . . . I like her."

"Okay. I'll make the calls for Twill, and I'll talk to your mother, too. But I need you two to keep in touch with me. You hear?"

"Uh-huh."

"I mean it, D. You've got to call me every day."

"I will. I promise."

It was the longest conversation I'd had with him since the birds and bees.

"Put Twill back on."

"He went outside."

I THOUGHT I WAS over the worst part about Aura and that kiss, but when I'd stripped down and approached the heavy bag the feeling returned. I worked that leather sack the way I would have liked to have beaten on Aura's pinstriped boyfriend. I threw punches until my knuckles were swollen and even the soles of my feet were slick with sweat. And I kept on until my balance was threatened. I was down on points, in a championship fight, in the last minute of the final round, and refusing to let my body rest.

I had been at it for nearly twenty minutes when I finally sank to my knees.

Another cold shower, followed by twelve minutes on the locker room bench, and I was ready to go. I dropped by Gordo's office on the way out. I was so preoccupied coming in that I didn't even say hello to my substitute father.

But the octogenarian wasn't at his desk. Instead a young cocoa-colored man was sitting there: Timmy "The Toy" Lineman.

He was a tallish middleweight whose limbs and torso were corded with long and lean muscles, containing no fat at all.

"Damn, LT," the youngster said. "You go after that bag like you wanted to kill somebody."

"Where's Gordo?"

"Search me. Said he had to go to a doctor or sumpin'. All's I know is that if I sit here from seven to seven I get three weeks off on my locker space."

"He say what was wrong?"

"No," the smiling kid said. "Hey, you know, LT, it's different hittin' a bag than fightin' a brother in the ring."

"Really? That heavy bag fights back more than any middleweight I ever sparred with."

Toy's smile dimmed almost imperceptibly. He knew better than to challenge me to a "friendly" match.

HALF A BLOCK FROM the Tesla Building my cell phone made the sound of a hyena's yip.

"Detective Kitteridge," I said into the phone.

I gave my regular callers special rings so I knew who was on the line. The bear was anyone I didn't talk to on a regular basis.

"What's up, LT?"

"Just feelin' my age, man."

It was an honest reply and so threw the special detective off balance. He was used to more banter with me.

"I hear you showed up at a murder scene last night," he said.

"My father told me that bad news skims over the surface while good deeds sink to the bottom."

"I need you to come in, LT."

"Not unless you got some paper on me."

"Refusing a friendly request only serves to make you look involved."

"Showing up at the goddamned door did that. But I didn't have anything to do with it and I told Bonilla everything else."

"I'll expect to see you in my office at three," he said before disconnecting the call.

9

I pondered Kitteridge's request on the elevator ride up to the seventy-second floor. Carson was a good cop, maybe the only completely honest senior cop in the NYPD. Turning him down would cause trouble, but walking into his office without a full grasp of the situation would probably be worse. *I* didn't even know why I was at the murder scene. I was sure that Alphonse Rinaldo didn't want me talking to the cops about his business, and crossing Rinaldo was a mistake that no one had ever made twice.

I realized that there was a scowl on my face because when the walnut elevator doors slid open on my floor I smiled. I almost always grinned upon the lovely features of the Art Deco hallway that led to my offices. It was a wide hall with light fixtures of polished brass and a multicolored, marble-tiled floor.

Obtaining the eight-room suite of offices in the Tesla was the one crime I never regretted.

WHEN I TURNED THE corner I saw her: pretty and pale, slender, and not quite of this world. Mardi Bitterman stood in front of my oak door, an apparition of her own suffering. She wore a green and black tweed business suit that would have been more appropriate on a woman of fifty—fifty years ago.

The teenager smiled when she recognized me.

"Good morning, Mr. McGill," she said softly. "I guess I was a little early."

If this was a job interview it would have been over then. A young employee who comes in early is a rare commodity in twenty-first-century New York.

"How are you, Mardi?" I asked.

"Fine, thank you. Twill helped me get an apartment from some friends of his in the Bronx. Me and Marlene moved in last week."

I was busy working keys on the seven locks of my door.

"And you want to work for me?"

"Yes, sir," she said. "Twill said that you always wanted a receptionist, and I studied office sciences in high school."

I pushed the door open and gestured for her to go in.

"Are you planning to go to college?" I asked.

"This is beautiful!" She was referring to the reception antechamber of my suite.

There was an ash desk backed up by a trio of cherrywood filing cabinets. The double window looked out over New Jersey, and the walls were painted a subtle blue-gray.

The desk even had a little plastic sign that read RECEPTIONIST.

"I thought Twill said that you never had a secretary," she said.

"I haven't. But I've always wanted one. It's just that the kind of work I do means that somebody would have to give a little extra effort. I mean, it's not easy working for a guy like me."

Mardi was running her pale fingers across the white wood.

"I'd love to have this job, Mr. McGill. The lady, Mrs. Alexander, who lives in the place downstairs, said that she'd look after Marlene if I was ever late, and I know about the kind of work you do."

"How old are you now, Mardi?"

"I turned eighteen last May."

Thinking of the terror and humiliation that Twill's friend had endured, the words of my father came to me: *Tragedy either makes or breaks the will of the proletariat.*

I had planned to pawn the child off on Aura when Twill made his request the night before. But now I couldn't imagine talking to my ex. And seeing the resolve in Mardi's face, I believed that she might well be made for a job like this.

"Let's try it out," I said. "We'll talk salary and hours later on. There's a laptop computer in the bottom drawer of the desk and an Internet connection in the wall. Why don't you set that up and make yourself at home."

I went to the fireproof brown metal door that led to my inner offices and entered a code on the digital keypad.

"There's a code to this door," I said before entering. "If you last two weeks I'll give it to you. For today I'll just leave it unlocked in case you need to come down and ask me something. And, oh yeah, whenever you walk in the front door three hidden cameras take pictures for about eight minutes. Just so you know."

I left the girl looking up at the ceiling, trying to find the secret eyes.

MY OFFICE DESK WAS made from ebony, its back to a window that looks south, on lower Manhattan. It was a clear day and you could make out the Statue of Liberty in the distance.

I tried my virtual answering machine but the growling bear from before had left no message.

For a while I counted my breaths, making it up to ten and then starting over. After maybe fifteen minutes I called information on my cell phone and they agreed to connect the call for no additional charge.

"Oxford Arms," a severe woman's voice said.

"Mr. Strange, please."

"One moment," she said, as if I were put on earth to irk her. And then, "We have no Mr. Strange in residence."

"Really? He told me that I could call him there at any time. Maybe you have another number for him?"

"Please wait," she said, managing to insinuate her agitation in the sound of the click that put me on hold.

Forty seconds later she was back. "Mr. Strange checked out this morning. He left no messages."

I paused there, wondering what this wrinkle meant for my involvement in Rinaldo's business.

"Is that quite all?" the woman asked.

"Aren't you supposed to be polite or something?"

The lady hung up.

I SHOULD HAVE FELT relief at Strange's departure. If he was gone, didn't that mean the investigation, whatever it was about, was over?

But when working around Rinaldo, loose ends were never a good thing.

I logged on to the New York news engine that the computer whiz Tiny "Bug" Bateman had written for me. This customized piece of software allows me to connect various newswire accounts of specific crimes and criminals—it even taps a special police website using keywords from newspaper and wire accounts.

Wanda Soa had been a cocktail waitress and student at the Fashion Institute of Technology. The man found stabbed to death in Wanda's apartment carried no identification and the police had yet to identify him. No one heard the shot that killed the woman, but the door had been left wide open and a passing neighbor got worried and called the super—a woman named Dorothy Harding. Police were asking for anyone with information to come forward.

There was no mention of the name Tara Lear.

The crime made very little sense. It was unlikely that Wanda stabbed the button man before he shot her, and she certainly couldn't have done it with half her face gone. From what I remembered, the door hadn't been broken open, so someone had probably let the killer, or killers, in.

And what was I doing there? That was my existential question, in hindsight.

A buzzer that I'd never heard before sounded—quite loudly. I nearly jumped out of my chair.

"Mr. McGill?" bodiless Mardi Bitterman said.

It took me a moment to remember the intercom box on my desk. I hadn't used it in the twenty-one months I'd had the office.

Pressing a button, I said, "Yes?"

"There's a man out here who says that he's the new financial officer for the building. He wants to talk with you."

I remembered the guards at the front desk telling me that there was a new bookkeeper who was going through everyone's overtime. They didn't like him, and I still had enough of my union-organizing father's background to side with the working class.

"Send him in, Mardi. Tell him to follow the hall to the far end."

10

There are no straight lines in the life or labors of the private detective.

In gumshoe fiction, the PI gets on the case at about page six and follows it through without a pause or distraction from his, or her, personal life. He certainly doesn't have to deal with accountants who have been charged by their bosses with the ouster of a suspect tenant: me.

At least he knocked.

"Come in."

Though I had not seen his face clearly, I knew Aura's lover by his height and weight, pinstriped suit, and oxblood briefcase.

The only hint revealing my murderous heart was a momentary flutter of my eyelashes.

"Mr. McGill?" he asked.

I nodded and started counting breaths again.

"My name is George Toller," he said. "I'm the new chief financial officer of the Tesla."

"Oh? I thought CFOs ran corporations," I said.

"May I have a seat?"

I gestured toward one of the blue and chrome visitor's chairs, and Toller sat down.

"You are correct, of course. I run the entire company for Hyman and Schultz. They own nearly three dozen New York properties—thirty-three, to be exact. They have sent me here to clear up some messes left by the previous owners and their representatives."

That was another thing about mystery novels: at the end of the story the crime is solved and that's that. The crook is caught, or maybe just found out. But, regardless, the crime is never carried on to the next book in the series. You rarely find the stalwart and self-possessed dick looking for a perpetrator from the previous story.

I wasn't so lucky. The crimes I dealt with lagged on for years, sometimes decades.

And in this case Toller was the investigator and I was the elusive criminal.

The previous manager of the Tesla, Terry Swain, had embezzled a large sum of money over twenty-some years. The new owners looked a little closer than the previous ones and tumbled to the misappropriations. Around the same time, I was between offices and had found out that there was a beautiful suite recently vacated on the seventy-second floor. I offered to muddy the waters of the investigation for a rock-bottom price on a fifteen-year lease. Terry leapt at the deal and I got him off, even saved his retirement fund for him.

Ever since that time the owners have had it in for me. First they sent Aura to get me evicted but instead we became lovers. Now they sent my ex-lover's lover.

There had to be some kind of meaning to that.

"How can I help you, Mr. Toller?"

"You could pack your things and move out," he said. "I'd be happy to tear up your lease."

He smiled without showing any teeth.

It struck me that he had no idea about the relationship between me and Aura.

"I couldn't give up this view," I confessed.

"Eight rooms and only one employee? Mr. McGill, this is a waste of space."

We hated each other without having ever met. What was interesting to me was that our reasons were so far apart. His sense of propriety was bent out of shape by my shadowy dealings with his masters' property. College had taught him contempt for me. Conversely, my abhorrence for him had a genetic basis. This man had stolen my woman. I wanted to cut out his heart right there on my African-wood table.

I wondered if there were wars between nations that had begun like this, if whole peoples slaughtered each other without even being able to agree on what they were fighting about.

"Is that all?" I asked pleasantly.

"I've taken an office on the forty-second floor," he replied. "My primary purpose here is to negate your contract and to have you evicted, maybe even incarcerated."

Toller was not a day over forty-five but he carried himself like a man of seventy. He was one of those men who came into the world with the weight of years on his shoulders. I could tell by the timbre of his voice and the cast of his eye that he felt he was being threatening. I expected that he could imagine the fear I felt at his words.

I smiled.

"Do they pay you well, Mr. Toller?"

"I do all right."

"'All right'? That's a lot of money to try and nullify a good-faith contract. Listen to me, man, these empty rooms are mine, just like the little place thirty floors down is yours. I'm not leaving, and you're not taking or sending me anywhere. Okay?"

Finally—a frown.

"I'm very good at my job, Mr. McGill. I have a background in forensic accounting."

And I have a pistol in my top drawer.

The image of Toller kissing Aura came back to me. I could feel the fingernails digging into my palms.

"I haven't broken any laws, Mr. Toller," I lied. "So you can take your red case and your blue suit and do whatever it is a CFO forensic bookkeeper does. I'm staying right here."

"I don't think you understand the seriousness of your situation," he replied.

"What a man don't know," I quoted, "he just don't know."

Something about the phrase inflamed the prig's aesthetic. His left nostril flared and he rose to his feet, hugging the briefcase under his arm like a pet piglet.

"You'll be hearing from me" were his last words before leaving.

THE IDEA OF TOLLER'S investigation didn't intimidate me. I was vulnerable, of course—all people are. Innocent or not, anyone can be made to look bad. And I had enough skeletons in my closet to make a death row inmate seem angelic. But I wasn't worried—not about Toller—just overwhelmed by the circumstances of my life.

Any good boxer can tell you that if you have a sound strategy, and stick to it, you always have a shot at winning the fight. And even if you don't win, you can make it through to the final bell, throwing at least some doubt on your opponent's claim to victory.

What beats a fighter with a good plan isn't power or a lucky punch, not usually; no, what beats a journeyman pugilist is the onslaught of an implacable attack. If your opponent throws so much at you that you get confused, you will necessarily be drawn away from your game plan and defeated by the complexity of your own (mis)perceptions.

I had a lot on my mind: everything from murder to the unexpected bouquet of wildflowers that Katrina had placed in our dining room.

I resolved to ignore any new information until I had answered at least one question.

At that moment the buzzer sounded again. I decided to have that wire disconnected.

"Yes, Mardi?"

"A Mr. Alphonse Rinaldo to see you, Mr. McGill."

11

how him in," I said, stunned by the impact of the soft words.

Alphonse Rinaldo.

I had never seen him outside his downtown offices. The Big Man didn't come to you; he never went anywhere, as far as I knew.

When the door came open I stood up. Mardi entered with a smile for me and the view. She moved a little awkwardly but that was okay—I was off balance myself. Alphonse Rinaldo was the most powerful man I had ever met. Seeing him follow the child into the room was unreal. His dark-brown silk suit cost more than most cars. He was five-nine, with a perfect complexion and black, well-managed hair. He nodded and then moved gracefully to the visitor's chair.

It seemed like a travesty that such an important man should sit in the same seat that was occupied by George Toller just a while before.

"Can I get you anything, Mr. Rinaldo?" Mardi asked.

"Coffee?" he said.

"There's a Coffee Exchange in the lobby," I said. "Get me one, too, will ya, Mardi?"

I handed her a ten-dollar bill and the key ring for the front door, adding, "The silver key works on the top lock."

She smiled and backed out of the room.

"Nice place," Rinaldo said. His voice was smooth and deep like a placid lake on just the right day.

"Thank you."

I sat down and frowned again. It was becoming less and less likely that I'd make it to the final round.

Like Toller, Rinaldo was carrying a briefcase. But unlike the so-called CFO, the Special Assistant to the City of New York wasn't bringing tuna sandwiches and condoms to work.

For a moment there I imagined Toller going to the eighty-first floor and rutting with Aura on her big metal desk.

"What's wrong, Leonid?" Alphonse asked.

"You came here all by yourself?"

"Yes."

"Then you must know why I look like there's something wrong."

Instead of smiling he took a small photograph from his breast pocket and leaned across the desk, handing it to me.

It was a snapshot of a raven-haired girl, no older than twenty-five, whose look was somehow both reserved and wild. She was facing the lens but not looking into it. The shot was taken when she was unaware.

"Is this the girl you saw last night?"

"I don't get it, Mr. Rinaldo, you could get any of a hundred people to show you the crime-scene photographs. As far as I know, the NYPD is an open book to you."

"I cannot be involved." His eyebrows furrowed one-sixteenth of an inch. It wasn't much, but a man that close to being royalty didn't have to do much.

"The face on the dead girl was pretty destroyed, but she had blond hair and one blue eye."

I could tell by the waver over his lips and the slight puffing of his cheek that he sighed in relief. I couldn't actually hear the exhalation, but it was there.

"What happened to Strange?" I asked.

"I pulled him off the job," Rinaldo said. "Told him that it was over."

"But it's not."

"I need you to find this girl, Leonid. It is very important to me."

In that fight—the one where you had a plan and stuck to it—you could be thrown off balance by any change in your opponent; for instance, if he were to switch from a normal right-handed stance to southpaw. I never expected to see vulnerability in this man who, for all intents and purposes, was beyond the reaches of pain.

"Did Strange tell you my caveats?" I asked, pretending that this was a meeting between equals.

"He records every conversation he has on my behalf."

"So what do you have to say?"

"If you hadn't voiced those restrictions I wouldn't be here."

Our eyes met. Rinaldo's gaze was unwavering. Even in obvious pain and defenseless he wouldn't look away.

"Excuse me," Mardi Bitterman said.

She was carrying a cardboard box that they use for large orders at the Coffee Exchange.

"That was quick," I said.

"I called down. They have a building delivery service," she said. "I didn't ask how you wanted your coffees, so I had them bring a cup of half-and-half, some sugars, and sugar substitutes."

She put the box down in front of Rinaldo, also placing my key ring and change in the center of the desk.

"Thank you," Rinaldo said, and then he touched her elbow.

She flinched, pulling her arm away.

"Excuse me," he said.

"It's okay. I, I just don't like being touched. I'm sorry."

Mardi backed out of the room again, half-smiling and looking as if she were about to cry.

Rinaldo took his coffee black, as I did mine.

"Whatever it costs," he said. "I need to find her and make sure she's safe."

"From who?"

"I don't know. Obviously someone is trying to hurt her. She's been hiding for a few weeks now and I have no idea why."

"That's not much to go on, Mr. Rinaldo."

He brought the briefcase to the desktop and pushed it in my direction, careful not to disturb our coffee cups.

"The information in here was gathered before all the problems started. Some of it might be out of date but a lot will be helpful. There's some money for expenses and special contact information for me. You are not to contact me through regular channels, Leonid. Do not talk to Christian or Sam, and know from me that I will not have them, or anyone else, call you. I will pay you personally."

He reached for his pocket again and I held up a hand.

"That won't be necessary," I said.

"No?"

"This is like any other transaction between us. A favor, that's all."

"That's it, then," he said.

"You don't have anything else to say?"

"I don't want you talking to her, Leonid. Whatever you do should happen in the background of her life. Find out what's wrong and fix it. If that proves too difficult, come to me."

"You wanted me to make contact with her last night. Why the change?"

"I didn't want her to know what you did or that you worked for me. And . . . and this murder makes things even more difficult. I want her to experience as little trauma as possible."

I didn't like it but his tone left no room for complaints.

"Anything you'll need is in here," he said, tapping the briefcase with the middle finger of his left hand.

"Was the man who killed Wanda Soa after Tara?"

"I honestly don't know. As I said, Tara disappeared three weeks ago—she only showed up at this Soa's apartment yesterday . . . maybe the day before."

"What's your relationship with the girl?"

"There is none."

I tried to come up with some kind of question that would have opened up a further dialogue but there were no words I could think of.

"So that's all?" I asked.

He nodded.

We both stood. I came around the desk to see him to the door and received my fourth or fifth shock of the day: Alphonse Rinaldo held out a hand to me.

"Thank you," he said.

I had to bite my lower lip not to repeat the words.

I WATCHED HIM WALK down the long aisle of empty cubicles, waiting until he exited through the brown metal door. At least he didn't hesitate and turn to see if I was there—at least that.

12

When a boxer's game plan is shot he has to come up with something new on the fly. The classic boxer turns into a brawler, the habitually offensive fighter goes into his shell.

I'm not a passive man by nature. Don't get me wrong—I have been devious and underhanded from time to time. Often, when I was still working for what seemed like half of the New York underworld, I'd taken down people who never even saw my face. But as a rule I'm usually more than willing to take on any job, or opponent, head-to-head.

I gave up my dirty tricks with the intention of doing the right thing in my business and my life. But that never changed my brawling style—a style that I knew instinctively would not see me to the end of this period in my life.

So I refrained from opening Rinaldo's briefcase right away. Instead I sat there, allowing the details of the past twenty-four hours to filter through my mind without feeling pressed by the need to impose my will on them.

I had learned a thing or two. For instance, I now knew for a rock-solid fact that I loved Aura Antoinette Ullman. Seeing her kissing George Toller made me lose control—something I never did.

That was a detail I could put to bed. It didn't matter if she came back to me or not—I'd still have that wild love inside me.

I smiled a real smile and then laughed a little. Small victories are sometimes the hardest earned.

I turned the briefcase around so that the front latches were facing me. But still I held back.

Twill, my excellent son, had put Dimitri on the phone and then left so that I couldn't question him further. That meant he was hiding something. Twill didn't have the little secrets of most adolescents. He wasn't smoking marijuana in the basement laundry room or worried about a girlfriend's missed period. Whatever he was concealing needed to be exposed before the two young men who shared my name, if not my blood, got too deeply into whatever mess they'd created.

And so another detail fell into place.

I called Gordo's cell phone but a voicemail recording in his raspy words just said, "Leave a message," and provided a span to do that in.

"I hear you got the sniffles, G-man," I said. "Call me if you need some chicken soup."

I turned my attention back to the briefcase.

And then, for no reason, I wondered what kind of flowers I'd get for my office if I were to buy flowers. Now that I had an assistant, I could send her to the florist downstairs and order orchids or roses . . . or wildflowers.

"Mr. McGill?"

She was standing at the doorway in her fifties business suit, smiling painfully.

"Yes, Mardi. Come on in and sit down."

Putting off the job at hand was becoming pleasurable.

The child moved quickly to the chair as if she were afraid I might rescind the invitation.

"I got online and went through all the drawers and stuff," she said. "I put all your take-out and delivery menus in order."

"Thank you."

"That's okay," she said, pushing her ash-blond hair over the left shoulder.

"How long have you been back in town?" I asked.

"Five weeks."

"Twill never told me. Did you just call him lately?"

"No. He came down to the airport and picked us up."

I remembered him borrowing my car.

"So you've seen a lot of him," I said.

"Yeah. Him and D helped us move into Mrs. Alexander's place."

"You see much of Dimitri?"

"Sometimes he comes around with Twill. At first I thought he liked me. I mean, he's a nice guy, but I don't like him like that. But now he has a girlfriend and I can see that he's just shy around girls and acts like that."

"Is the girlfriend nice?"

"I guess. I've only seen her a couple'a times. I think her name's Tanya—something like that. She's Russian or something."

"You met her yesterday?"

"No. She came over with D a few weeks ago."

Mardi squirmed a bit in her chair. I leaned back, raising my hands.

"So," I said. "What can I do for you?"

"I've never had a job like this before."

"And I've never had a receptionist," I said.

"But Twill was always saying how you had this big empty office and the only thing you ever wanted was somebody at the front desk."

"Dimitri won't talk to me, and Shelly never shuts up long enough for me to get a word in," I said. "But Twill, if nothing else, pays attention."

"What do you want me to do?" she asked.

I took out the reddish-brown leather wallet that I bought at Macy's in 1976. It was old, nearly shapeless, and falling apart. But I loved that billfold. I took out the credit card that I had gotten for my little corporation.

"Take this and start an account with one of the online office-supply stores. Get what you need to do anything secretarial that I might ask. Spend the next few days going through the files and putting them in order.

"There's a number for Zephyra Ximenez in the Rolodex. You spell her last name with an X instead of a J. She's been my girl Friday from her office for a while now. You two should get to know each other. You'll also find a card for Tiny Bateman. He's my software expert. Trouble with the computer or anything electronic and he'll set you straight. If anything doesn't make sense, just ask me."

A true smile from Mardi Bitterman was like the kiss from any other young woman. I could see in her pale eyes that she was going to be perfect as my assistant—the wounded leading the wounded, as it were.

MARDI LEFT THE OFFICE with an extra set of keys for the front door. I had no more distractions to keep me from opening Rinaldo's briefcase. I tapped the coal-gray leather and winced, placed my thumbs on the latches, and was about to flip them when my cell phone made the sound of migrating geese.

"Have you spoken to them?" was Katrina's response to my hello.

"No," I lied, "but Twill left a message on my voicemail half an hour ago. He said that he was up at school with D and that they were going to some kind of party tonight. I think he's afraid to talk to either one of us."

"But he sounded okay?"

"Oh yeah. They're just boys on the prowl, honey."

The ensuing silence was her relief.

"I got some business I have to take care of, Katrina."

"Tell me when you've spoken to either one of them," she said. "And tell Dimitri to call me."

I PHONED THE ATTENDANCE office at Twill's school to report that he had an intestinal flu. After that I told his social worker the same lie.

"How is he doing?" I asked Melinda Tarris, assistant subagent in the Juvenile Offenders office.

"I've never met anyone like your son, Mr. McGill. He could become the president of the United States if we got his record expunged."

13

Her full name was Angelique Tara Lear.

She'd turned twenty-seven on October 7th. The address Rinaldo's briefcase had for her was different from the one where the murders occurred. Tara lived on Twelfth Street, on the East Side, at the edge of the Alphabet Jungle. There was a photograph of her sitting at an outdoor café. It was probably taken with a tele-photo lens without her knowledge. I say this because she seemed to be in the middle of a conversation.

She was a raven-haired wild-eyed thing in spite of her pedes-trian, almost reserved, attire. She wore a white blouse that but-toned up like a man's dress shirt. I imagined that she had a navy skirt that came down below the knees to go with that blouse. But no matter how much she tried to be normal and reserved there was an abandon to her expression and also the kind of carelessness that drives the male animal, of all ages, wild.

I looked at the picture for a long while. She was leaning for-ward, laughing. There was mischievousness in her gaze and a tilt to her head that was saying, *Am I hearing something else behind your words?* After a while I came to believe that the wildness wasn't that of a party girl—she would have been wearing makeup and some-thing more provocative if that were the case. No. Angelique was just happy—almost, and hopefully, unsinkably so.

There was another picture that caught my attention. She was all in black, at a funeral, crying. She stood next to a fair-sized head-stone that read IRIS LINDSAY. True sorrow is hard to gauge, but I believed her pain.

The young woman, however, was less interesting than the fact of the photographs. Someone had followed Angelique and taken many dozens of pictures—these being only a few. And if those two shots were representative of the whole roll, or memory card, then the surveillance wasn't about who she was with but the woman herself. Someone seemed to be studying her.

Was that Rinaldo? Had he hired a private detective to take pictures of her on the street, at work . . . in the shower? Was he her protector or her stalker?

She had an undergraduate degree from Hunter College and an MBA from NYU. The latter diploma would have cost a hundred thousand dollars, minimum. There was no credit report on her. Was that left out on purpose or didn't it matter? I could get a credit report on my own, of course, but I wanted to tread softly around Tara until I knew why Wanda got half her face shot off.

Tara had been recently hired as a "fellow," whatever that meant, at Laughton and Price, an advertising firm on Lexington, not Madison. Her mother lived, at least at the time of the report, in Alphabet City proper, east of the East Village. Her brother, named Donald Thompson, was only a name with no address, or even an age.

Under the neatly typed pages was a layer of cash wrapped into bundles. Twenties, fifties, and hundreds that stacked up to thirty thousand dollars—money for my expenses. This told me that Mr. Rinaldo would spare no resource in finding the woman with whom he claimed to have no relationship.

I went through the pages again. There was no criminal record included.

It wasn't much but it was enough to go on.

When the buzzer sounded I was no longer surprised.

"Yes, Mardi?"

"A Miss Aura Ullman?"

"Uh . . . send her in." I wanted to stay focused, to keep my mind in the world of Tara Lear, but just the mention of Aura's name and I was at sea, in a fog, with no sense of direction.

"LEONID," SHE SAID.

"Aura." I managed to get some lightness into my greeting.

She frowned a bit. Every other time she had come into the office I stood up and, if we were alone, kissed her.

Now, however, those lips would have tasted of George Toller.

Aura was a woman of the New World. Golden-brown skin, natural and wavy dark-blond hair, and pale eyes that Nazi scientists tried to create in what they called the inferior races. She was forty and beautiful to me; of African and European lineage, she was completely American.

Aura lowered into the closest chair, giving a wan smile.

"How are you?" she asked.

"Thankfully busy," I said.

"A case?"

"A whole shipload."

She smiled. Aura liked my jokes.

"Who's that at the front desk?"

"Mardi Bitterman."

"The child who was raped by her father?"

"Yes." In the days when we were passionate lovers, and then platonic lovers, I told Aura everything.

"I thought she moved to Ireland with her sister."

"Where there's heat," I said, "there's motion."

"I came to see how you're doing."

"I'm fine."

"You didn't look fine yesterday when I, I told you."

"Listen, honey," I said. "You're a gorgeous woman and you deserve to have real love in your life."

"I wanted you."

I tried to start counting my breaths but got lost after one.

"Leonid."

"Yes?"

"Will you forget me now?"

"No."

"Will you ever talk to me again?"

"Yes."

"When?"

"You can give me a week, right?" I asked, once again managing a jaunty attitude.

She looked into my eyes and, after a moment or two, nodded. Then she stood up and went out the door.

If my father had been there I would have asked him how that particular moment was a product of the Economic Infrastructure unfurling through history.

I COULD SWITCH OFF the pain of Aura's departure by turning back to Angelique. She was a mystery and missing, the object of attention of a man who was as dangerous as any terrorist or government-trained assassin.

I honestly believed that Alphonse Rinaldo could bring down a president if he set his mind to it.

And now he had set his sights on this young woman. Whether he meant her harm or not was a question for later. Right then I had no choice but to follow my nose.

I decided that I was going to do my best to save Angelique. After all, she was the one in trouble. I'd call her Angie and believe in her innocence until proven otherwise. *She* was my client, and Rinaldo was the devil I had to deal with.

History guides all men's hands, my father's voice whispered from any of a dozen possible graves.

"Bullshit," I said aloud in my seventy-second-floor office.

And then the office phone rang.

Instead of answering I remembered reading a line in an article where a man somewhere in Africa had said, "In the lowlands, where I make my home, it never rains, but the floods come annually."

After two rings the phone went silent. Soon after that the intercom sounded.

"Yes, Mardi?"

"It's a Mr. Breland Lewis on the phone for you."

"Tell him to hold on. I'll be on the line in a minute."

14

I don't like getting calls from lawyers. Just hearing Lewis's name, I shuddered and shrank.

And this is in response to my own attorney. If somebody asked me for a list of a dozen friends, Breland would have been on it. But still, he was representative of the law, and law, regardless of its mandate to protect the people, is no friend to man.

"Breland," I said into the mouthpiece.

"How are you, Leonid?"

"You tell me."

"It's Ron Sharkey again."

Ron Sharkey was the metaphor for well over twenty years of criminal activity on my part. I had torn down the lives of well over a hundred men and women in the years I was a fixer for the mob. Most of those that I destroyed were criminals themselves and so I could console myself saying that I was just another means of retribution for what was right and good in the world.

But I had taken down innocents along the way, too. Ron Sharkey was one of these. He lost everything because of my machinations, and he never heard my name or saw my face.

After Sharkey was released from prison I had Breland keep tabs on him. Years in stir had bent the once honest businessman. On the outside again, he had become a drug addict and petty thief.

The police arrested him on a dozen different occasions, and every time Breland was there with bail money and representation before the court.

"What's he into now?" I asked.

"It's kind of complex. Maybe we better sit down and talk."

"Yeah," I said, "okay. Listen, I got a lot on my plate right now. Can you give me a day or so?"

"Sure. It'll hold for a day or two. But it can't wait a week."

BRELAND LEWIS'S PHONE CALL was the beginning of one long headache. It blossomed behind my left eye, a bright-red rose of pain. It wasn't Sharkey in particular, or even my oblivious client, Angie. It was more like everything, all at once.

"When you hit your fifties life starts comin' up on ya fast," Gordo Tallman said to me on the occasion of my forty-ninth birthday. "Before that time life is pretty much a straight climb. Wife looks up to you and the young kids are small enough, and the older kids smart enough, not to weigh you down. But then, just when you start puttin' on the pounds an' losin' your wind, the kids're expectin' you to fulfill your promises and the wife all of a sudden sees every single one of your flaws. Your parents, if you still got any, are gettin' old and turnin' back into kids themselves. For the first time you realize that the sky does have a limit. You comin' to a rise, but when you hit the top there's another life up ahead of you and here you are—just about spent."

The time for sitting on my butt on the seventy-second floor, playing like I could avoid my responsibilities, was over.

I hit the street at a good pace, moving north toward my home. On the way I thought about my duties to an unknowing world.

MY INTUITION WAS THAT the thing with Angie and Alphonse was not about sex. The details and photographs had intimacy but no heat to them. It seemed to me that Angie was like a family member, maybe even a daughter, who had somehow become estranged from the Big Man—after which she got into trouble. Or maybe the rift between them caused the trouble in some way.

I wasn't flat-out rejecting the notion that they were lovers. And even if they were related, he might still have had bad intentions toward her.

The problem was that I knew so little about Rinaldo. He was an honest-to-goodness twenty-first-century enigma. No one knew what he did or where his entry was on the chain of command. I'd only met a few people who'd ever heard of him.

"Rinaldo?" Hush, the retired assassin, had said when I'd asked him. "Yeah. I did work for him a couple'a times."

From the age of fifteen until his retirement, the only work Hush had ever done involved homicide.

"Funny thing, though," the serial-killer-for-hire opined. "I never met him in person. He was one of the few clients I ever had who I didn't look in the eye."

"Why's that?" I asked. We were in my office late one Tuesday evening. I was guzzling Wild Turkey while Hush sipped on a glass of room-temperature tap water.

"You can piss on a cardinal in his Easter suit but if the bush starts burning you have to lower your head and pray."

Remembering those words, rendered in Hush's deep voice, I stopped there in the middle of Broadway foot traffic. I was fool enough to be a friend to the killer-for-hire—but now to even consider investigating a man that Hush feared . . . that just had to make me stop and laugh.

"What the fuck's wrong with you, man?" someone said.

He was standing behind me, a young black man whose attire I could only call modern-day Isaac Hayes: light-brown leather from head to toe, his hat and shoes, pants and vest, and of course the open jacket. The only thing on that young man that wasn't bovine in origin was the golden medallion that spelled out something. The lettering was so ornate that I couldn't make out the word.

"Say what, brah?" I asked him in the accepted dialect of the street.

He was taller than me, of course, and skin—not so dark. The brown in his eyes was light, unnaturally so. I guessed that they might have been covered by cowhide-colored contacts to make his image complete.

The synthetic eyes looked me over, saw my big scarred hands and slumped, strong shoulders. He beheld in me the immovable object—though he might not have known the physics term. I saw in his fake eyes that he had been stopped before.

"I almost run you down, man," he said, allowing a constrained belligerence to express his ire.

I just looked at him. Any word I said would have led to a fight, so I left it up to him. I was ready to go to war—I almost always am. Combat was how I made it through childhood; it was what kept me alive.

The young man in leather gauged me.

Finally he said, "Fuck you," and walked around. After a few moments I went on my way, thinking that he was smarter than me.

He knew when to avoid an obstruction in the road.

15

It was three o'clock when I reached the front door of my apartment building—3:01, to be exact.

The hyena yipped in my yellow pocket. That was Detective Kitteridge, of course. I was supposed to be at his office. I guess he expected me to answer his call. But I didn't have the sense of the city fop who knew to skirt around a threat when he saw one.

I ignored the call—creating at least a temporary antagonist by my inaction.

MY LIFE IS A series of trials testing whether or not I am capable of maintaining my perceived place in the world. One of these perennial auditions is the staircase of my apartment building. I live on the eleventh floor. There are fourteen steps between each stage— one hundred forty little ascendancies. Unless it's late at night I almost always walk up.

I take the stairs at a fair clip.

The first four floors are no problem. I'm breathing at a good pace between five and eight. It's only the last two flights that are a real strain. The only reason I walk up is for those final twenty-eight steps. If I'm not breathing hard by then I go faster the next time. When I'm no longer able to make that run I'll know it's time to quit the game.

The stairs are not my only test. There's the heavy bag at Gordo's Gym, and how frightened I get, or not, when a man pulls a gun on me. There's sitting in the same room with Hush, who, if he were to have put a notch in his gun for every man he'd killed, would have whittled off the entire handle in the first half of his career.

Life is a test, and the final grade is always an F.

THAT YEAR I HAD a black key made for the front door. Except for the color it looked like a regular key, but it also contained an electronic component. The physical device did indeed turn a mechanical lock, but the electronics flipped another switch throwing back a bolt that came up through the floor. The door itself was reinforced with a titanium plate.

In a drawer in my office I had a few key rings that had masters for almost every lock in New York City. And for those that were "unique" I had illegal masters that were able to adjust to the cylinders they encountered.

Just because I was aware of dangers that other people were ignorant of didn't make me paranoid. I didn't feel bad about having the locks on my front door changed at least once a year.

My enemies would have to work to get at me or mine.

BECAUSE THE LOCK IS always new it didn't make much noise. I was halfway down the hall to the dining room when I heard the voices.

It was a man and Katrina speaking in normal tones. There was no urgency or conflict there—no feeling.

"Dimitri?" Katrina called. "Dimitri, is that you?"

"It's me, Katrina," I said and then I entered through the open door.

My wife was sitting at her end of the rustic hickory-wood dining table and a man somewhere in his late thirties was sitting on the side, a place away from her. They both had teacups in front of them.

He was a brown man with straight dark hair and a small, Caucasian nose. His face was too boyish to be called handsome or plain. His eyes were brown also and more mature than the rest of his physiognomy.

"Leonid," my wife said.

She stood and walked toward me, past the pickle jar of wildflowers. She kissed my cheek and took my arm.

"This is Bertrand Arnold," she said. "He's one of Dimitri's classmates."

Arnold, who was as many years older than Dimitri as he was younger than I, stood up and put out a hand.

"It's an honor to meet you, Mr. McGill. D has told me a lot about you."

"You're kidding, right?" I said.

"No."

"How the hell's a kid who never says more than three words to me at a time gonna be singing my praises to somebody else?"

The look on the brown man's face was one of bewilderment. He had no prepackaged answer. That told me something.

"I . . . uh . . ." he said.

"Leonid," Katrina said in her maternal voice. "You're going to scare the young man."

"What did D tell you?" I asked Bertrand. "About me, I mean."

"He ssssaid that you were a detective. That, that, that he once saw you knock down two men at the beach."

CONEY ISLAND, FIFTEEN YEARS before. Two redneck Brooklynites got it in their heads that a beautiful young white woman like Katrina could find somebody better than a fat little black man. All three kids were with us. Dimitri, the oldest, was not yet eight.

The two guys had a brief span of time in which to retreat. I stood up, walked over to them, and time was up.

"HE REMEMBERED THAT, HUH?" I said.

"Yes," Bertrand replied, vehemently.

"Let's sit down, Leonid," Katrina, the peacemaker, said.

"You look kinda old to be one of D's classmates," I suggested to Bertrand as we sat down.

"My parents own a bakery. Arnold Bakery in Astoria. I wanted to open up a branch store in SoHo. But when the bank asked me for a business plan I realized that I didn't know enough to start a business on my own. So I decided to go back to school. At first it was just an extension course at CCNY. But then I began to realize that I really liked business and so I decided to get a degree. I met Dimitri last year."

It all sounded very plausible. Generation X and their heirs took longer to mature than their elders. I knew nothing about Dimitri's life, but he must have had friends and schoolmates.

"Is D in his room changing or something?" I asked.

"No," Katrina said. "He still hasn't come home."

"Then why are you here?" I asked the boy-faced man.

"I haven't seen Dimitri for a few days," he replied. "He's not in class. He doesn't answer his phone. So I decided to drop by to see if he was okay."

My breathing was normal again. The rage I'd felt at my own helplessness was lessened by the trial of the stairs.

But the headache was getting worse.

"I was asking Mr. Arnold if he knew anybody I could call to get in touch with Dimitri," Katrina said.

"Do you know a friend of D's," I asked Bertrand, "a girl named Tanya—something like that. She might be Russian."

"I've seen him with a blond girl once or twice over the last couple of weeks. I don't know her name. She never spoke and Dimitri would always hustle her off if I was around. I think he was a little jealous."

"Why? You makin' eyes at her?"

"She's very pretty, but I wouldn't go after a girl that he was with."

"I'm very worried, Leonid," Katrina said.

"I talked to Dimitri on the walk back home," I said. It wasn't completely a lie. I *had* talked to him. "He said that he and Twill were with these Russian girls. Mardi told me that Dimitri's friend was maybe called Tanya."

"Mardi Bitterman?" Katrina said.

"Yeah. She's my secretary now. Twill wanted me to hire her and I think she might work out."

"Do you really want a girl like that working for you?"

"A girl like what?"

"You know what . . . her history. You were the one who told me."

"She gets raped so now that means she can't work?"

Katrina's stony silence was a throwback to the days when we openly detested each other.

"I should be going," the baker said.

He stood up.

"Could you write down your phone number?" I said. "I mean, if D doesn't show up I might want to ask for your help."

"Sure," the helpful baker replied.

"I'll get pencil and paper," Katrina said.

She didn't want a confrontation with me; not over Mardi Bitterman, at any rate.

Bertrand stood there uncomfortably while I studied him. He could see that I didn't trust a stranger in my home. And he was right. I didn't know what trouble Dimitri was in. Maybe Bert was trying to get the lowdown on my son.

No words had passed between us while Katrina was gone. She returned with a Bic and a wire-ringed notepad.

"This was all I could find," she apologized.

Bert took the notepad and started scribbling.

"The first number is my cell phone," he said. "The second is the bakery, and I put down my e-mail address, too."

"You got a home phone?" I asked.

"No. Just the cell."

He shook my hand and my wife's hand. Katrina walked him to the door.

I remained in my seat, wondering if we lived on the eighteenth floor would I be retired by now.

16

My thoughts slowly merged with the pain behind my eye. I pressed a thumb against the bridge of my brow and the ache lessened maybe three decibels.

"Leonid," Katrina said.

The headache flared back.

"Yes?"

"What's wrong?"

"Nothing. It's just a twitch."

"I was hoping that we could talk," she said, lowering into the chair next to me.

"I swear Dimitri's fine," I said. "The only trouble he's got is girl trouble. And you know young men been runnin' after that since buckskins were in style."

"About us."

"What about us?" I said, wondering at the brightness of the pain.

"I've been back home for over a year now, Leonid."

"Yeah?"

"You're still so . . . distant."

I looked at my wife then. She was a few months past fifty-one, but regular exercise, spa treatments, and minor cosmetic surgery had kept most of her youthful beauty intact. Those pursed red lips could whisper the nastiest things in the dark of night.

It had been a long time since those lips had been next to my ear.

"It's not you, Katrina," I said. "It's, it's . . . you know how you read sometimes about men going through midlife crises?"

"Yes."

"I'm having a goddamned lifelong catastrophe. The ship is sunk and white-tipped sharks are headed my way."

"I don't understand," she said.

"You see these hands?" I asked, holding up my mitts.

"Yes?"

"They look normal, don't they? Just some big hands on a stout man. But if you look close you can see the blood on them. Blood and shit and, and, and maggots turnin' into flies. I wash 'em every night, and every morning they're filthy again."

"Is it because I left you for Andre?" she asked.

"No, baby, no. That's the dirt on you. That's your guilt."

"Why did you take me back if you don't love me?"

"Because you asked me to forgive you."

"But you never have."

The pain broke through some kind of barrier and now it was behind both my eyes. I lowered my face into those hands and grunted.

I stayed like that for a minute or two, and when I sat up Katrina was gone from the room.

I HAD THREE TABLETS of Tylenol with codeine in the medicine cabinet. A dentist gave them to me after a tooth extraction. I took one and sat in my office chair with the shades drawn, the lights turned out, and my eyes closed.

Thirty-seven minutes later, by my father's Timex, the only physical thing he left me, I opened my eyes.

The pain was still there but it was as if it had been sent to another room. I felt it through the wall, pulsing and singing red. But I could think again. I could concentrate through the bifocal lens of the medication.

I KEPT RON SHARKEY'S file in a locked cabinet next to my desk. It was quite thick, as it went back all the way to the time that I framed him and he was sent to prison.

I opened the folder to the first page but realized that thinking about Sharkey at that moment would break down the fragile wall the drug had erected. So instead I pulled out a file from Rinaldo's briefcase that I had not yet perused. It was labeled RELATIONS.

There were fourteen single-spaced typed pages, most with photographs paper-clipped to them, detailed synopses of Angie's friends, family, and daily acquaintances.

Paging through these names, I was even more aware of how dislocated I felt. It was as if the codeine had snagged in that moment of alienation that characterized my life.

Focusing on the subjects' professions, I decided on the one I was most likely to catch at that time of day. I studied his history and habits, his relationship to Angie, and his picture, taken without his knowledge.

"LEONID," SHE SAID AS I was about to go out the door.

"Yes?" I tried to sound friendly, open.

She had changed into a beige dress that accented her figure. Katrina had a figure that any man from twelve to a hundred and twelve could appreciate. The hem came down to the middle of her calf and the neckline did an arc just under the beginning of her cleavage.

"I'm sorry for what I said about Mardi. It's really very nice that you want to help her."

"That's Twill for you," I said. "He knew that Mardi needed a job to take care of her little sister, and that I needed someone to sit in my receptionist's chair. You know, his social worker told me that he could be president if he didn't have a record."

Usually Katrina loved talking about the virtues of her children. But she wasn't going to be sidetracked that afternoon.

"Will you at least try, and keep trying, to talk to me?" she asked.

That question was another kind of test. No . . . a final exam.

At first my body was facing the door, only my head was turned toward Katrina. But I rotated the full hundred and eighty degrees to appreciate her aggressive question. I could have apologized and said I'd try. But what difference would that have made? She wasn't going to leave and neither was I.

"What if I were to tell you that I came up behind a man and shot him in the head?" I said. "Left him leaking blood and brains in some back alley somewhere. What if I told you about a grieving widow and three little kids with no father or life insurance or friends to help them out? Is that the kind of talk you want to hear, Katrina? Is that what you want to share with me?"

My words were both truth and metaphor. I had never been an assassin. But I had destroyed whole families, regardless of that.

Katrina was testing me as I was going out the door to earn our rent and food. Instead of taking the exam, I gave her my own questions to ponder.

She winced at me. Behind her was the nimbus of my headache, some lost soul haunting me for reasons that put fear into my wife's eyes.

"You should go," she said. "We'll talk about this later."

BEING A BOXER, EVEN an amateur like me, one learns to deal with manifestations of pain and concussion. I walked down the street toward Central Park, dragging the headache and the drug-induced mental bifurcation behind me like the chains of lifelong servitude. That's why, for so long, black men dominated boxing. That ring encompassed our entire lives. We were in training from the day we were born.

I entered the park at Eighty-sixth Street and found my regular route. It was a bit off the beaten path, mostly quiet. There were a couple of teenagers getting high on a boulder, and two lovers, whom I heard but did not see, coming to the partially stifled climax of their lovemaking as I walked by.

A big white guy in tattered clothes came up to me when I was almost to the East Side.

"Gimme a dollar, man," he said.

There were arcane tattoos on his hands and face, and probably the rest of him too; old blue and red and yellow stains that had begun to fade and spread.

"Say what?" I asked.

"I said gimme a dollar. And hurry it up before I make it five."

"I tell you what, mothahfuckah. You come here and take it from me."

"I got a knife in my pocket," he warned.

I couldn't help but smile.

17

I emerged from the park without having to resort to physical violence. The big white guy read my smile the way Barack Obama
read the hearts of the American people.

The torch had passed. The old intimidation and fear-mongering
had given way to a kind of diplomacy . . . with teeth.

ON SIXTY-NINTH, ON THE far East Side, was a twelve-story building that
had a tennis court on the roof. There well-heeled men and women
rented one of the three courts for $120 per half-hour to play tennis
under a Manhattan sun or moon.

Shad Tandy taught those who could afford his rates how to
strengthen their backhands and their serves.

According to the records given me by Rinaldo, Shad was the
son of a woman who once had been wealthy. She was poor now
but somehow had managed to get her son into the right schools
on scholarships and spit. He had the pedigree and manicure of a
young Kennedy and the bank account of the man who tried to take
my dollar in the park.

Shad was a shade under six feet, with sandy hair and deep-brown
eyes. He had the lithe body of a tennis player, with strong legs and
lean arms.

The middle-aged woman he was teaching was thrilled to have

him hug her from behind to show how the backhand felt in its execution. I was sure that she paid the four dollars a minute just for that physical closeness once, or maybe twice, a week.

I sat at a table which stood upon a synthetic patch of grass reserved for those waiting to use the courts. I had paid for an impromptu lesson from the thirty-year-old Tandy. The country was going through a serious recession and there were many gaps in the schedule of the courts. I had a briefcase full of money, and so the $120 was nothing to me.

"Can I get you something to drink, Mr. McGill?" Lorna Filomena asked.

The twenty-year-old brunette wore a fetching white tennis outfit replete with short-short skirt, white tennis shoes, and bluish ankle socks.

"You got some cognac in that cabinet?" I asked her.

"No, sir," she said, still smiling, "we only have bottles of water."

"Sparkling?"

"Flat."

"Why not?" I said. "Man cannot live by bread alone."

She went to the door that led to the elevator and bent over. From somewhere she came out with a small bottle of Evian.

Handing me the chilled plastic container, she asked, "Are you really here to play tennis?"

"Why? Don't I look like a tennis player?"

"People don't usually play in a suit and street shoes."

"Don't you like my suit?"

"It's really very nice," she said, putting a spin on the third word to show that she meant what she said. "But it's just not tennis wear."

"Why would I have given you all that money if I didn't want to learn?" I asked.

"I don't know," Lorna speculated. "You asked for Mr. Tandy by name, and I've heard that he's had trouble with people he owes money to."

The playful tone didn't disguise the girl's dislike of Shad Tandy.

"I look like a leg-breaker to you?" I asked.

"I don't know." She leaned against the wall and cocked her head. She really was *very* pretty. "You sure don't look like a tennis player."

"Who does he owe money to?" I asked.

"Shad's mother is a total bitch," Miss Filomena said. "She has to live like she's rich, but her family lost their money before Shad was born. His father's still in jail. Shad's always doing something to get money. Sometimes maybe he goes too far."

"Did you and Shad have a thing?"

She thought for six seconds or so, decided that she didn't have anything to lose, and said, "Yeah, we did. He gave me all kinds of trinkets and told me even more lies. Then his mother said I wasn't good enough, and he cried when he told me it was over."

"So if I was here to beat a few dollars out of him you wouldn't exactly mind?"

"It would probably take me ten minutes to get to the phone to call the police."

I like honesty in the people I talk to. Nine times out of eleven, truth trumps good intentions.

"Hey, Lorna," Shad Tandy said.

He was running up to us. His middle-aged student had disappeared from the court.

"This is your next lesson, Shad," she said in a very friendly, even perky, tone. "Mr. McGill is a walk-in but I knew you wanted the classes."

They had certainly been lovers. Shad heard the threat in her pleasant voice. He looked at me, saw what she had seen, considered running, and then decided I might catch him, or shoot him in the back, if he tried. He glanced at Lorna, hoping that she just wanted to see his sweat, not his blood.

"Have a seat, Mr. Tandy," I said. "They serve a good water here."

The cell phone vibrated in my pocket but I ignored the request.

"You're here for a lesson, Mr. McGill?"

A door closed and Shad looked up quickly. Lorna had gone and shut us in on the roof. There was no one else there.

When he turned his attention back to me I was staring daggers.

"You owe a lot of money, son," I said.

"I got it. I got the whole twenty-five hundred. He, he, he said I had to the end of the week. Mr. Meeks said I had till Friday."

My gaze didn't waver.

"I don't have the money on me," he said. "It's in a safe deposit box. But I can get it."

I looked so deathly certain to the tennis pro he must've thought that I was planning to push him off the roof.

"Where is Angelique Lear?" I asked.

Shad's tanned white skin went suddenly pale. His fear deepened with a sense of the unknown.

"I don't understand," he said.

"Angelique. I want to know where she is."

"But, but . . ."

He leaped from his chair. I lunged, too, hitting him on the cheekbone with a schoolbook right-hand lead. Shad fell and stood . . . then fell again. It was the kind of punch that catches up with you as the moments click by.

Shad was on his back with his hands up over his face.

"I don't understand," he said. "I already told Grant. That's where I got the money to pay Meeks."

"Mr. Meeks," I reminded.

Shad's lips trembled.

The phone vibrated in my pocket.

"What did you tell Grant?"

"That, that, that Angie had broken up with me a few weeks ago. . . . But then she called me the other night to borrow some money. She said that she was at her friend Wanda's house."

It bothered me that this coward would call Angelique by the nickname I decided on.

"Stand up," I said.

He did so.

I knocked him down again.

"Do you know what happened at Wanda's place?" I asked the bleeding young man.

"No. What happened?"

I answered him with threatening silence.

"Angie had been moving around a lot," Shad whined, "and Grant said that he had the answer to a scholarship she'd applied for. I didn't see anything wrong with that."

"Did you call her to tell her that he was coming?"

"He said that he wanted it to be a surprise."

"Stand up."

"No."

"Where is this Grant?"

Shad tried to crawl away on his back, looking very much like the worm he was.

"I can get down on my knees to beat you, boy."

"He met me here. Paid for a lesson, just like you did, only he had the right clothes. After the lesson he bought me a drink and asked about Angie."

"Didn't that make you suspicious?"

"I needed the money. He said it had to do with a grant. That wasn't unusual. Angie was always getting grants and stipends. She's the luckiest person I know."

"What did he look like?"

"Bald, white, maybe forty."

"What was his first name?"

"I don't know. Maybe Grant was his first name."

I could have broken his jaw with a well-placed kick. I certainly wanted to.

"Have you heard from Angelique since last night?"

"No. No."

"If you do," I said, "and you tell anyone—anyone—I will come back here and throw your sorry ass off the roof. Do you understand me?"

Shad nodded, sniffling some of the blood back up into his nostrils.

18

Lorna was waiting on the other side of the door.

"Do I have to call an ambulance or something?" the sweet young thing asked.

"He can walk and talk all right," I said. "He might need an ice pack and a towel."

"Let his mother give him that," she said.

ON THE STREET I looked at the fancy phone that my self-titled telephonic and computer personal assistant (TCPA), Zephyra Ximenez, had provided me with. Breland Lewis had called four times.

I went into a chain coffee shop and ordered herbal tea. I needed something calming so that the violence coursing through me didn't overtake my good sense. Six sips after sitting at a small round table I inhaled deeply and sat back against the wall.

I missed smoking . . . very much. A cigarette calmed me down more than a quart of chamomile tea and thirty minutes of zazen sitting combined. But tobacco also cut down on my breath, and a good wind was a necessity in my line of work. The kind of situations I got into could run a regular guy ragged.

Twenty minutes or so after I bloodied Shad's face I entered my lawyer's ten digits.

"Breland Lewis, attorney at law," a mature female voice recited.

"It's Leonid, Shirley."

She didn't even say hello, just patched the call through.

"Leonid?"

"What's the big deal, Breland?"

"It's Sharkey. I think you better see him tonight, or at the latest by tomorrow morning."

"Why's that?"

"I need you to get some feel for what we're getting into. These new charges have a federal spin on them. He's expecting you."

"You told him about me?"

"I said your name was John Tooms. He thinks you work for me, that I'm sending you over to help out."

RON SHARKEY WAS PART of the past that I'd never shake.

The first time I heard of him was from a man named Bob Beam. Beam offered $7,500 to get his business partner in trouble with the law.

"All I need is for him to get fouled up on some charge that would make him have to come up with ten thousand dollars or so," he told me in my office—I was set up on an upper floor of the Chrysler Building at that time.

Beam was a squat, wide-faced white man. He smiled like a satrap sitting on a mound of silk pillows.

"Why?" I asked.

Beam was suggested to me by a technology smuggler named Frog Cornbluth. It was a valid reference but Frog's endorsement didn't come with any insurance and so I wanted specific details in case it blew up in my face.

"Ron and I own a company that imports chip boards," Beam told me. "The last time I did a run to Beijing I was told by a reliable source that a large company there was thinking of buying us out. That could mean millions. I'm still in deep debt from my last business and I'm only a junior partner in the company. My profit would be gone before I got the chance to count it."

"So how will getting Ron into trouble help that?" I wasn't outraged by the suggestion. This was business as usual for me.

"Just enough trouble to make him have to get a lawyer. I happen to know that money's tight for him. I'll offer to buy some of his stock at a cut-rate price and then enjoy the windfall when the company's sold to Wing Lee."

It turned out that Ron made regular trips to Toronto to visit a small computer company that they supplied. I wondered aloud if there might be a way to secrete an illegal substance in the toe of a shoe in his suitcase. Bob, smiling broadly, said that that would be no problem.

I had a friend who had a friend who worked a regular job in international airport security. A call was made and Ron Sharkey's bags were searched. The drug was discovered. But it was closer to a pound than the agreed-upon two grams.

Ron signed a power of attorney over to Irma, his wife. She attempted to make the deal with Bob but something about his financial status scotched the trade before the money made it into Irma's account.

Bob didn't tell me that he was having an affair with Ron's wife. Irma told Ron that she couldn't raise the money and that she didn't want to threaten their son's future by selling the only property they had—their house. Ron, being a good sort, said he understood and made a deal with the federal prosecutor to accept an eight-year sentence—with no chance for parole.

By that time I was out of the loop but I learned what happened after the fact.

Bob was hired by Wing Lee to stay on as president of the company, keeping his junior share. Irma divorced Ron and married Bob. Three years later Bob died of a heart attack and Irma remarried. This third husband embezzled from the thriving new chip-board company and ran down to Brazil.

In the meanwhile, Ron had been broken by a system that produced more hardened criminals than it ever took in. The one-time honest businessman had been the bitch of half a dozen lifelong criminals. The monotony and terror of incarceration had made him a drug addict. On the outside he became a low-level dealer and half-assed burglar.

After I saw the error of my ways I started keeping tabs on the innocents that I'd torn down. When Ron got out I hired Breland to go to him, give him a little money and his card. Whenever Ron got into trouble, Breland was there to represent him in court. I had spent over ten thousand dollars keeping Ron from going back to prison.

"WHAT'S HE INTO NOW?" I asked my lawyer as I sipped the lukewarm tea.

The headache was playing in the background like a Wagnerian intermezzo.

"I don't know all the details yet. I was busy and had one of my associates go down to bail him out. But it seems like he was caught driving a car with a small amount of drugs in his pocket and some serious guns in the trunk."

"Who would trust Sharkey with something like that?"

"He says that he found the car parked on the street with the key in the ignition. That he was going to pick up his girlfriend and drive to Cape Cod because she used to live out there."

"Did the car have any registration?"

"No. Nothing. It was NYPD that picked him up to begin with, but you can bet that the feds will be on the trail before too long. If he goes to court it will be long and drawn out. You'll spend a hundred thousand dollars and he'll go to prison anyway."

"Where is he now?"

"At his girlfriend's place, way over on Avenue C."

I took down the address and stayed in my seat, wondering if there would ever come a time when life would get easier and I could relax.

19

It was somewhere between five and six but the night had already come on under the domination of daylight savings. I definitely did not want to go home. And so a train ride down the East Side was called for.

I had never met nor had I even seen Ron Sharkey. I knew him by his picture and his predilections, his choices and mistakes. Ron Sharkey was a part of me, the man I had to save in order to look at myself in the mirror in the morning. He wasn't the only one, but he was certainly one of the squeakiest wheels.

WILMA SPYRES LIVED ON the top floor of an eight-story brick building that had been painted turquoise for no apparent reason. The buzzer was broken, as was the lock on the downstairs front door.

Some doors to apartments were open down the hall. TV shows, food smells, and voices assailed me as I made my way to the elevator. It was broken, too, and so I took the stairs. I ran across a young man and woman injecting each other with what I assumed to be some kind of opiate on the fourth-floor landing. She was dirty blond and probably white, while he had a New World Hispanic tint to his skin. They gauged me as either a threat or a mark and finally decided to ignore my passing.

Wilma's door was a dingy white. The paint upon it was thick

and cracked. I imagined that every time it got too dirty the super just whitewashed over the filth.

"Who is it?" a woman said in answer to my knock.

"John Tooms. Breland Lewis sent me."

"Who?"

I repeated my words.

"Who is it?"

It felt as if I were in a Cheech and Chong skit.

"I'm here to speak to Ron Sharkey for his lawyer. My name is John Tooms."

Muted voices sounded from down the hall. Smells of cooking rose from the floors below. Four different kinds of music came from a dozen sound systems of varying quality, and now and then traffic sounds broke through from the street below.

The door opened.

A woefully frail and slender woman stood there before me. She wasn't a day over twenty-nine but her brown hair was already shot through with gray. Her breath came in laconic gasps and her green eyes hadn't been clear in a very long time. For all that, you could see that she was once quite fetching.

"Can't you people leave him alone?" she asked without much conviction.

"I'm here to help Ron, Ms. Spyres. I'm working for his lawyer."

The skin of Wilma's face pulled back, creating a scowl intended to express her disdain for lawyers and their toadies. I couldn't, in all conscience, disagree. The wordless grimace told me that no one had ever wanted to help her, or any man she laid claim to.

"May I come in?"

"What do you want?"

"I just need to go over a few details with Ron. That's all."

Her shoulders shook. The scowl was trying to obliterate me.

"Will," a man said.

Ron Sharkey came up from behind her.

He was on the short side but still two inches taller than Wilma and me. He wore gray slacks that were too big for him and green suspenders to hold them up. His grayish-white T-shirt was frayed, and his feet were bare, pale creatures.

He rested his hands on the woman's shoulders and said, "Lewis sent you?"

I nodded and maybe frowned some.

"What was your name again?"

"John Tooms."

"Come on in, Mr. Tunes. Don't worry about Will here. She doesn't bite."

The living room was furnished with mismatched couch and chair, both covered over with dark-colored and stained sheets. The coffee table was a rude wooden crate turned upside down. There was a bong and a hypodermic set on the makeshift piece of furniture.

"Give me and Mr. Tunes a few minutes, will you, honey?" Ron said to his woman.

She snorted and then lurched through a doorway that I supposed led to their bedroom.

Ron closed the door after her.

"Have a seat, Mr. Tunes," he offered.

There was a fold-up wooden chair leaning in the corner. Thinking about the apparent stains and hidden needles, I took that for my seat.

"Tooms," I said.

"Say what?"

"My name is Tooms, not Tunes."

"Sorry. How can I help you, Mr. Tunes?"

He tried to sit on the crate but it cracked a little and so he moved to the couch. There he sank deeply in the dark-maroon fabric.

"I do specialized work for Breland," I said. "He thinks you might need some help getting out of the trouble you're in."

"No. Naw. Not me. He got me out on bail. I'll just do a plea or something. I won't even get any time. I mean, it wasn't even my car."

"Whose car was it?" I asked.

"Listen, Mr. Tunes. I'm okay. Nobody's gonna worry about a little fish like me. All I have to do is tell the judge that I found that car with the keys inside and took it for a ride. That's the way it happened. I'm really okay."

"There was contraband in the trunk," I said.

"Not mine."

"But we can safely say that it belonged to someone," I replied. "From what I understand, there was a lot of money wrapped up in that property."

Sharkey began pumping his left heel up and down like a sweatshop seamstress working a mechanical sewing machine.

"I didn't know about what was in the trunk."

"Somebody does," I said. "And the feds will want to get hold of that information. They're gonna lean on you . . . heavily."

Ron had a boy's face. It had aged many years past what it should have been but he still had that innocent, adolescent look.

"Look, man," he said, "somebody in my position can't worry about what might happen. I mean, look at me. Somethin's bound to get to me sooner or later anyway. I mean, I don't even know how I ended up like this. I was supposed to be an entrepreneur selling computer components and spending my summers in Bermuda or Bimini. Now I'm rolling my own cigarettes and lookin' up to Wilma because at least she can put the rent together almost every month."

I wanted to say something but had no words.

"You could do me a favor, though," Ron said.

"What's that?"

"My wife. My ex-wife. Irma."

"What about her?"

"I asked Breland to find her for me but he said he couldn't do it. You know, I'd really like to find her . . . to tell her how sorry I am for destroying her life. She has my son. I'd like to see Steven before I die."

How would it help, I wondered, to tell him that his loving Irma had betrayed him and put the drugs into his shoe?

"Her last name is Carson now," Ron was saying. "Her maiden name was Connors, then Sharkey, Beam, and finally Carson. I guess that's why it's so hard to find her."

"I can look into it, I guess." What else could I say?

"Hey, man," Ron said with deep feeling. "That would be great."

20

I left Wilma's apartment in a foul mood. The young lovers were still on the fourth-floor landing. They were huddled in each other's arms, pressed into a corner. His eyes were closed as she watched me walk by. Looking into her distant eyes, I tasted blood.

I'd been biting my lower lip that hard.

ON THE STREET I looked at my watch. The blue iridescent hands told me that it was 7:07. I figured I was on a roll and so trundled over to a liquor store I knew on Bowery and picked up a pint of cheap scotch. When buying scotch I always looked for the lowest price. Why spend good money when you hate the taste? For me, bourbon was king, while scotch was a mere pretender to the throne.

I CAME TO A building a little farther down on C that was dark even for the buildings in that neighborhood. There was a buzzer, though.

"Yes?" a mature woman said through the speaker.

"Mrs. Lear?"

"Yes?"

"My name is Tooms. I'm looking for your daughter."

"What do you want with her?"

"A man named Spender asked me to find her," I said, using a

name from Rinaldo's files. "She hasn't been to work in a few days and he's worried."

"Did you call her?"

I rattled off her home number. I had, of course called it; no answer, no answering machine.

"I also went by her place on Twelfth," I added. "So I'm here to ask you."

For a while silence ruled our conversation. In the heartland of our nation, I've been told, people are happy to meet you and sit and talk. But in New York, a stranger's voice is, at the very least, a potential threat—definitely possible.

"Why are you looking for her?" Mrs. Lear asked at last.

"May I come up, ma'am?"

"I don't know who you are."

"Tooms, ma'am. I'm working for Larry Spender . . . Angelique's boss."

"Yes," she said, "Spender." Her "S" got stuck for a second more than she intended.

A buzzer sounded and I pushed the door open.

It was a much tidier building than the one Ron Sharkey inhabited. The halls smelled of mold, but I found no people shooting up in the stairwells. On the fourth floor there were small welcome mats in front of each apartment door. When I got to 4C, a willowy woman in her middle forties was standing there, peering out, ready to slam the door at a moment's notice.

She was wearing an off-white dress that fit her slender form from habit—not intention. Her face had aged past the forty-six years that Rinaldo's records said she was, but you could see hints of the beauty that once was there.

"That's a nice gold suit you have," she said as I came to a stop.

"Thanks. My wife made me buy it." I glanced down at the

sleeves to see if any of Shad Tandy's blood was there—none that I could see.

"She has good taste."

"In everything but men."

"Come on in," she said, charmed by a joke.

The living room was small and well lived in. The furniture had been new when the deliverymen hefted it up the three flights, but it would be called secondhand now. There were small moth holes in the curtains, a lot of them, and three dead plants in as many pots.

The floor was swept and the walls had no dents, scars, or other markings. The once white paint had faded and darkened, but uniformly so.

There was no sofa or couch, just three stuffed chairs that faced each other across a small glass-topped table.

"Have a seat, Mr. . . . ?"

"Tooms."

"I wish I could offer you something to drink, Mr. T-Tooms. But my bar is empty."

Before sitting I pulled the pint bottle out of my pocket and set it on the glass table. This brought a light into the senior Lear's murky brown eyes.

"Oh," she said, straightening her shoulders. "I'll go get us a bucket of ice and some crystal."

She left the room, and I silently thanked Christian Latour for his diligence in collecting information on the people Rinaldo had him look into. It was the fruit of his research, I was sure, that had said Mrs. Lear was a *heavy drinker who preferred scotch.*

The lady's living room was filled with warm, dark color. It was like another time; not the past necessarily, but a period that only certain people inhabited—not my kind. My world smelled of sweat and smog, while Lizette Lear's was a world of potpourri, peach pie, and mothballs.

"Here you go," she said, bringing in two squat glasses and a white plastic bucket on a silver-plated tray.

She seemed to have some trouble with her left hip so I helped her set the platter down on the table.

"Ice, Mr. Tooms?" There was color in her cheek and the beauty that had shriveled over the years now seemed to be blossoming once more.

"A lot of it," I said. "Please."

The ice clinked and Lizette's smile threatened to become a laugh. She cracked the seal, poured my drink and hers. She drained her glass, sighed, and poured another.

Along with the relief flowed beauty. I had never seen anything like it. Lizette curled back in the chair and her body seemed to become young again, supple, even enticing. She looked into my eyes and for a moment I forgot why I was there.

"Angelique," I said, as much to remind myself as to pull away from Lizette's instantaneous charms.

Mrs. Lear smiled, downed the second glass, and tossed her mouse-brown hair.

"She's an amazing human being," she said. "Pretty, smart, certain about what she wants. And she always gets it."

Lizette poured a third drink.

"Do you know where she is?" I asked.

"No. No, I don't. But you can be sure that wherever she is she's another step closer to something else she wants."

You couldn't help but note the jealousy in her words.

"You aren't worried that she's missing?"

"Not at all." She finished the third shot and poured another. "Angie makes silk from straw, sows' ears, and bad boyfriends. . . . If I wasn't a good Christian I'd say she was a witch. She doesn't approve of me. Doesn't like my drinking. Blames me for her father leaving."

"Where is her father?" There was no mention of him in Rinaldo's files.

"I don't know," Lizette said, gazing up at the ceiling. She was rounding pretty and making a run for beautiful. "He rolled into my life, made me jump for joy, and then was gone before I hit the ground. Angelique doesn't have an ounce of him, and less than a pound of me, in her makeup. She has an old soul, that one."

"Do you know her boyfriend?"

"Johnny," Lizette said with a smile. The mention of this new name brought her into full blossom.

"I thought his name was Shad. Shad Tandy."

"Shad Tandy?" It was as if I'd shoved a sour lemon against her teeth. "He's just a momentary mistake for my girl. Her true love is a young man named John Prince. He's an architect. Probably walks on water, too. He and Angie break up now and again, but they always get back together."

"Do you have a number for him?" I asked.

"Sure." She finished her fourth shot, stood up, none too steady, and lumbered toward a door.

While she was gone I allowed myself a smile. There was no John Prince mentioned in Rinaldo's files. I liked that. It let me feel that I had a leg up on the Big Man.

When she returned, Mrs. Lear had forsaken the off-white dress for a flimsy robe. She was only in her forties, after all. She liked drinks, and men; I represented both.

"I can't seem to find it. Must have thrown it out in one of my cleaning binges. But you can probably look it up."

"Do you know where he works?" I asked as she slumped back into her chair.

"For an architectural firm. I'm sorry . . . I don't know which one."

"That's okay."

"You haven't touched your drink," Lizette chided.

"On the job," I said. "What do you do for a living, ma'am?"

"Lizette."

"What do you do for a living, Lizette?"

"I haven't had a job for a while, Mr. Tooms. What's your first name?"

"John."

"I haven't had a job in a while, John. My nerves, you know. Angie helps me out with the rent, and she has groceries delivered every Monday and Thursday. She doesn't give me any cash, though. If I want a cigarette I have to bum one on the street."

"She must do very well at her job."

"She told me that someone gave her a grant or something, and she's using part of that to help me. You'd think she could give me a few bucks, though. A bottle of wine now and then isn't such a sin. . . ."

"Maybe you and me could go out for a little swizzle."

"Maybe some other time," I said, rising to my feet.

"Do you have to go already?"

"I need to find your daughter."

"Angie's fine. She's like a cat."

Lizette wanted to stand up but her body wasn't accommodating the desire.

"Will you come back again?"

"When I find Angie I'll come back and tell you."

"Angie," Lizette said with a sneer.

As I went out the door I heard her mutter, "Bitch."

21

It wasn't much after eight when I left Lizette's hungry cave. From there my feet took me down the street to the Naked Ear.

The Ear was busier that evening. Large groups of young and not so young people hovered around the bar, drinking and talking, laughing and trying to get the bartender's attention.

I wedged my solid bulk between two women in identical blue dresses, said *Excuse me* to a man who was laughing so hard that he couldn't take a sip from his glass.

Finally I sidled up to the bar next to a middle-aged man who was reading *The New York Times*.

"Anything happening?" I asked.

"Not yet," he said, refusing to look at me. "Everybody's waiting for January twentieth like early Christians waiting for the end of time."

There are very few rules I adhere to. In my line of work you can't let something from yesterday keep you from right now. But one thing I never do is talk politics with strangers in bars.

"You're McGill, right?" a woman said.

The bartender that night had black hair and shocking cobalt eyes. She'd been the runner-up to beauty her entire life, but the judges always left the party with her.

"Cynthia," I said, reaching back into my memory.

"Cylla," she said. "You were close."

"Not bartender close."

"Lucy said to tell you that she had to take off tonight but she'd be back on duty tomorrow."

I felt the twinge of unrequited infatuation where instinct told me my heart was.

"Three cognacs, right?" Cylla said.

"Yeah."

"Find a seat and I'll bring them to you."

THE OUTER CIRCLE OF the bar was never heavily inhabited, even on the busiest nights. When the Ear got going, ninety percent of the clientele thronged around the bar like youngsters in a mosh pit.

I found a small round table near a couple of young smoochers. Their love transported them. The beers were glasses of red wine and the table was outside on the Champs-Élysées *en été*.

Ignoring the lovers, I tried to understand the life of Angelique Tara Lear. Her boyfriend had betrayed her. Her mother, whom she supported, called her a bitch. Her friend had been murdered, maybe in her stead, and the most powerful man in New York seemed to be obsessed with her every move and acquaintance. Few people did that much living in an entire decade.

My phone made the sound of Chinese wind chimes.

"Hey, Zephrya. Guess where I am."

"Looks like the Naked Ear."

"'Looks like'?"

"You got the GPS turned on on your phone again," she said. "I could tell you exactly where you were in Beijing or Timbuktu."

Zephyra Ximenez was my lifeline in the electronic dimensions. I rarely saw her. Ninety-nine-point-nine percent of her work was on the phone or online. She had a Dominican mother and Moroccan father—lineages, when combined, that gave her dark red-black skin and the kind of look that defines rather than trails after beauty.

I had met her at the Ear and tried to pick her up, but she didn't have a father complex. When I told her about my work she offered me her professional services.

In the long run that was a much better deal for both of us.

"The police are after you, Mr. McGill," she said.

"Say what?"

"Lieutenant Bonilla—the last time I talked to her she was a sergeant—and Detective Kitteridge have both called and demanded your presence."

"What did you tell them?"

"That I would pass the information on as soon as possible."

"I hired a receptionist," I said. "A young woman named Mardi Bitterman."

"Really? Wow. With me, Bug Bateman, and now this Mardi, you almost have a real office."

"Yeah. From now on you can call her during business hours when you can't get me."

"Your drinks," Cylla said.

She had brought them on an old-fashioned dark-brown tray that was lined with cork.

"Is that Cylla?" Zephyra asked.

"It is."

"Let me speak to her a minute, will you, boss?"

While the young women chattered, I took my first nip of brandy and wondered at the zinging feeling in my chest. It made me happy to see Cylla laughing with Zephyra. I wanted the same youthful abandon for Angie but didn't have high hopes.

I LEFT THE BAR about midnight and walked for a while. I honestly didn't realize that I was headed for Lucy's block until I was standing there in front of her building.

The light was on in her apartment. There was jazz coming from somewhere else. I was a teenager, drunk on his first forbidden bender and smitten with passion for a girl.

At my age this feeling was better than love. It was the moment before you really knew the object of affection. Her nipples and the sounds she made in her sleep were still in the province of the unknown. She had no secrets because she was, in herself, a mystery. I had no hold on her because she hadn't yet offered me one.

Standing outside her place, I had two choices: one of them was to ring her bell.

I took out my phone, disengaged the GPS, and entered a number.

"Lieutenant Bonilla," she answered on the third ring.

"You wanted to see me, Lieutenant?"

WE MET AT A little after-hours joint on Eighty-first. The bar closed at one but the owner stayed open for cops and special regulars.

Bonilla was already there when I arrived. She was sitting in a faded red booth, wearing a steel-gray pants suit that had a definite masculine flair.

I sat down across from her and nodded.

"Have you talked to Kitteridge?" were her first words.

"Not since a while ago. He wanted me to come in this afternoon but I demurred."

"You know, you shouldn't take Carson lightly."

The lady cop was offering me good advice. She was intuitive, working outside the rote demands of her profession. She understood that there was a conflict going on in me.

Carson Kitteridge was the only innately honest senior cop I had ever dealt with. It was in his job definition to bring me to justice, whatever that meant. For all that, he played by the rules. He would never take somebody down except by the letter of the law. But Bethann Bonilla was even more rare. She had empathy for me; no love, or even real concern, just a feeling for what I was.

"What do you have on the murders, Mr. McGill?"

"I'm not on that case, Lieutenant. I don't even know what the papers say about it because I haven't had the time to sit down and read them."

"What are you working on?"

"Nothing criminal."

"Does it have to do with Wanda Soa?"

"Not that I know of."

"Then what were you doing at her apartment?"

"I've already explained that."

"Do you expect me to believe that you haven't wondered?"

"Listen," I said. "If you come to work tomorrow and nobody in the city has committed a crime, you still get paid. You could get shot in the leg and have to take six months off and they will send you a check every two weeks. I, on the other hand, have to sweat over every dollar. I don't have time to worry about some woman who called me. I don't have the luxury to be inquisitive."

"This case has Charbon very worried," she said.

That was a threat. Captain James Charbon was oil on my water. He was my own personal ton of bricks. Kitteridge just wanted me in the jail; James Charbon wanted me under it.

"What is it you're trying to get from me?" I asked. I had to.

"Anything you know."

"Okay. I want you to listen to me. I had never heard of that woman before you told me her name. I got a call but I can't be expected to identify a dead woman's voice. Maybe if you explain to me the problem I could try to find out what you need."

"There's nothing but problems. Soa's apartment was party central. We lifted eighty-six different prints from the living room alone. On the walls, on the floors, under the couch. Women and men, maybe even children. Prints everywhere but on the knife. It was wiped off with some kind of cloth that we didn't find at the scene. The gun was gone, too."

"Do you have a scenario of how the man was killed?"

"We figure that the John Doe was pointing the gun at Wanda when someone blindsided him, stabbing him in the chest. Problem was the gun went off, killing the girl. The killer fell dead right after."

"And," I continued, "the second killer wiped their prints off the haft and then took the pistol . . . maybe for protection."

"That's how we see it. The guy was a professional. No ID. He didn't even have labels in his clothes."

"Not much to go on," I said.

"And if I don't come up with something you can bet that Captain Charbon will dump it on you."

"If anything comes up," I said, "anything at all, I will tell either you or Carson."

"It's my case."

"Then I'll tell you."

22

It was after two when I got home. I couldn't imagine subjecting myself to the test of the stairs, so I took the elevator and opened the front door quietly, hung the hideous yellow suit on the rack in my den, and then lay down on the daybed, sighing like a black bear on the first day of hibernation. I'd only had five little glasses of cognac, but at my age, and at that hour, it was enough to make the world around me jiggle and spin—on the verge of flying apart.

Bonilla presented me with a serious problem that I identified with my seemingly permanent headache.

Captain James Charbon didn't like the stink of me. He was a hardworking official who had many open cases, and so most of the time he left me alone. But when there was an investigation on his desk—one that had my name anywhere attached—he became hell-bent on getting me charged with something, anything.

This passion was brought about by extraordinary conceit.

When Charbon was a detective working the street he prided himself on a nearly perfect success rate.

I was the one exception.

A woman I knew named Lana Stride had been indicted for her involvement in the murder of a Park Avenue psychiatrist. She was guilty, the police said, of finding and giving to Brooks Sanders the name of the mental-health professional who had persuaded Brooks's wife to seek a divorce. If Lana had considered her actions she would have probably known what Brooks would do. But Lana was a lush and didn't remember what she'd done.

Sammy Stride, Lana's brother, offered me $2,500 to find Lana an alibi. It just so happened that I had once done a barely legal job for a state senator who Lana told me she knew when she was a cocktail hostess. Using the chit for a job done gratis, I asked the good legislator to tell the police, on behalf of our mutual acquaintance, that he was with her on the afternoon that Brooks had said she told him about the shrink and his wife.

State senator trumps confessed murderer 12,341 times to 1.

The senior officer on the case, James Charbon, had been looking to return the favor for seven years. From the moment he found out, from Carson Kitteridge, that I was a close confidant of Lana's brother, he made it a lifelong goal to hobble me.

Luckily I was mildly inebriated and exhausted from a frustrating day of weak leads, so Charbon felt like a faraway threat that could be managed—later.

I turned on my side.

The killing of Wanda Soa was a mistake, but it was professional, still and all. The killer had been paid by somebody. And that somebody, I was pretty sure, was not Alphonse Rinaldo. It could have been a man named Grant, who paid good money to Shad Tandy, but maybe not. Grant could have been working for Rinaldo. He might have gotten the address to be passed on to me.

I closed my eyes and lay deathlike in my wife-beater and boxers. I thought about Lizette Lear leaving her house every night for some neighborhood bar where there were cigarettes and men and alcohol, all variables in an equation that often altered but never changed.

After a night of carousing, Lizette would find herself coming back to consciousness in a hospital, the drunk tank, or, if it was a lucky night, maybe she'd awaken to nausea in her own bed. But whenever she opened her eyes, Angie would be there to wipe her face and hold her hand.

I so closely identified with the feeling that I opened my eyes to break the hermeneutic connection.

Katrina was sitting next to me in a chair that she must have pulled up. I hadn't heard the movement. I had been dreaming, not thinking.

"What's wrong?" she asked.

"Bad dream," I said.

"Why are you sleeping out here, Leonid?"

"I didn't, I didn't want to wake you."

"How do you feel?"

I sat up, experiencing a host of physical symptoms: my hands were hot, feet cold, head still hurt, and my stomach felt like a child's balloon filled with water and ready to burst.

"I'm just fine," I said.

Neither of us spoke for a time. I could hear the folding alarm clock ticking on my desk. Those were the seconds of my life creeping sideways into a vast unknown.

"I'm worried about Dimitri," Katrina said. She was worried about a lot of things, but our brooding son was always the most important.

"Not Twill?" I asked.

"Don't bait me, Leonid."

"Twilliam is the one risking getting thrown back into kid jail in order to be with his brother," I said. "He's the one taking chances."

"Dimitri is your son." It was the closest she'd ever come to admitting Twill and Shelly were other men's offspring.

"I have to lie down."

"I'm going to call the police."

"And what will you tell them?"

"That our son is missing."

"I spoke to him today."

"He hasn't talked to me."

"If you call the cops the least that will happen is that Twill will be sent back to juvie. If they're into something shaky, they both might go."

"Dimitri is a good boy," Katrina intoned.

"He's with Twill, honey, and you know what Twill is like."

Silence reigned for a while. I put a hot hand on my cold, bald, aching head.

"Come to bed," Katrina said, capitulating.

"I don't think that's a very good idea. Let me just lie back down here and I promise I will get your son to call you as soon as possible, hopefully tomorrow."

With that I lay back on the daybed, a vampire lowering into his coffin, a mummy into dust.

I WAS SICK IN the shower the next morning but stayed under the icy November waters until the hangover was filed into memory with all its hundreds of brothers.

Shelly and Katrina were still asleep when I left the apartment at 7:47.

I had fried pork chops, scrambled eggs, and two triple espressos at a diner on Fifty-seventh. The wonderful thing about knowing you won't die of old age is that you can enjoy the wrong things in life without trepidation or guilt.

I ARRIVED AT THE advertising agency of Laughton and Price at 9:17. Their main offices are a few blocks south of Hunter College, on the seventh floor of an old stone building.

I was feeling pretty good but not yet ready for stairs.

The elevator opened on a glass door that was watched over by a young caramel-colored receptionist who sat at a desk, which, in turn, sat behind a short copper wall.

I waved.

She glowered.

I smiled.

Her resolve faltered.

I hunched my shoulders and she pressed the buzzer.

"Good morning," I said, pressing my thighs against the copper wall.

"May I help you?"

She was American, no doubt, but at least one of her parents, I was sure, had come from a British island in the Caribbean. One of the joys of living in New York is that there are so many types of black people here. Africans, Islanders, upper and lower classes, professionals, southerners, and any combination of the afore-mentioned.

"Saint Lucia?" I said.

"What?"

"Your parents. Are they from Saint Lucia?"

"My, my father was born there. Who are you?"

"My name is John Tooms."

"And what do you want with me, Mr. Tooms?"

"Nothing, Babbett," I said, using the name on her nameplate. "I'm here to speak to Larry Spender about Angelique Lear."

"But how did you know about me?"

"Elocution," I said. "The way you hold your shoulders. And there's something about people from your father's island—they make you feel friendly."

Babbett smiled, and so did I.

"Have a seat, Mr. Tooms. I'll tell Mr. Spender that you're here."

THERE WAS A LITTLE grotto of pink chairs around a chrome table upon which were piled expensive design and fashion magazines that I'd never heard of. They were the kind of magazines that could have naked women with exposed nipples on the cover without the censors going crazy. This was art, not pornography . . . but the women still warmed my brandy-soaked blood.

"Mr. Tooms?"

He wore a nice yet inexpensive suit that was medium gray. His brown eyes, which clashed with the color of the suit, were sad, but still he managed a smile. This was one of the small braveries of the modern world: people who were able to remain civil even while they suffered depression, cancer, and losses that could never be recouped.

"Mr. Spender?"

"You have news about Angie?" He was in his late forties but aging fast. Though he had more hair than I did, people still would call him bald.

And though he was more white than anything else, you could see by Mr. Spender's varied features that his people had been in America for a very long time. His rounded nose and small eyes, fleshy cheeks and wavy brown hair spoke of the many races that crossed Europe, Africa, and then the Atlantic to set up a life in the melting pot that very few call home.

"Can we go to your office?" I suggested.

"Sure."

23

At least Laughton and Price was modern enough to have disposed of the cubicle mentality. The brunt of the workforce was situated at a couple of dozen desks in a very large room. The ceiling was low but there were windows on three sides and enough space between the desks so that the workers could lean back without bumping into each other.

Most of the employees were young and earnestly engaged with their papers, phone conversations, computer screens, and drawing boards.

Larry Spender led me through the modern-day white-collar sweatshop toward the corner office door that had his name on it.

"HAVE A SEAT," HE said after closing the door behind us.

There was a comfortable brown leather and chrome chair facing his desk, behind which was a window that looked south down Lexington Avenue. The November light, even on a clear morning like that one, seemed to carry darkness in its womb.

"So what do you know about Angelique?" he asked.

"I didn't say that I was bringing information, Mr. Spender. I came here looking for her, or at least for how to find her."

These words set Spender back in his swivel chair and even

pushed his face in a little. These aspects of suspicion came naturally to him.

"Who sent you?" he asked.

"I was hired by Lizette Lear, Angelique's mother. She, Lizette, relies on her daughter, financially and emotionally, and is at her wits' end." I find that proper diction is a balm for suspicion among the professional classes; reminds them of favorite professors or something.

"Her mother hired you?"

I nodded and smiled.

"But, but, but Angie says that her mother doesn't, um, isn't very friendly with her."

"That might be true," I said. "My father was a union-organizing socialist who hated banks as much as a good Catholic hates the devil. But you better believe that if he ever misplaced his passbook he'd have torn our little cold-water flat down to the ground looking for it."

I also find it useful to tell the truth now and then. There's a special timbre to the truth coming out of one's mouth. If you mix that in with the lies it helps lubricate the dialogue.

"I guess, I guess her mother might ask someone to help," Larry said. "Angie is a wonderful person."

"That's what everyone seems to be saying," I agreed. "All the people I've spoken to, her mother included, have talked about how perfect she is."

"Who have you spoken to?"

"Lizette, of course, and Shad Tandy, her fiancé—"

"No," Larry said. "They're not engaged. Actually I think they broke up a month or so ago."

"No? But he said—"

"He lied. That bum was just using Angie."

Bum?

"You sound like a little more than just a boss," I suggested.

His fingers were picking imaginary lint from the desktop.

"Angelique is a very natural kind of person, Mr. Tooms. I run this office, supervise everyone who sits out there. Most of them want things from me and at the same time talk about me behind my back. They secretly tattle on each other and cheat the company in a hundred different ways. They can't be trusted, most of them. But Angie is just, just different. She's always at her desk half an hour early and she doesn't have a bad thing to say—period. I like her very much. She, she . . . you don't feel like she's trying to get you to do anything for her, and then you find yourself wanting to help."

"I also went to speak to a Wanda Soa," I said, deciding it wouldn't be profitable to comment on this middle-aged man's puppy love.

"Who?"

The murder, partially due to the cops, I was sure, hadn't made it to the front page of any New York paper.

"Just another friend. Have you heard from Angelique?"

He shook his head and pulled his lips into his mouth.

"Can you think of any way to get in touch with her?" I asked.

Again the sad sway of his head.

"Any work friends who might know?"

"I'm her closest friend in this department. You know, Angie has an MBA but she wants to be more, more creative. We're working together on an ad campaign for an Indian tea company that wants to start importing their brand. We convinced them to set up a bottling plant in the Northeast in order to make them seem more American."

"Do they have any contact with Angelique?"

"I wish I could help you, Mr. Tooms," Larry Spender told me.

"I really care about her. But she just stopped coming in two weeks ago. She doesn't answer her phone. She hasn't called."

He raised his hands to the level of his shoulders in a perfect expression of helplessness.

"Maybe you could do one thing for her," I said.

"What's that?"

"Do you have an HR department?"

"Yes. Of course."

"Introduce me to someone there. You can tell them that I'm representing her mother."

TRUTH IS THE AGREEMENT between me and you about something, anything: the world is flat, all Arabs are terrorists, the future is predicated on the past. It is true if we agree that it's true.

I was John Tooms representing Angelique Tara Lear's mother, Lizette. This was a fact presented by both Larry Spender and myself to Ms. Sharon Weiss, assistant head of HR.

The HR department, which occupied a moderate-sized space on the ninth floor, had real offices for the six employees situated there. These offices were small and the walls were amber-tinted glass, but you couldn't hear their private conversations.

Ms. Weiss's desk was a blue plastic plank held in place by a black stalk that was anchored to the floor. Weiss was blond to the world, if not by birth, and voluptuous in the way that made Hugh Hefner's millions. Her body, wrapped in a furry tan cashmere dress, looked to be in its late twenties, but her face was almost forty.

Sharon's expression told me that she had not yet been convinced by Larry's and my corroboration of the true. By that time, the office manager had left for his floor filled with real and, I'm sure imagined, backstabbers.

"You say that you, um, represent Mrs. Lear?" Ms. Weiss asked.

I leaned forward in the hard chair she had for guests and penitents, placed my elbows on the blue plastic, and laced my fingers. When she saw my hands, Ms. Weiss's expression changed. I have very big hands, a workingman's hands, a prizefighter's hands, virtual baseball mitts. A certain breed of woman, raised under working-class fathers, is very impressed with hands like mine. It's a meta-sexual response, not about romance, or even touch.

While Sharon was trying to get her nostrils under control I used one of those hands to bring out my wallet.

Breland Lewis hadn't pulled the name John Tooms out of a hat. That was one of my primary aliases. I took out a card that read JOHN TOOMS—PERSONAL INVESTIGATIONS.

"Not private investigator?" she asked after reading the lie.

"I do mostly family work," I said. "Missing kids, wayward spouses. I never use a camera or tape recorder."

Placing her elbows on the desk, Sharon Weiss asked, "What can I do for you, Mr. Tooms?"

"Angie Lear is missing," I said. "Her mother is a sick woman who relies completely on her daughter. She's very worried, for many different reasons. I came here to look for her, and also to find out if she's been let go."

"I'm not allowed to give out personal information," Sharon told me. There was a lot of yellow in her brown eyes. I wondered if the reflection of my suit brought out that hue.

"I won't tell anyone," I said. "And as long as you don't give me any specific information, there would be no reason to question you."

She believed my hands.

Opening the folder that she had retrieved when Larry Spender called, Weiss paged through, slowly. As she read a frown came across her face.

"Hmm."

"What?" I asked.

"This is very unusual."

"What is?"

Sharon looked up at me.

"I've never worked on Miss Lear's file," she said. "It's, um, strange."

"In what way?"

"She didn't go through the usual interview process. Upper management simply sent down the word to hire her. And, and there was a note attached, just a few days ago, that says to keep her position open regardless of her absence. I've really never come across anything like it."

"Is the note signed?"

"No. But it's stamped with the executive board's seal. No one, not even the president, can revoke that."

"Damn," I said. "Are there any other abnormalities?"

"No. She has good attendance and no behavior reports. All in all, except for her recent absence, she's an exemplary employee."

"I see. Well . . . thank you, Ms. Weiss. You've been a great deal of help. And don't worry. I won't pass any of this information on to her mother. I'll just tell her that as far as I know she hasn't been fired."

"Thank you."

We both stood and she came around the blue plank as I opened the glass door. I extended a hand that she took with both of hers.

"You have very strong hands, Mr. Tooms."

"Do you have a card?" I asked. "I might want to call you."

24

The day was bright and chilly. It wasn't yet noon but the sun, I knew, would set in less than five hours. The next step for me was to go down to Angie's apartment. First, though, I had to visit my office to prepare myself for that leg of the investigation.

When I didn't see Aura and her beau making out on the street I recognized that I was nervous about going to the Tesla. This trepidation was deeply disturbing to me. My office is the center of my life. The seventy-second floor of that Art Deco building is the one place where I feel secure and almost happy. It was bad enough that Aura had taken love from my life, but now . . .

JUST THE TOP LOCK of my outer door was engaged. The only thing I could imagine was that Aura was in there. She wanted to talk, and so did I.

I pushed the door open eagerly but the excitement quickly faded. I'd forgotten about Mardi, my new receptionist. She stood up when I blundered in. She was wearing a rose-colored dress that seemed more appropriate for a girl her age.

"What's wrong?" she asked.

"Nothing," I said. "Why?"

I come from a long line of slavery, second-class citizenship, revolutionaries, orphans, and crooks. Put all that together in a man's heart and you make ordinary circumspection look like careless abandon. My face rarely gave away anything that I felt.

"I just thought," Mardi said. "Nothing."

"That's a nice dress," I said to cover up the odd discomfort we both felt.

"Thank you. I bought it yesterday when I saw that you thought my Mrs. Alexander's dress was too old-fashioned."

"I didn't say that."

"I could tell, though," she said. "I'm pretty good at picking up on how people are feeling. Sometimes Twill brings me along when he wants to know if somebody is lying to him."

"Have you heard from Twill in the last twenty-four hours?"

"He called last night to find out how the job was going."

"How did he sound?"

Mardi's smile could only be called knowing. She said, "Twill's one of the only people that I can't read very well. He's always the same no matter what."

"And how was your day yesterday?" I asked.

"Real good. A Detective Kitteridge called. He was nice, said he needed to speak to you. I organized all the files and phone numbers. I started going through your notes. I'm trying to figure out a good way to put them in your files."

"That's great. You know, I think you'll be a real asset to me, Mardi. We should set you up with a payroll company. You'll start at five seventy-five a week. Then find out the best medical insurance coverage for you and your family."

Mardi's smile was so wide I could almost see her teeth.

BACK IN MY INNER sanctum I went through a closet at the opposite end of the hall from my office. There I kept all my various disguises.

I decided on the drab workman's overalls. A man in work clothes rarely needs ID. I put on some funked-up work boots and a cap that had *ConEd* stitched over the visor. I picked out a red metal toolbox and lumbered toward the front.

"I'm going out for a while, Mardi," I said as I moved toward the door.

"Okay, boss," she said, seemingly oblivious to my change of clothes.

I stopped to smile at her.

The attention made her beam.

"LAWRENCE DOLAN," I WAS saying to the super of Angelique Lear's building on Twelfth Street, two blocks up from the northern border of Tompkins Square Park. Angie lived on a sedate block straddling the northwestern fringe of Alphabet City. The rickety edifice was six stories high and slender, with only one apartment on each floor.

"How can I help you, Mr. Dolan?"

"We got a call on a gas leak. I'm here to check it out."

"I haven't made any report," the hunched-over white man said in perfectly executed English.

"I don't know who made the call," I said. "All I know is that they sent me paperwork on this address and I'm supposed to check it out."

"Where's your truck?" the man asked. He would have been tall except for the slouch. His hair was gray and his white skin stained from many years of working with dust and dirt.

"They got us two to a truck nowadays," I said, pretending to harbor resentment. "Trying to cut costs. Merwin's gone to a place down on Sixth Street."

"You have to understand, Mr. Dolan," the man who had given me no name said. "I didn't call, and so I'm hesitant to let you in."

"Hey," I replied, hunching my shoulders with nonchalance. "It's nuthin' to me. I'm just gonna shut off the gas and electric and you can work it out with my supervisor when she wants to turn it back on."

"What? Turn off our power?"

"There has been a gas leak reported," I explained patiently. "If I can't tell my boss yea or nay I have to shut you down. I mean, they could be sued for millions if there's an explosion or a fire."

"But why the gas *and* electricity?"

"When people refuse to let us in we shut 'em down. That way we got a reason to come back . . . one day."

I reached into my breast pocket and handed him an official-looking business card. It had my alias and a few phone numbers printed in dark-blue ink.

"My boss is Janey Markus," I said. "Her number's at the bottom but you can get to her through any of these. She'll tell you the same thing I'm saying."

The number actually went to a machine I kept at Zephyra Ximenez's apartment. If he called he'd get one of a dozen specially designed recordings telling him that Ms. Markus was not in but that she would return the call as soon as possible.

"This is crazy," the nameless super said.

"Are there any good Indian restaurants around here?" I replied.

Anger flinched in the super's face.

"Go on up," he said. "If the tenants let you in then I guess you can do what you want. But I will tell you right now that there isn't any leak."

I smiled.

He grimaced.

I went up to the locked front door and pressed a buzzer at random.

"Yes?" a tremulous woman's voice inquired.

"Con Ed."

25

"Regular as clockwork," Isabella Katinski told me as I pretended to study the back of her stove.

After a pleasant conversation concerning the history of the building, I had asked her about the absent upstairs neighbor, Miss Lear, on the pretext of needing to check out her gas line.

I'd already cleaned the pilot lights on the stove.

". . . she's out her door at eight-ten every morning and back at six on Mondays and Wednesdays, eight on Tuesdays and Thursdays, and nine on Fridays unless she doesn't come home that night."

"Fridays are for the boyfriend, huh?"

The diminutive septuagenarian smiled at me with pearl-gray teeth. Her dress was hippie vintage turquoise-and-plum-colored flannel that had her covered from shoulder to ankle.

"She's out late if there is no boyfriend," Isabella told me. "When there is one, she's on the clock there, too."

"How so?" I asked.

"Can I get you some ice water, Mr. Dolan? I only have tap and cubes. If you're one'a them that needs your water from a plastic bottle I can't help you."

"WHAT WAS I TELLING you?" she asked when we were seated at the small triangular table that took up a good part of her Lilliputian kitchen.

"You were saying how your neighbor's got some kind of pattern with men."

The window we perched near looked down on the cavernous area between the buildings north of Twelfth and south of Thirteenth. There were fire escapes and tiny little sun-starved gardens, clotheslines strung between the buildings, and tatters from nameless things left outside too long.

Angelique's building was one of the smallest structures among its huge brick tenement brothers.

"When she first meets a boy you can hear 'em from ten to about two every Friday for the first month," Ms. Katinski said. "After that there's a couple'a months of creaking from ten to midnight. Then there's only footsteps for a month or so more. After that the boyfriend moves on and she stays out all night now and then again."

"She's a wild one, huh?" I said.

"Don't get me wrong, Mr. Dolan," Ms. Katinski proclaimed. "She's a very nice girl. When I had trouble with the noise downstairs she took care of it for me."

"SHE COMPLAINED ABOUT MY music even though Mrs. Katinski's apartment is between me and her," Seth Martindale told me while I drained the rusty water from his decades-old radiator. "Said that the old lady was hard of hearing or something."

"I was just in Katinski's apartment," I said. "She seemed to hear me all right."

"You see?" the sixty-something retired insurance adjuster said. "And here she almost got me evicted from my apartment. I've been living in this place for thirty-eight years, longer than she's been breathing."

"She almost got you evicted? How'd she do that?"

"City marshal came over with papers. I didn't even know we had a city marshal, but there they were, all dressed up in uniform. Told me that I had gone over the allowed decibel level and if they got another complaint the city was going to evict me."

"SHE'S A GODSEND," NYLA Winetraub, on the second floor, told me.

Nyla was Isabella's age but a bit more shaky. Her eyesight was going, nearly gone, and she liked to be near a wall to grab on to if she started to fall. She wore dark clothes and only had a single lamp on in the living room. I didn't know if she was trying to save money on utility bills or if maybe it was just that electric light no longer did much to illuminate her world.

"She helps me fill out all of my forms and answer correspondences," Nyla was saying. She was a dark-skinned white woman with lots of ageless character in her thin face. "She writes checks for me and even put in an answering machine so I can tell who's calling. You know, there's so many salesmen on the phones nowadays."

She paused and cocked her head, as if listening to faraway soft murmuring.

"You aren't really a Con Ed man, are you, Mr. Dolan?" she said.

"No, ma'am."

I wasn't surprised that it was the blind woman who saw through my disguise. Winetraub, I would have bet, was almost as perceptive as my new receptionist.

"Why are you here?" the old woman asked.

"I'm surprised that you don't just ask me to leave," I said.

"Why would I do that?"

"Well, I am a stranger in your house under false pretenses."

"If you were going to hurt me or steal from me I couldn't stop you," Nyla said reasonably. "And if I cried out you might hit me.

Anyway, you're here to find out about Angelique, and I'm worried about her. She's been gone for over a week. Do you have any news?"

"No, ma'am. But I am here looking for her . . . for a friend of hers."

"John Prince?"

"No."

"John's a nice boy. He called here looking for her a few days ago. But I couldn't help him."

"Do you have his phone number?" I asked.

"No. I forgot to ask," she said. "Sorry."

"Do you have any idea of what happened to Angelique?" I asked.

Nyla turned her gaze, such as it was, toward my voice. We were sitting across from each other in front of a window that was completely covered, ceiling to floor, by dark-brown drapes. It was clear to me that her nearly sightless eyes were struggling to make sure of my intentions. Her hands reached out toward me and so I took them gently in my paws.

"You have strong hands," she told me.

"My father was a union organizer," I said. "Before that he was a sharecropper's son."

Nyla smiled. "You have your father's hands."

For some reason my throat closed up a moment. Nyla seemed to intuit this physical response and squeezed.

"Angelique came down to me just before she left," the elderly woman said. "She told me that she was in trouble and would be gone for a while."

"Did she say what kind of trouble?"

"There were men who wanted her to do something, but either she didn't know or wouldn't tell me what. She is in deep trouble, though. Angelique is a very responsible girl with both feet firmly planted. If she's hiding, it's from something real. I'm afraid for her welfare."

"Did you call the police?"

"What would I tell the cops? She's not my daughter. She's an adult."

I was surprised at the word "cops" from the old woman's mouth and reminded myself that I shouldn't make assumptions.

"Did she give you any other details?" I asked.

"No. Nothing. Have you heard anything about her?"

"She hasn't been to work, and her most recent boyfriend, Shad Tandy, doesn't know where she is. She might have been staying with her friend Wanda for a while there."

"Wanda Soa," Nyla said with a smile. "One night, a few months ago, Wanda and Angelique came down and made dinner with me. Wanda is from South America somewhere. They once traveled down there together, for Carnival. Have you asked Wanda about Angelique?"

"She isn't answering her phone," I said.

"Oh."

"You think the super might know something?" I asked, to pass on from any suspicions I might have aroused.

"Mr. Klott? He's a piece of work, that one. He tried to get me put out, on the part of the landlord, when I went to visit my daughter in Florida—told the city that I had a residence out of state. It was Angelique who helped me get the right aid."

"Can I do anything for you, Ms. Winetraub?"

"Find Angelique," she said. "Make sure she doesn't come to harm."

26

Prominent in my red metal toolbox are three huge key chains that have the masters for ninety percent of the locks in New York. I update my stock every six months. For those locks that take a little more I have special lock-picking keys that were designed by my personal engineer and hacker, Bug Bateman.

I used one such special key on Angelique Lear's lock. It was a simple mechanical adjustment, and I made it into her top-floor apartment in under a minute. All I had to do was insert the key mechanism and rotate a bolt on the base until the tumblers fell into place.

The first thing I did was go to the kitchen, blow out the pilot lights, and turn a couple of the burners up high for thirty seconds or so. Then I went through the place quickly, looking for immediate clues.

I gathered all the mail I could see and secreted the envelopes in the false bottom of my red toolbox. Then I cruised through the apartment, scanning bureaus and tabletops, going through any drawers as I came across them.

Two of Angelique's bedroom walls were hung with many framed photographs. The wall to the left of her bed had photos of her with either a blond-haired, olive-skinned, blue-eyed woman or a slender and pale young man with black hair and piercing eyes. She was laughing with Blondie at Carnival in Rio, and arm-in-arm with the intent young man in Rome. My unaware, maybe even unwilling, client was smiling or laughing in every photograph. Not one picture looked posed or insincere.

Across from the foot of her bed were her diplomas—from elementary school to her master's from NYU. The bed was neat and made. The orange-and-yellow bedspread was frayed here and there from many years of use.

The night table held some tissues, a box of condoms, and a fuzzy pink pair of handcuffs—no useful clues there.

The floors were bare oak except in the bathroom, which was covered in off-white linoleum flecked with tiny squares of bright and shiny confetti colors.

Her bookshelf was small and crowded with the classics, from the Brontë sisters to Melville, Shakespeare to Flannery O'Connor. The pockets of the clothes hanging in her closet had nothing in them. The purses and suitcases on the shelves above were likewise empty.

I didn't have the time for an in-depth search but after twenty minutes or so I was pretty sure that Angelique lived the uneventful life of most young women her age. She was just a happy-go-lucky girl with an education and a job, biannual vacations, and a healthy interest in men. There were no antidepressants or sleeping pills in her medicine cabinet, no secret stash of hashish, or any harder substance, that I could find.

I wondered how such a normal young woman could be mixed up in murder—or, even worse, with Alphonse Rinaldo.

"Hello?" came a voice from the front doorway.

I pulled a shiny black plastic box from my pocket. It was half-again the length and three-quarters the width of a classic BlackBerry. I pressed a button on the side and a yellow light appeared at the front end of the little faux machine.

I scooted into the hall, situated myself in front of the bathroom door, and said, "In here."

A few heavy, hurried footsteps and Klott was at the entrance of the short hallway.

"What are you doing in here?" he demanded.

"My job." I was holding the little box out in front of me, taking readings.

"How did you get in here?"

"Door was unlocked and I smelled gas. Don't you?"

Klott sniffed the air and turned toward the kitchen. I followed him, holding the box out in front of me like a uranium prospector with a new-century Geiger counter.

When I entered the kitchen I pressed a button underneath the box with my baby finger and the yellow light slowly turned red.

"You see?" I said, pushing the box closer to the stove and secretly pressing the button again. Now the red light started blinking.

"What's that?" Klott asked.

"The newest thing. We use it to detect escaping gas. When it's white everything's okay. I got an amber light outside the front door."

"How did you get in here?" Klott asked again.

"It was open."

"I check every apartment every night. This door's been locked for the last week and the tenant hasn't been here."

"She must've come in when you weren't looking and left in a hurry 'cause the door was unlocked, and you can see that it wasn't broke or anything."

Klott went out to inspect the front door.

"What were you doing in the other part of the house?" he asked.

"You use the detector to make sure the gas is not coming from multiple sources," I said, pretending to be paraphrasing some manual.

"Let me see that thing," he said, reaching for my box as he did so.

I stiff-armed him with my left palm. He went backward eighteen inches. Now that we knew who had the muscle in the room, he wouldn't try to get physical again.

"Don't be grabbin' at me, man," I said, reverting to the dialect he expected of my skin color.

Klott's eyes tightened but he stayed put.

"Are you finished?" he asked.

"Just gotta check out the stove and I'm done."

"You didn't do that first?"

"I save the obvious for last."

I pulled the stove away from the wall and for the next eight minutes or so pretended to check the connections. After that I pushed the unit back into place and relit the pilots.

"That's it," I said.

"I'm calling your supervisor," Klott replied.

"And what are you going to tell her?"

"That you broke in here."

"Lock's not broken and I haven't taken anything," I reasoned. "My boss'll tell you to call the cops, and they'll ask for the proof. You won't have it and the next time you call them they won't come."

A shiver went through Mr. Klott. He'd been living in his little real estate fiefdom for so long that he honestly believed that he was king of the mountain.

"Nice doin' business wichya," I said with a smile.

After that I picked up my red box full of master keys and letters and made my way down to the street.

27

Back at my office I found Mardi reading through the files I kept of my honest cases. She looked up and gave me her soft impression of a smile.

"Hi, Mr. McGill."

"Mardi. How's it goin'?"

"I've been reading through your files."

"And?"

"I thought the life of a private detective would be romantic, or at least exciting," she said.

"Not hardly."

"I can see that. In this case you sat out in front of a woman's apartment for nearly two weeks and in the end you say that nothing happened."

"Thomas Lavender," I remembered. "Got a job in Boston and was sure that his wife was entertaining some lover whenever he was gone. With his approval I bugged the phone system, put mikes in the bedroom, living room, kitchen, and even the bathroom. Then I sat out in front of the house eighteen hours a day. She never so much as sang in the shower."

Mardi giggled, hearing a joke I might not have made.

"She was looking for a couple'a bucks six months later and found my card in Tom's wallet. She called and asked me why her husband needed a private detective."

"What did you say?" Mardi asked.

"I told her that I'd never heard of her husband or her for that matter. She wanted to know how he got my card if I didn't know him. I asked her was anything written on the card. She said yes, that someone had written a phone number on the back. I said someone had probably used my card to write him some note, that it happens all the time."

"How did you know there was a number on the back?" Mardi asked, much more interested in my story than she was in the file.

"I always scribble some number on the back of a card when I give it to a spouse who shares space with the target of my investigation. I asked him what he liked to do and he said he went to museums a lot, so I wrote down the information line at the Frick.

"Didn't work, though."

"Why not?" my clear-eyed receptionist asked.

"A week later Thomas called me. He wanted to know what I'd told his wife—her name was Laurel. I told him about the call and he said that she must have figured out the whole thing. She said that she couldn't live with a man who would even consider having a detective follow her."

"They broke up?"

For a moment I thought about those long days that Lavender spent over five thousand dollars for. On three different occasions I saw her run into her downstairs neighbor, a Mr. Clinton Brown. I could see by the way they'd talk to each other that they harbored a subterranean passion. But they didn't act on these feelings. I was sure about that. Lavender hired me to tell him if his wife was cheating—she was not. But when she found my card in his wallet she left him, and Mr. Brown and Laurel moved in together.

"A few months later, Lavender called me in order to gather some ammunition for the divorce. I told him that he didn't want me in the witness chair."

"Why not?" she asked.

"Because the only thing I could do was corroborate his wife's claim."

In essence, Lavender had hired me to scuttle his marriage. I did just that.

"I'm going to change and go out to a meeting," I said.

"Okay," Mardi replied.

Back in my office I sorted through Angie's mail. Three bills, four requests for money from floundering nonprofits, six advertisements for shows and performances, and a postcard from San Francisco.

Hey Ang,

I'm Out Here On Business For A Few Days And I Remembered The Time We Walked Across The Golden Gate Bridge. I Miss You.

Love, John

DETECTIVE CARSON KITTERIDGE was keeping a desk in the precinct office in the West Twenties that month. I dropped by, hoping that he wasn't there. But even if he was it didn't matter much. I hadn't come to see him on the day he asked because the police have to be reminded now and again that this is America and the people's rights are the rock bottom of the law.

They knew me at the station and didn't care for me much. I was like a werewolf or griffin to most of the NYPD—a mythological demon that did everything from eating babies to shitting on the souls of virgins.

"Detective Kitteridge in?" I asked the buck sergeant at the front desk.

The brown-eyed, pale-skinned man looked at me, sneered as well as he could, and pressed a button.

He motioned with his head toward the waiting area and I went to sit on the solitary bench that the department kept for their visitors. It was made of hard wood and had many stains and gouges from long use and little upkeep. I rested my elbows on my knees and laced my fingers, an apologetic sinner at the gates of the house of damnation.

Breathing in through my nose and out through my mouth, I began counting breaths up to ten, and then started over. I kept that up until I lost count and drifted. When I felt myself drifting, I went back to counting.

Through it all my headache was pounding. But I was getting used to that.

I kept up that regimen for quite a while, over an hour. I did it to keep my mind calm and keen, because I couldn't afford to get angry.

Detective Kitteridge wasn't beyond petty revenge. I had refused to come to him when he said and so I was going to have a long wait. That way he could have his payback while at the same time he could weigh my interest in the double murder. If I stayed I must have needed something. Maybe that something would indict me in some way.

The cop had his customs and I had mine. So I sat there counting parcels of air and remembering that breath was the most precious moment in any mammal's life.

"LT," he said.

I looked up and smiled.

This mild response was unexpected. Carson Kitteridge, my own personal city-assigned tormentor, grimaced.

Carson's skin was bone white and he had about as much hair as I did—very little. His eyes were pale blue, like an overcast afternoon in late summer. He was even shorter than I. I wouldn't say we liked each other, but, as with so many people in the modern world, our work brought us together more times than we would have preferred.

"A day late and a dollar short," I said. "But I'm here."

"Come on back to my office."

CARSON ENTERED A CODE on an electric lock and led me into the secure section of the precinct. We passed a few offices, made our way through a locker room. From there we went through an exceptionally slender doorway, entering a stairwell that was narrow and steep. We went down four floors, finally coming to a long, dark hallway. If I had been under arrest and in chains that hallway would have had a sense of finality to it.

I've known quite a few advocates of The Life who had entered halls just like this one and were never seen again.

And I knew that I wasn't special.

I could die just like anyone else.

Carson led me to the end of the hall and turned left, continuing on until we came to another turn. Along the way we passed not one door.

"Here we go," the police detective said as we made the second turn.

We had come to a shiny yellow portal for which Carson produced a key.

It was a small office that smelled of mold and stale tobacco smoke. The desk was green metal, as were the straight-back chairs in front of and behind it. The light was very bright and it felt warm and humid in there, like the heat radiating from a wet dog.

"Sit down, LT," Carson said.

He went to the chair behind the desk.

When we were both seated, but not necessarily comfortable, Kitteridge lit up a cigarette.

I smiled and then grinned. A laugh was not far off.

"What's so funny?" he asked.

"You went to all the trouble of gettin' an office down here just so that you could smoke at work."

He didn't want to but Carson Kitteridge smiled.

"Some people are just too smart for their own good," he said, tamping down the smirk with the words.

"Not me, man. I just see a kindred spirit, that's all."

"We don't have a thing in common, McGill."

"If we didn't I wouldn't be sittin' in your chair now, would I?"

"Why are you here?" he asked.

"Didn't you call me? Call my answering service and my office?"

"Who's the girl answered the office phone?"

"My new receptionist."

"As long as I've known you you've never had an employee, LT."

"Mardi Bitterman."

That stopped him momentarily.

I had given Kitteridge a lead on a website that Bug Bateman and I created using the pornographic photographs that Leslie Bitterman had taken of himself and his daughter—Mardi.

That bust got Kitteridge a commendation.

"I thought your son just happened on that website," Carson said.

"It's hot down here, man. What do you want from me?"

"All right," the little cop said. "You want to get tough, that's okay with me. What do you know about those killings?"

"I thought this was Bonilla's case."

"The killings are hers, but your ass is mine."

"I guess I might have enough to go around."

"What were you doing there?" Kitteridge asked.

"I already told Detective Bonilla."

"I don't believe it."

"Why not?"

"Because if it was just circumstance like you said, then you wouldn't be here."

"Captain James Charbon," I said, clearly and slow.

Once again the detective's aggression was stymied.

He knew the good captain. The reason Kitteridge didn't have his own bars was James Charbon.

Carson at one time had a partner—Randolph Peel. Randy was bent. He took payoffs in cash and in kind from all sorts of crooks, big and small. And there were two things you had to know about Carson: (1) that he was what I liked to call an Extra-Logical, a breed of human who could see beyond the physical world into a dimension of pure logic—there he could perceive things that normal *Homo sapiens* could not; and (2) Carson was as honest as the day is long on June 22nd a hundred miles north of Stockholm.

Carson was bound to find out what Peel was doing, and he was therefore obligated to turn him in.

That was all good and well. But the problem was that Peel was James Charbon's brother-in-law. So Randy's downfall meant that Carson would never get a serious promotion as long as Charbon was ambulatory.

Kitteridge took a deep breath and sat back in his chair.

"You fuckin' with me, LT?"

"He told Bonilla that he wanted daily reports on my involvement in the crime. She told me about it, thinking that would light a fire under my butt. She was right. That's why I'm here."

Carson nodded. That was all he needed to do. The law, and its expectations, would be suspended for the while.

"I don't know who the button man was, and neither had I ever met, or consciously spoken to, Wanda Soa. But you better believe I have to find out something about both of them, because Charbon hates me more than you hate him."

For what seemed like a long time Carson and I stared into each other's eyes. He believed (and I did, too) that he could tell if a man was lying just by looking at him. I was giving him the opportunity to ply that talent.

28

"I don't know what's going on here, Carson," I was saying.

We were walking north on Eighth Avenue, looking to all the world like two down-on-their-luck salesmen in bad suits. He had called Lieutenant Bethann Bonilla—they were on a first-name basis—and learned that what I was saying was true.

Once he knew for a fact that Charbon was involved, Carson got fidgety. He didn't want to sit in the station anymore. Even in his underground bunker he felt vulnerable.

"So what do you want from me?" he asked.

The sun was going down again, taking with it, it seemed to me, my tentative connection to Reason.

"I don't really know," I said. "I mean, I get a call summoning me to a murder scene. I agree that's suspicious. But I never heard of Wanda Soa, and the button man was a stranger to me, too."

Neither one of us had an overcoat and the temperature was below fifty, for sure. I was certainly feeling a chill, but that was also the scrutiny I was under.

Kitteridge was so good at getting the truth out of suspects that he was on call to all the major precincts in New York. They sometimes lent him out to other cities for convoluted interrogations. If he was freelance I would have used him myself.

"I still don't know what you want," Carson said.

"Yeah. Well . . . what about Soa?"

"What about her?"

"Why is everybody so upset?" I asked. "I mean, I know that it's murder and all, but there usually isn't this much pressure put on a single case, especially if the press doesn't grab on to it."

"I don't know," Kitteridge said. It was a simple declarative sentence, one that I rarely, if ever, heard come from his lips.

Rather than show my surprise, I said, "Let's go in that diner, man. I'm freezin' out here."

There was a coffee shop with a counter and a few tables across the street. If I had been with any other one of the eight million New Yorkers, even those confined to a wheelchair, we would have plunged across the avenue, making our way through the traffic by bravado and stealth. But Carson went to the crosswalk at the corner and patiently waited for the light. I do believe that if his mother was having a stroke in that diner he would have done the same.

His adherence to the law was both laughable and frightening.

SEATED AT THE COUNTER, sipping black coffees, we continued our clandestine talk.

"Is someone putting pressure on the case?" I asked.

Carson stared at me. His left eye nearly closed with the concentration.

"You don't know Soa?" he asked.

"Never heard of her before I got to the crime scene."

"Then why were you there?"

"I got a call."

We waited again for him to redigest my words.

"There's an ADA named Tinely," he said. "Broderick Tinely. For some reason he's got a bee up his butt over the murder. He's been leaning heavily on Assistant Chief Chalmers, and the shit filters down from there."

"Why?"

"I don't know," Kitteridge said again. "I got a call from downtown telling me to lean on you. I didn't know about Charbon. He'd rather cut off his left nut than bring me in on anything he's doing."

I sipped my coffee, thinking that it tasted of metal and the chemical cleaners used on metal.

"What's the deal?" I asked.

"Are you involved with these killings or the people killed?" Carson asked.

"If I am I don't know how."

He thrummed his fingers on the countertop.

"It doesn't make any sense," he said at last. "None of it. The killer has no name, his fingerprints don't show up in any database. He had a wad of thirty-seven hundred dollars in his pocket and that was all. His last dinner was tilapia, brown beans, white rice, and plantains fried in peanut oil. The residue on his left hand and sleeve says that he probably fired the shot that killed the girl, but there was no gun in the apartment. There's no way in the world that he could have stabbed himself. The knife was shoved in just under his left armpit, all the way to the handle. They say that the killer wiped off his prints but it looks to me like the shooter probably jerked away from his assailant when he was stabbed and any prints were wiped clean."

"Did anybody hear anything?"

"A young man in the apartment upstairs might have heard a girl screaming around the time the killings occurred."

"And Soa?" I asked.

"Can I get you anything else, gentlemen?" a young Hispanic man with a sparse mustache asked.

"You got an espresso machine?" I asked him.

"Yes, sir."

"Make me a triple with some steamed milk."

"You don't like your coffee?" Carson asked.

"Do you?"

The young man smiled and moved off to fill my order.

"What's wrong with the coffee?" Kitteridge demanded.

"It tastes like toxic waste."

"I don't taste anything."

"Do you have something on Soa?" I asked.

"I could fill up a phone book on her. Her father's a businessman from Colombia and her mother's a Parisian socialite named Jeanne Ouré. Mother splits up her time between Nice and Salvador."

"Bahia?" I said.

"Say what?"

"Salvador is either a country or a city in the state of Bahia in Brazil."

"Brazil," Carson said. "She—Wanda—went down there pretty often. For a while there they thought that she was smuggling drugs."

"Was she?"

"Depends on how you look at it."

"What's that mean?"

"They had fourteen agents on her—city, state, federal. Scoped out four trips she made in a nine-month period. Didn't find a thing. Finally they grabbed her at customs coming into the country and searched her down to the spaces between her toes."

"They find anything?"

"Less than a gram of hashish wrapped up in some chewing gum aluminum foil in the back pocket of a pair of dirty jeans. She said somebody gave it to her at a concert and she forgot it in the pocket. But by then they had spent over eight hundred thousand investigating the girl, and so she was facing prosecution in three different courts. Three different courts."

"So she was on trial when she was killed?"

"No."

"No?"

"Somewhere along the way a lawyer named Lamont Jennings gets involved. High-priced attorney. Knows all the right people. Three weeks before she is to be indicted, all charges are dropped."

"Just like that?"

Carson nodded. "I'd say maybe that someone put a hit on her because they thought she might have given information to the feds or something, but I doubt it. Her folks have money, and she had no drug connections at all."

The waiter delivered my espresso and milk.

"Damn," I said after the server had gone. "It doesn't make any sense."

"No, no it doesn't. But there's power behind the investigation. Tinely wants somebody to go down for the murders. His assistant calls me every morning for an update."

Carson Kitteridge glanced at me while bringing the rancid coffee to his mouth.

"I have no idea who the hit man was or why he'd kill Wanda Soa," I said. "Those are facts."

"I didn't think so. Tinely said that you probably knew something. I told him that this wasn't your M.O., but he doesn't care. He wants to burn somebody, and if you're anywhere around, he'll set fire to you."

"So . . . you're protecting me?"

"That's just not the way I do things."

29

Kitteridge left me to drink my espresso and consider his words—also to pay the check when it came.

No one was safe where the upper echelons on the NYPD and the prosecutor's office were concerned. The government, even in a democracy, has the power to indict and condemn with impunity—below a certain income bracket, that is. And even though I was working for Rinaldo, that didn't mean he would protect me. My independent status made me expendable, and if I tried to bring him down with me I'd end up one of those lamentable suicides hanging from the bars of a subterranean cell.

They don't call them "the Tombs" for nothing.

As if to accent these dark thoughts, a cold breeze wafted across my neck.

"Hey, Juan," a tall black man said. He was standing to my right, wearing clothes that would turn into rags in most people's homes.

"Chester," my waiter said. "Wait a minute."

Juan reached under the counter and came out with a medium-sized brown paper bag. This he handed to the man he called Chester.

"Thanks, brother," Chester said.

"Go on now," Juan replied. "The boss is in the back."

Chester grinned—he was missing a couple of amber teeth—and mimed the motions of running in slow motion as he made his way back toward the door.

I suppose I was staring because Juan said to me, "He lives in my neighborhood in the Bronx. When nobody's looking I give him some soup and bread."

"What's he doing around here if he's from the Bronx?"

"This time of year people usually give," Juan said, "because of Christmas and Thanksgiving. But not so much this year. This year there isn't enough to go around."

I TOOK A CAB back to my office. Mardi was gone by then.

Hunting up Broderick Tinely using Bug's special browser, I discovered that his specialty was prosecuting real estate cases against abusive landlords mainly. He hadn't tried a violent case in eight years. He was getting on in age, fifty-two the previous April, and wasn't making much headway in the prosecutor's office.

That had to mean something, I just didn't know what.

Lamont Jennings didn't need to have a website. The cases he was related to in the news always concerned wealthy, high-profile clients. In a practice covering everything from DUI to murder, he represented the children of wealthy magnates, and wealthy magnates who lived like children. He rarely lost. His clients were never convicted of the worst crimes they had been charged with.

Neither Tinely nor Jennings had anything to do with Angie, at least not on the World Wide Web. And they had nothing to do with each other. As far as I could see, Tinely was just trying to change his position in the DA's office and Jennings was the right lawyer for a young woman being railroaded by the law.

AT TEN I DECIDED that there was nothing else for me to do, so I pulled an extra trench coat out of my closet and headed down to the street. I took the 1 train uptown to Eighty-sixth and Broadway. From there I walked north and then west to our apartment building on Ninety-first Street, only a stone's throw from Riverside Drive.

I was just getting the key out for the outside door when somebody yelled "McGill!" with a slight Eastern European accent.

As I turned I saw two men—one large and the other of medium build—walking hurriedly in my direction. I dropped the keys and shook out my arms.

When they were two and a half paces from me the smaller man spoke.

"Where's the girl?" he demanded.

They were both still coming fast.

The big man had a longer stride and so stepped within striking distance first. His hand darted out, intending to take me by the arm, no doubt. I squatted down below the hand and came up to hit him in the gut with a right uppercut. He grunted like he meant it and I stood up, hitting him in the nose with my bald crown.

Head-butting is illegal in the ring but there was no referee around to take a point away. The big guy wasn't down but he was hurt enough for me to take into account his smaller friend.

This guy was wearing black trousers and a thin sheepskin jacket. In his left hand was a pretty frightening-looking knife.

"Where's the girl?" he asked again.

In boxing they call it ringmanship—that's when you master the canvas better than your opponent does. In life the concept is pretty much the same.

I turned toward the big fellow in the army jacket and hit him a few more times—twice in the gut and once on the jaw—while the little guy took another step and a half toward us. I grabbed the big guy's arm and flung him at his partner.

They both went down.

I walked over the larger man's back and fell upon the knife-wielder, hitting him more than twice. I wrested the knife from his grip, picked him up by his sheepskin, and threw him against the wall. Using my left forearm, I held him steady while pressing the knife under his throat. I took a quick glance at the other guy. He wasn't moving. There was some blood pooling next to his left arm. That's when I noticed that there was blood on the knife.

"What do you want?" I asked my attacker.

"It vas mistake," he replied, his accent getting deeper.

"So what the fuck you jumpin' on me about?"

"Ve vere looking for a boy, a young man. He knows where is a friend of ours."

"What friend?"

"You do not know her."

"What's her name?"

"Tatyana. She is our friend. Our friend."

The big man on the ground groaned.

"Who sent you?"

"Gustav. Ve vork for Gustav."

"Where can I find this Gustav?"

My attacker hesitated, so I let the tip of his knife break the skin next to his Adam's apple.

"He owns pool hall on Houston. Shandley's Billiards. He is there every day."

I dropped the knife and hit my informant with a so-so left hook; more force than a jab but still less than a power shot. He fell to the sidewalk, dazed by the blow. I went through his clothes, and then his partner's, but neither one of them had a gun.

The big guy was bleeding from his arm but wouldn't die.

So I retrieved my keys and left the men to gather themselves and go make their report to Gustav.

KATRINA WAS SITTING IN the dining room, having a cup of chamomile tea and humming to herself.

On the way up in the elevator I had gone through all the actions I had to take in order to get to the desired end for me and my wife. Dimitri was in trouble. There's no way that the Russian leg-breakers would mistake my physique for Twill's. Dimitri was mixed up with a girl, and there were thugs who were willing to bruise and cut him until he gave up her whereabouts.

But the Russians didn't know where to look, and as long as Dimitri was with Twill they probably wouldn't find out. I had at least until morning to come up with some kind of plan.

I knew that the Eastern European gangsters couldn't find my sons because I made it a full-time practice keeping up with Twilliam, and two times out of every five I failed.

"Hi," I said, entering the dining room.

"Have you heard from them?" were her first words.

"Yeah," I said, "just when I was downstairs. I stayed out of the elevator to keep the connection."

"Why hasn't he called me?"

"He" was Dimitri. Katrina loved Twill, but he wasn't the kind of child you worried about. It was an odd feeling I had whenever I realized that my only blood son was my faithless wife's favorite.

"I don't know if it's love, honey," I said. "Probably isn't. But he must be getting some kind of great sex. His nose is open like the Midtown Tunnel at three a.m. I don't think he feels comfortable talking to his mother when he's feeling like that."

"He always comes to me," she said.

"A man has to let go the apron strings sometime."

A flash of anger went across the gorgeous Scandinavian face.

"Those flowers are getting kinda dry, aren't they?" I said to get her mind on something else.

"I like them."

"Just get some fresh ones, why don't you."

"A woman's husband is supposed to buy the flowers."

"The last time I bought you flowers you put them in Shelly's bathroom."

"That was nine years ago."

"Eleven," I said. "And in all that time I haven't let you down once."

"If you don't like them I'll throw them away."

"You got me wrong, baby. I like the arrangement. It's, it's wild. I'm just saying that they're getting dry and maybe you should replace them."

Katrina squinted at me. I could see that she was trying to decipher the symbolic content of our conversation. Maybe she thought that I was telling her something.

I wasn't. I liked the flowers. They distracted me and somehow transformed the room.

"You aren't lying to me, are you, Leonid?"

"About what, Katrina?"

"Dimitri."

"No. He's a young man lost in his first love. He doesn't want to come down, and wouldn't be able to if he tried."

"He's safe?"

"No man is safe when he's in love, Katrina, you know that. But I can promise you this—nothing will happen to our sons, either one of them, not as long as there's breath in my body."

My wife's bosom rose, hearing that truth and vow from me.

She stood up. Clad in her coral robe and nothing else, she gave me a look that was unmistakable.

"Are you coming to bed?"

My heart actually skipped. The shock of this feeling pushed the thugs and their threats almost out of mind.

"I can't, babe."

"Why not?"

"There's a job I got and it's really very serious."

Again Katrina studied me.

"Did you mean what you said before?" she asked.

"About what?"

"About shooting a man in the head."

"No," I said and then I told her about coming upon Wanda Soa's apartment without mentioning any names.

"I didn't do anything, but there it was," I said. "That's the kind of weight I have on my mind sometimes."

Without a word Katrina approached me, planted a wet kiss on my cheek, and then caressed my neck with her left hand.

I watched her walk away, thinking that I had missed an entire life somehow and wondering was it my fault or just fate.

30

When I was nine years old my father started taking me to firing ranges. We practiced with pistols and rifles on legal ranges, semiautomatics and explosives down on secret Appalachian retreats in the summer. We hunted bear and deer with bow and rifle and I learned how to set traps for beasts and men.

"There's a war coming, boys," he'd tell me and my younger brother, Nikita. "It's being fought right now in South America, Southeast Asia, and Africa. Most Americans don't think that the battle will ever make it to these shores, but they're wrong. Keeping the struggle away from our cities and our borders is like trying to make sure your kids never get sick—if you spend all your time isolating them, then later, when they grow up and go out in the world, the infections'll kill 'em."

I felt about my father the way a spider feels about the dark corner where she is drawn to build her web: he was fundamental and gave me no choice.

By the time I was twelve my father was gone for good. At the age of thirty-seven Nikita was sent to prison for an armored-car robbery and multiple murders in Michigan. At that time we hadn't spoken to each other for over a decade.

I was sitting at my desk, considering what weapons I had to bring to Shandley's in order to assure my own sons' survival.

Tolstoy, my self-named father, was right about the war. When

I look at the newspapers today I wonder why the pundits don't acknowledge that we're in the middle of World War III. I'm sure that some future historians will say so.

My father was a brilliant man, but what good was it to spend a life questioning false happiness and peace?

I don't know.

I can't know.

All I could do was strap a slender dagger to my left ankle and practice using the release on the wrist holster that held my custom-made four-shot .38.

I didn't sleep that night. There was too much chatter in my head. Twill was giving his innocent brother criminal advice in one corner while Angelique was sobbing behind the closet door. Gordo was somewhere making plans that would prepare me for a big fight—a fight I was bound to lose. Ron Sharkey was knocking on the ceiling below, asking for twenty bucks for his fix. And I was that spider, suspended in her dark corner—waiting.

WHEN THE SUN CAME up, at 6:37, I donned a blue suit that had finally made it home from the cleaner's. Then I walked down to my office, hoping not to see Aura swabbing George Toller's molars with her tongue.

I made it to my desk without heartbreak.

There was a job to do and a life to live and even though that was more than I could handle, there was nothing I could accomplish at 8:39 that morning.

So I logged on and started reading about the world war my father predicted.

It was mid-November 2008. There were pirates taking ships with impunity in African waters, terrorists punching holes in Indian security, China sinking toward depression because Americans were afraid to buy cheap goods for Christmas, and the richest nation in the history of the world talking about how to keep to a budget.

The buzzer of my front door sounded a few minutes shy of nine o'clock. I saw Aura on the screen of the four monitors in my desk drawer, her African and European heritage from the front, back, and both sides. The dress suit she wore was off-white working overtime to complement her ecru skin. Her big eyes looked up into the camera she knew was there.

She pressed the button again but I could see no benefit in answering.

She had the keys to my door, the combination to my inner locks, but she wouldn't use them.

I closed the drawer and picked up the office phone.

After seventeen rings he answered.

"Who the fuck is this?" Luke Nye bellowed into my ear.

"I wake you up, Luke?"

"Oh, hey, LT. What's up, man?"

The pool hustler wasn't intimidated. We just had an understanding like fellow soldiers from the same regiment fighting the good fight on foreign soil. Day or night, we were on call, and there was no use making any kind of big deal out of it.

That's the career criminal way of life—you're always behind enemy lines, you're always at war. And even though I was trying my best to go straight, I couldn't erase years of training.

"A guy named Gustav who works out of a pool hall down on Houston—"

"Shandley's," Luke said before I could get the word out. "Pretends like he's a Russian gangster but he's from Rumania. Got some Russians workin' for him, though. They say he's got the biggest dick in the tristate area. I don't know for a fact, I'm just sayin'."

"What about him?"

"He runs the pool hall as a kind of office. Asian kids come there to sharpen up their skills, but the real action is a few blocks east, where he's got a warehouse filled with foreign ladies just waiting to please."

"Pimp?"

"Sex-slaver. Brings 'em in from all over the world promising freedom, a hundred thousand dollars, and papers if they make a million on their backs—or thereabouts. Some of them make it but he has a lending policy for clothes and drugs; charges interest. Most of the ladies work until he sells them to less reputable thugs."

"Dangerous?"

"Smart. He knows that there's no more cowboys. He tries to keep it steady and nonviolent as long as no one messes with his product. But he's willing to go as far as necessary to protect his offshore accounts. . . . You got a problem with Gutsy?"

"You could say that."

There was a short silence on the line. I could hear faint, indefinable music in the background.

"You don't need Hush or anything like that," Luke said at last. "I mean, Gutsy knows a player when he sees one."

"Thanks, Luke. I'll pay you when I see you."

"Soon?"

"Day or two."

I TOOK A TAXI down to Shandley's. It was on Houston, a few blocks east of Elizabeth, on the north side of the street.

It was a clean place with a few youngsters shooting pool, trying their best to look cool without the benefit of cigarettes dangling from their lips. Most were Asian, none were black. I wondered what that meant.

It was a long, shallow, and dark space with sixteen tables, two deep.

At the back of the room was a set of double doors guarded by the big guy that I'd wailed on the night before. I didn't recognize his face but the bruised cheekbone, swollen nose, and bandages on his left wrist were definite clues.

The tough guy bristled when I approached. He made a forward move with his shoulder and I held up a finger.

"I'm not here to fight," I said.

"I need to search you before you can go in."

"Touch me and I'll touch you back," I said.

He didn't quite understand the phrase but he got the meaning.

"Tell Gustav I'm out here alone and if he's not scared or nuthin' maybe we could talk."

The sentry went through the right door, closing it behind him.

I stood there feeling like I was wasting time. There was a lot to be done, but your kids come first. That was a lesson I got in the negative space of my father's abandonment.

The door opened and the big guy waved me toward him.

Approaching, I stopped at the threshold and gestured for him to precede me.

It was a medium-sized, windowless room filled with the smoke of foreign cigarettes. There were five men in attendance. Four bullets, I figured, was more than enough for that crowd. After all, one of them was already wounded, and I had a knife, too.

My other assailant was sitting next to a red-faced guy who looked big even sitting down. This, I was sure, must be Gustav. Behind them stood two slender guys in nice suits. They might have been brothers but one was ugly with bad skin and exaggerated features, while the other could have been a matinee idol.

"Have a seat," Gustav said.

Eyeing the banged-up guy next to me, I said, "No thanks."

"If you don't want to visit why are you here?"

"I was going to see my girl last night and these guys jumped me," I said by way of explanation.

"Vassily lost two teeth," Gustav said, patting the shoulder of the man sitting next to him. "And Bruno had to have thirty-six, what you call them, stitches, on his arm. It is me who should be mad at you."

"I can't help it if you got pussies workin' for you."

The one called Vassily tried to rise but Gustav put a hand on his shoulder again.

"What is your name?" the big boss asked me.

It's funny how a simple thought put into words, or even just an intonation, will affect you sometimes.

My response to his question was unexpected fear. It wasn't that I minded telling him some name, or that he might somehow catch me in the lie. It was the weight of all the moments that led me into this closed room with rough men who hated me for reasons that were older than America. I was afraid of being killed by them. And also of killing them.

These men are not your enemies, my father whispered into my right ear.

Thou shalt not kill, my mother said in my left.

"John Tooms," I stated with certainty. "And I don't want to think that I got to be lookin' over my shoulder because these guys are too stupid to go after the right mark. I mean, if you and me got trouble we settle it right here, right now."

I meant every word I was saying. I had a license for a concealed weapon, and the men in that room were all criminals. They were after my son. I had to hold back from attacking them right then and there.

Hubris.

Gustav smiled.

"Calm down, Mr. Tooms," he said. "You are not our enemy. It was mistake. My men made mistake. Two mistakes, by the look of their faces. You like girls, Mr. Tooms?"

I said nothing, pretending not to understand the question.

"Joe," Gustav said to the matinee idol. "Bring out Diamond."

Joe opened a door behind him. I moved my thumb in such a way that the pistol could be in my hand in no time.

For the next few seconds my shoulder listed imperceptibly to the right. Gustav would be the first to die, or maybe Joe. Bruno would probably be last. I'd get shot, at least, but that didn't have to be fatal.

When Joe came back into the room he was accompanied by a white teenaged girl. Completely naked, she had all the so-called charms of a woman, but I could see the vestiges of adolescence in her face.

"This is Diamond. You could take her in back room or she could go with you somewhere," Gustav said. "She just has to be back by two. I give this to you for apology."

Diamond, without being asked, turned around slowly so that I could further appreciate her beauty. The only blemish was an angry bruise on her left buttock.

"No thanks," I said.

"You want boy?" the boss asked.

"No," I said, forcing a smile to my lips. "No. I got my own girl. All I need to know is that you're gonna leave me alone when I'm over at her house."

"I have no business with you, Mr. Tooms."

"Because the next time I see any'a your men near me I'll do more than loosen some teeth."

31

I walked eight blocks north, wandered a little to the west, and stopped at a rare phone booth I knew of on St. Marks Place. There I dialed a number that I shouldn't have known.

"Hello?" he said on the second ring.

"What's this shit about Russian gangsters, Twill?"

"Pops?"

"Answer me."

"Where'd you get this number?"

Twill had gotten a friend of his to buy a pay-as-you-go cell phone with a Utah area code nine months before. That was his *secret* line. The only problem with the secret was that Bug Bateman had built me a shadow Internet ID that could read any e-mail that the boy sent or received—all without his knowledge. One of those e-mails had passed on the secret number.

"I'm a detective, boy," I said. "It's my job to know things. Now tell me about this Gustav dude."

"Uh . . ."

I had to smile. It was a rare event indeed to catch my son so unawares that he was speechless.

"You got it, Pops," he said then. "Bulldog fell for this girl named Tatyana, and she was tied to this dude. She's Russian—kinda. But you got it wrong about Gustav—he's a Rumanian.

"Tatyana says that she did everything Gustav said but he got kind of a thing for her and wouldn't let go. So D tried to run with her but they got in too deep and called me."

"I thought we agreed that you'd come to me if there was serious trouble," I said.

"That was if *I* got in trouble, Pops. This was D's mess. You know Dimitri, Dad. If I called you he might'a done somethin' stupid."

"Where are you?"

"Up in the Bronx."

"At that gambling house?" I dealt out another secret so that Twill would worry.

"You know about that, too?"

"I need to see you, Twill. And your mother needs to see Dimitri. She's used to you runnin' around like you do, but she never saw D do anything like this."

"D's upstate with Tatyana. I got a friend up there put 'em up. I'll call him but he probably won't even get the message till tonight."

"Then you," I said.

"I'll meet you at Takahashi's at four, Pops. I swear."

AMERICANS BELIEVE IN STRAIGHT lines. They think that all you have to do is get out there and get the job done, one step after the other. If you don't do that then you're either lazy or incompetent. American men especially, and more and more women all the time, seem to think that life is like a mission. That's how they approach sports and war and sex—even love. That's what they think about when somebody's credit goes bad or there's an accident on the road: somebody veered off the straight and narrow.

Years of orphanages and foster homes, uneducated teachers and corrupt officials, from crossing guards to the presidents of entire nations, have shown me that Einstein was right: the connection between A and B is questionable at best, and there's no such thing as a straight line.

I couldn't wait for Angie's problem to be resolved while Dimitri and Twill were in trouble. And that was true for every other problem I was dealing with.

I FOUND OUT FROM a guy I know in the City Planner's office that the building Angelique lived in was owned by Plenty Realty. Plenty had their office on Hudson in the West Village. It was a one-room affair on the fourth floor of a building a few blocks south of Christopher Street.

I called the office, looking to speak to the owner, a Mr. Jeffrey Planter.

"Old Mr. Planter's dead," the young woman said in a flat tone, "and Jeff Junior is in Florida for the winter."

"It's not winter yet," I said, more in response to her tone than her words.

"Is that all you wanted?"

"Is there somebody in charge?"

"Mr. Nichols."

"May I speak to him?"

"He's not here. And he's old, anyway. His hearing aid always messes up when he holds the phone to his ear."

"When will he be back?"

"I don't know exactly. He's showin' somebody a place right now."

"Will he be back by noon?"

"That's when I go to lunch."

"I'm not coming to see you."

The nameless receptionist hung up on me. I couldn't blame her.

I GOT TO PLENTY REALTY at ten past twelve. The fourth-floor door was unlocked so I walked in without knocking.

It was a small office with three desks in a line against the far wall. Only the center desk was occupied. An older gentleman, a gray-haired white man, stood up when I walked in. He was barely taller and a lot thinner than I. He wore a baggy, dark-green suit, a brick-red-and-white-checkered shirt, and thick-lensed glasses rimmed with dull steel.

"How can I help you, Mr. Trotter?" he asked after I identified myself as a private detective working for Nyla Winetraub. "This doesn't have anything to do with that mix-up when we thought she'd moved to Florida, does it?"

"No."

"Because we were going on the information we received," he said, blundering on in spite of my assurance. "We were acting in good faith."

"You know that Ms. Winetraub is nearly blind."

"Yes," Mr. Nichols said. He smiled. I wondered at that. Was he happy that he had some kind of knowledge about his tenant? Or was it that he was relieved that he was almost as old as Nyla but still managed eyesight?

"Well," I said. "Miss Lear from upstairs takes care of Nyla's correspondence and other incidentals, but Lear's been missing for more than a week and Nyla is worried about her friend as well as herself."

"I don't see how I can help you, Mr. Trotter. I mean, I haven't seen Miss Lear for three years, not since she signed the papers on her unit."

"I tried to speak to your super, a Mr. Klott . . ."

Nichols grimaced when I mentioned the name.

"...but he wouldn't tell me anything."

"Klott is a sourpuss if ever there was one," Nichols told me. "But I still can't see where any of this concerns our office."

"I was wondering if Miss Lear had moved, or maybe that she was evicted."

"Oh no. Not at all. The rent on that unit is very low to begin with, and she doesn't pay full price anyway."

"No? The landlord supplements her?" I asked. "Maybe she's with him down in Florida."

"How did you . . . ?" Nichols waved his hands around and then clasped them, the grin back on his lips. "Certainly not. And you shouldn't try to call him. He'd get very upset with me for divulging tenant information."

"I don't want to cause any trouble, Mr. Nichols. I'm just trying to do my job. A young woman is missing and nobody seems to want to help. Now, if there's somebody paying Miss Lear's rent, maybe a family member, then I could have something to give poor Miss Winetraub."

"There's really nothing I can do to help you there, Mr. Trotter. The money, sixty-six-point-six percent of her rent, came from a bank in Delaware. We've been told to keep that knowledge from her. They contacted us just after she called to see an apartment. They asked us to quote only the portion of the rent she was expected to pay. I'm just telling you this because I've said too much already. I do hope that you will keep the confidence."

"I'm working for Winetraub," I said. "And all she wants is for me to assure her that Miss Lear isn't in any trouble. I don't care who's paying the rent unless that leads me to the information I need."

"There was one thing," the nervous little man said.

"Yes?"

"A couple of weeks ago we got a call from Mr. Klott telling us that there was an incident in front of the property. It seems that two men accosted Miss Lear. I'd forgotten because nothing really happened."

"They tried to pick her up or something?" I asked, trying to seem as dense and as coarse as I possibly could.

"No. At least I don't think so. Two big strong men in suits tried to make her get into their car."

"What happened?"

"There's a building down the street tenanted by some, uh, long-haired men with tattoos and the like. They work on cars." Nichols sounded excited by these men. I was sure that he could describe the scent of their sweat. "They saved Miss Lear . . . drove the attackers off."

"That sounds promising," I said.

"Yes. Their place is three buildings east of our property."

"You seem to know a lot about that building, Mr. Nichols. Are you this familiar with all Plenty properties?"

"The senior Mr. Planter owned quite a few buildings," Mr. Nichols said wistfully. "His son has sold almost everything. Now we . . . I . . . am mostly a real estate agent for rentals and sales here in the West Village. But I go out to look at the three buildings we still own . . . at least once a month."

He took off his glasses and rubbed them clean with his blue-and-white tie.

"Can you think of anything else, Mr. Nichols?"

"No."

"There's no name associated with the money from the bank?"

"No."

"Maybe if I spoke to Jeff?" I suggested.

"The transfer was made electronically, and the original communication was made by phone—with me. Jeffy . . . Mr. Planter doesn't spend much time in the office even when he's in New York. It was a woman's voice but I'm sure it wasn't her money."

"How much is Lear paying?"

Nichols hesitated but then said, "Six hundred, but you can't tell anybody that."

"Wasn't she surprised that the rent was so low?"

"No," the elder man said, wincing at the memory. "She might have even tried to talk me down. I'm pretty sure she did. But when I wouldn't budge she accepted the price and signed a five-year lease."

"Five years?"

"The bank wanted it that way. They paid the full balance of their share up front. It was a good deal. We needed to do work on that building, and so it was all tax-deductible."

Nichols was looking very nervous. I got the feeling he wasn't used to having visitors and didn't really know how to converse without letting out too much.

"Don't worry," I said. "I'm not here to cause trouble for you. I'll go talk to the hippies. I'm sure that they'll be able to tell me something."

"Yes. Yes, I'm sure they will." But he didn't look very confident.

32

Three lots down from Angelique Lear's apartment was a three-story building that had once been a single-family residence, had then been converted to apartments, and now was, once more, tenanted by a single group—related by interest if not by blood. A few windows were open on the south-facing wall. From each of these some kind of music was blasting. I could make out heavy metal, hard rock, and some punk. No R&B, blues, or rock and roll proper.

I didn't need a tour guide to tell me that the two men working on the '64 Chevy in the open garage had done time and spent almost every moment of it in the company of their white brothers.

They both had long hair. The younger of the two had greasy red tresses, while his heavier friend's hair was salt-and-pepper, with a bald spot toward the back. They wore overalls and T-shirts in spite of the November chill. They had more tattoos than a lot of merchant marines, and almost every one represented a crime, sexual act, or violent wish fulfillment.

They seemed to be enjoying their work, until the younger one looked up to see me standing at the threshold of their garage.

"What the fuck you want?" he said, mimicking perfectly the dialect of people he probably detested.

The older ex-con hefted a twenty-four-inch wrench and stared at me. There were letters on the patches of skin between the knucklebones and finger joints of his fist but I didn't have the leisure to look closely enough to read what was written.

"Excuse me, gentlemen," I said in my best English, "but I have come here today to find out what happened to a young woman named Angelique Tara Lear."

"Huh?" Red said.

"Get the fuck outta my garage, man," the older one warned as he approached me with the bludgeon, held at waist level.

"I respect a man's domicile," I said, wearing the disguise of language. "That's why I am standing on the sidewalk."

"In my fuckin' driveway, motherfucker," he corrected.

By now he was almost upon me—his mistake. The ten or twelve pounds of stainless steel would be of little use to him in such close quarters.

"I was told that you saved the lady in question," I said as if we were gentlemen in a Sherlock Holmes story. "Miss Lear has disappeared and her father hired me to make sure that she's all right."

Even though I hadn't actually used the word, money was now a part of the conversation.

Red had moved up to flank his brother in life and in crime. He had an uneven green *X* tattooed on the left side of his neck. It was a jagged cry of illiterate emotion.

"What you want her for?" the younger man asked.

"Angelique and her father are estranged," I explained. "He only found out from her landlord yesterday about the attack. It seems that she's late on the rent and her mother, the cosigner, didn't have the money to cover it. She called the father, the father called Plenty Realty, and they told him about the attack. I guess a Mr. Klott told them."

"Klott," the balding white man spat. "He's a piece'a shit."

"Mr. Lear hired me to make sure his daughter was all right,

and so I came to the people who saved her. He's willing to pay for information that will lead to his peace of mind."

"It was me was there," the kid said.

"But this is my house," the elder added. "My rules."

"Hey, Pete," the younger man objected. "You don't own what me and Figg did. You wasn't even there when those men jumped that girl."

Pete turned his head, placing his free hand on the kid's chest.

"This is my house, Lonnie. You live here for nuthin'. You eat and sleep on my dime. So you wouldn't even'a been here if it wasn't for me."

The kid's light-blue eyes were considering the words—also the big piece of steel in his benefactor's right hand.

The younger man needn't have worried. I wouldn't have let Pete break his skull. That cranium contained information I needed.

"Yeah, sure, Pete. You right," the kid said.

For a long moment Pete stared at Lonnie. Then he turned to me. "You still here, blood?"

"Mr. Lear doesn't care who he pays for the information," I said simply, unperturbed by the elder's display of personal power.

"I told you to leave."

"You don't want the money?"

"I want to crack your head open with this wrench."

Most people will explain their jobs to you with surprising accuracy. They were, let's say, given a hundred tasks and they accomplished that number. Or, if only ninety-seven jobs were completed, they'll have a good excuse for the gaffe—which is usually something or someone else's fault. The generator blew, they might tell you. Or their associates, underlings, or bosses failed to make good on their promises or deadlines.

Even the president of the United States claimed that his war was a mistake based on misinformation he received from those whom he expected to supply him with the truth.

People who work within systems can avoid their own short-comings because they are surrounded by people who are just as flawed.

I have never had that luxury. I work for myself and according to my own rules. When I was a crook, working for crooks, I had better know my weaknesses because a misstep meant at least prison and at worst death. And once I decided to go straight, my options became even more restricted. No one was going to protect me. No one was going to cover for my errors.

One of my most serious flaws is physical overconfidence. I'm rarely afraid of any man or group of men who threaten me. That's why when I was faced by Gustav and his Eastern European goons I was, mostly, fearless.

This fearlessness, by the fact of the absoluteness of the word in a physical world, is unfounded. I can be hurt. I can be killed. And, worse than all that, I can lose. But somewhere in my true being I am unaware of these facts. And so when Pete threatened to smash my skull, I smiled.

It wasn't a broad grin. I didn't show any teeth, but a bare flicker of disdain did cross my lips, and therefore the line that Pete had, in his mind, etched in the concrete at our feet.

Most people who glance at me see a short, bald, overweight, middle-aged black man. Not much of a threat to anyone. But prison had taught Pete to look closer.

After that smirk, he studied me like a religious scholar carefully perusing an original leaf of the New Testament, scrawled upon crumbling parchment.

It took him a minute but finally he said, "Show me some ID."

John Tooms had a detective's license with my picture on it. It was laminated and stamped, official to even the closest of inspections, and as counterfeit as a hundred-thousand-dollar bill.

If there was any flaw in the document Pete would have found it. He studied the card with an expert's eye. He tested everything from the texture of the photograph to the edges of the lamination.

Handing the card back to me, he asked, "How much?"

"Thousand dollars if I get any information that I should be able to chase down."

"Thousand dollars," Lonnie whispered.

"Let's see it."

"Let's hear what your friend here has to say first."

"Okay," Pete said. "Come on upstairs and we'll talk over a beer."

"I would prefer to take a walk down to the restaurant on the corner."

"You scared?" Pete asked, giving me a triumphant grin.

"I never enter the living quarters of a man who has threatened me."

"How can I be sure you'll pay if I let Lonnie talk to you?"

"You know my name and you know the location of my office. I'm not stupid enough to try and cheat a whole house full of ex-cons."

The three of us stood around for a few seconds more. Everything had already been decided, we just needed a short time for that decision to settle.

33

The Cisco Kid Café was a dilapidated restaurant-bar with posters of old westerns on the walls. The strawberry-blond waitress wore a very short cranberry skirt over stout shapeless legs and sported clashing tattoos that bore witness to a life of rebellion and failure.

"Hey, Lonnie," she said to the youngest of us.

"China," he responded.

"What can I get for you guys?"

"I'll take whatever you got on tap and they can have anything they want," I said, making it clear that the bill should come to me.

Lonnie ordered a beer, while Pete asked for a double margarita without salt.

"So this is how it works," I said to the men once China had gone. "What I need is information I can work with. Descriptions, license plates, things they said or that Angelique said about them. I need something to help me find her. That's what I'll base the payment on. If you can't give me a few things like that then we can just have our drinks and move on."

Lonnie and Pete looked at each other. It was straight talk and they accepted it.

Pete nodded. "What if you can't find her with what we give you?"

"That's my problem. I'll pay for good intelligence. But I don't want to hear about some black Lincoln and two guys in suits."

"What if you're workin' for the guys after her?" Lonnie asked. He was still an innocent, in spite of his associations.

"Do you know where she went?" I asked.

"No."

"Then anything you give me the guys who tried to grab her probably already know. I need to get to them."

China came back with our drinks and served them. She and Lonnie exchanged a few pleasantries before she wandered off to the bar to chat with the young bartender—who sported a bright-yellow Mohawk.

"I wrote down the license-plate number," Lonnie said when the girl was gone. "It was a dark-green Lincoln . . . pretty late model."

"You got the number on you?"

"In my wallet."

"Anything else?"

"Figg—Figgis—an' me heard the girl screaming when we were workin' on his motorcycle," Lonnie said. "We run out and see these two white guys in business suits tryin' to drag her into their car. They didn't look like cops, so we run over there. Figg took a tire iron. He got there first and told 'em to let her go. They said he better get away and he cracked the passenger's side of their windshield. One guy reached into his pocket and I hit him in the jaw."

"What'd they do then?"

"Figg broke a headlight, and I think they were worried that a cop would pull 'em over, even if they got away from us. There was people stoppin' to look by then. They let her go and took off. That's when I memorized their license-plate number . . . at, at least long enough to write it down."

"What did Miss Lear say?"

"She thanked us. We asked what did they want and she told us that she didn't know but that they were probably workin' for some guy that'd been hasslin' her. We asked her who the guy was but she didn't say."

"Did she say what it was they wanted with her?"

"She said that she wasn't even sure what it was about."

"Anything else?"

"Uh-uh. She just thanked us and went up to her place."

"How long ago was this?"

"Two weeks today. I remember 'cause we had a party that night. We invited Angelique, and she said she'd come by, but she didn't."

"You call the cops?" I asked.

"We don't talk to cops, man," Pete said. "Not never."

"Then why take down the plate number?"

"I gave it to her," Lonnie said. "I thought she might call the police herself."

"Can I have it?"

Lonnie looked at Pete and the elder nodded. The kid had a green wallet made from desiccated plastic that was cracking. From this cheap billfold he produced a grayish-white scrap with a number written on it.

"It was a New York plate," the kid said.

I reached into my right-front pocket and came out with a roll of cash that I had prepared before getting to the house.

"Who do I give this to?" I asked the men.

Pete reached for the wad and Lonnie didn't complain. I let go the money and watched it disappear into Pete's overalls.

"Anything else?" I asked, just to say something.

"Yeah," Lonnie said. "She said that her luck had run out."

"What did she mean by that?"

"She told Figg that she'd had a run of real good luck for seven years, just about. Now she figured she had to pay for it."

I digested that little piece of secondhand editorializing and then stood up.

"You not gonna finish your beer?" Pete asked me.

"Strike while the iron's hot," I replied. "I'll leave fifty with China. You guys have a good time."

34

I walked westward toward the Village proper, thinking about luck. Wanda Soa was unlucky—definitely. The man who probably shot her shared the same ill fortune. Ron Sharkey and a few dozen others that I'd focused my attention on were luckless bastards who were blindsided by disasters while they planned vacations, retirement, and weekends with their grandkids.

In this way Angie and I had something in common: we were descendants of Typhoid Mary, passing over earth that would one day soon inter the bodies of our luckless victims.

My cell phone sounded, proving to me, for at least that moment, that providence favors the arbiters of evil.

"Hey, Breland," I said into the phone. "What's up?"

"They arrested Ron Sharkey. Have him in that special federal facility down south of Houston on the West Side."

"What's the charge?"

"They don't have one yet, but I was told by the agents who arrested him that they were considering terrorism."

"You're kidding."

"That's what the man said."

"Can I get in to see him?"

"I'll work on it. You in the city?"

"Call me when you got something."

TAKAHASHI'S IS A JAPANESE coffee house on the third floor of a nondescript building between University and Fifth. Twill had found the place when he was only twelve and truancy was his pastime. He liked the people who owned and ran the odd establishment, even learned a few phrases in Japanese. They served good coffee and great tea, had a small menu, free bowls of rice crackers, and various performances in the evening, from workshop poetry to Asian string music.

During the day not many people came around.

It was the perfect place for surreptitious afternoon meetings.

I arrived at 3:53. Twill was already there, seated by the window that looked down on the street.

I waved to the owners, who were at the opposite end of the long, unpopulated room. Angel and Kenji smiled and waved back.

"Hey, Pops," Twill said as I took the seat across from him. "S'happenin'?"

I gazed into my son's dark, handsome face and shook my head. I wanted to be angry with him, but that would be an uphill task. He might not have been honest, but he was a good boy—no, a good man in a boy's body.

"Been down so long," I said, "looks like up to me."

"That's a book, right?"

"Yeah. How did you know?"

"Mardi got me readin'," he said. "One day I told her that I didn't read much because there's millions of books and I never know which ones I should be studying. I mean, teachers talkin' 'bout Mark Twain and Charles Dickens and shit. But I don't understand what they got to say got to do with me. But then Mardi says that it's not what's in the book but just the fact that somebody reads that builds up the mind, like. That sounded good, 'cause then I could read whatever I want and still be ahead of the game."

One of the pitfalls presented by my son was how engaging he was in conversation. He knew how much I loved to play with ideas, especially when those ideas had to do with thinking that ran contrary to everyday beliefs. He knew how much I liked to read.

"Talk to me, Twill."

That brought a broad grin to the young man's face.

"Her name is Tatyana Baranovich," he said. "Baranovich. She comes from a place called Minsk and has won every award that CCNY has to give to an undergraduate. She's a senior, about to graduate. D been talkin' about her for almost a year now. You know how shy he is. Every now and then they got coffee together, and that'd keep him smilin' for two weeks."

"So she didn't feel the same?" I asked.

"I don't know what she felt. I tried to get Bulldog to ask her on a date. I told him we could get your car and I'd take somebody, too. But he said that he just liked talkin' to her. But you should see this girl, Pops. I mean, she got it workin' every which way. Damn."

I felt like a dirty old man cackling at Twill's leering sexual expression.

"So what happened?" I asked.

"One day he sees that Tatyana is all upset. She tells him that she can't go back to her apartment because the man who paid her rent wanted her to do something that would mean she couldn't go to graduate school."

"Gustav."

"Yeah, right." Twill was a little discomfited that I was ahead of him in the story. "Gustav's a pimp. Tatyana is in the country illegally. And she's a hot number with some of his clients out west. He tells her that she can go to graduation but after that she has to work full-time for a few years."

"Did she make good on the million?"

"Damn, Pops, you *are* a private detective, huh?"

"Did she make her nut?"

"She says so," Twill allowed. "And I believe it, too. She doesn't have real fancy clothes or no habit. City College don't cost that much.

"D came to me and I talked to the girl. She told me about Gustav but not how connected he was. It was only later on that I found out he had people all over the place lookin' for her. D been thinkin' that maybe they could go down to New Orleans and start over, like."

"And you were going to help him?"

Twill admitted his involvement with a slight motion of his left shoulder.

"If Gustav is so connected like you say, then you know New Orleans would probably only be a temporary fix."

"Yeah, I know. But when they were gone I knew I could tell you, and then it would only be a matter of time before it was all smoothed out again."

It was the first time I had seen the boy in Twill for at least three years. He showed an unshakable faith in my ability to save him and his brother. I was so surprised that it might have shown.

"So D and this Tatyana are together now?"

"Oh yeah. All night, every night. He thinks they're in love."

"Are they?"

"He is."

"Twill, if you suspect that this girl is playin' your brother, why help?"

"Tatyana's okay. She in trouble, and she a ho' through no fault of her own. Somebody got to break D's cherry, an' you know he will remember that girl till the day his grandchildren die."

"Hyperbole," I said.

"Poetic exaggeration," he corrected.

"What am I going to do with you, Twill?"

"Me? It's D in trouble, Pops."

"Without meeting you she would never even be with him. You're the one that convinced her something could be done."

"Oh, come on, man. Don't put that shit on me. Bulldog's my brother. He asked me to help him. I couldn't say no."

"No," I admitted, "you couldn't."

"So what do you want me to do?" Twill asked.

"Tell Dimitri that two men from Gustav were laying for him out in front of his mother's house. His mother's house. They saw me in the dark and thought it was him. They attacked me, threatened me, pulled a knife on me. You tell him that and then say I figured out what was going on. Then you tell Tatyana that I intend to do something, but she has to come meet with me first."

Twill nodded, a wry twist to his mouth.

"Convince her, Twill," I added. "I can't do this neatly without talking to her."

His assent was in his eyes, even more subtle than the shifting of a shoulder.

When we got up to leave he put a ten and a five on the table. He never ate and rarely drank at Takahashi's, but he always left a tip.

We separated on the street. Him, a boy walking off into a man's life, and me wondering, What if the Gordian knot was someone you loved?

35

I was already taxiing my way toward the federal detention center when Breland called and said that I had been granted permission to visit the prisoner.

The so-called holding facility was on the seventh floor of a building that had once been a warehouse. Instead of bars there was thick metal grating over every door and window—laced with razor wire along the seams.

The first person I met was a brown woman with a skinny body and a huge round face. She was standing on the opposite side of a small, iron-latticed window that was set toward the left side of a large wall. The waiting room, where I was standing, was nearly empty. The only other applicant was an Arab woman, surrounded by three small children. She was slumped in a chair. The feeling she radiated was that of intense hopelessness.

"Can I help you?" the bureaucrat asked through the haze of crisscrossed metal.

"Leonid McGill for Ron Sharkey."

"Purpose of visit?"

"His lawyer sent me."

Name? Occupation? Relationship to inmate? Citizenship? Weapons? Other contraband? (This was followed by a long list of everything from cash to chewing gum.)

"Any and all actions, comments, and utterances may be recorded while you are here," she said when the list was through.

Utterances?

"But I represent his lawyer," I said.

"If you do not wish to continue we can stop the process here."

"No," I said. "You can knock yourselves out recording me. Just remember my left profile is my good side."

The brown woman—who had short, straightened hair—almost smiled.

"Have a seat, Mr. McGill," she said. "You'll be called in the order this application has been filed."

The morose Arab woman didn't seem to want to commiserate, so I sat five metal chairs away from her and her oppressed children—waiting my place in a line of two.

Seventeen minutes later a man's voice said, "McGill."

The woman had yet to be called.

I looked around and saw that a door-sized panel to my right had slid open. After a moment that might have seemed like hesitation I stood up and went through the makeshift doorway.

The hall was short, ending at a larger-than-normal metal door replete with a metal screen window.

A man stood on the other side of that door.

"I'm Agent Galsworthy. How can I help you?" a tall white man in a gray-green suit asked me. His eyes were the color of lemons and pecans, giving the impression of small, dusky oranges. He was slender and should have been tall except for the fact that he was a little stooped over, which was odd because he wasn't a day over forty.

"McGill for Sharkey," I said.

"How did you know he was here?" the official asked through the grating. He was my own personal antagonist-confessor.

"His lawyer."

"Who's that?"

"Breland Lewis."

"What's your relationship with the prisoner?"

"His lawyer—Breland Lewis."

It was then that I detected a strong smell of human sweat on the air.

"What is your connection to the prisoner?"

"Can I just say ditto, or is there some reason I got to say the same words over and over?" I asked.

Galsworthy was like the cop in front of Wanda Soa's building; he thought that an evil stare would break me down to jelly. But he was just another bean counter. The only difference was that he counted skulls instead of legumes.

I smiled politely.

"What do you do for Sharkey's lawyer?"

"PI."

I have learned over the years that you never give a lawman or a bureaucrat any more information than they ask for. If you do, they get confused, and then they get angry.

"You aren't on the visitors list," the pen-pusher told me.

"Lewis said that he called."

"The call has to be followed by a fax."

"You're telling me that he didn't send the fax?"

"We check the machine every three hours."

"And so I have to wait until that time is up and someone looks?"

"That will be after visiting hours are over."

"So what are you telling me?"

"Procedure," Galsworthy said, as if I were a dog trying to understand the true intentions of the man who called himself my master.

"Thomas," another voice said.

Through the haze of metal crosshatching came a broad man in a slate suit with the jacket open, his shirted belly hanging out. This man was in law enforcement. I could only hope that he had more power than the hunched-over inquisitor.

"Yes?" Galsworthy said to the new arrival.

"Let Mr. McGill in."

"We haven't received the fax yet."

The slightly disheveled man took a key from his pocket and approached the door that separated us.

"I have to finish the paperwork before you can allow him to enter," Galsworthy complained.

"You go do that, Tom. Mr. McGill and me will be in my office."

While speaking, the cop, whatever kind of cop he was, unlocked the door and swung it inward.

"Stop!" Galsworthy shouted.

Heads shot up at desks in the small office behind the two men. Two uniformed federal officers came in through a door with hands on their holstered pistols.

I stepped across the threshold as the pudgy cop held up his hands for the guards.

"No problem," he said to everybody but Thomas Galsworthy. "Just a question of jurisdiction."

The uniforms sighed and went back to their office. The heads went back down, and the cop offered me a welcoming hand.

"Jake Plumb," he said. "I'm in charge of the Sharkey case. Don't pay any attention to Tom here. It's his job to make sure that nobody ever gets in to visit their clients and loved ones. He's kept one poor woman and her kids outside for the past three weeks. Her husband isn't even here anymore, but the rules are we can't say that he's been shuttled down to the deportation detention center in Miami. Ain't that right, Tom?"

Agent Galsworthy sneered in silence.

"What do you do, Mr. McGill?" Plumb asked me.

Jake was three inches taller than I but his loose girth made him seem a bit shorter.

"PI," I said, "here to see, as you already seem to know, Ron Sharkey."

"Come on down to my little office, Mr. PI. I'd like to talk to you before you get in to see the junkie."

Thomas Galsworthy stared at us with what he must have thought was an evil gaze. But he kept silent, I guessed, because of having been humiliated by the way Jake had usurped his power in the office. The fat federal cop was moving toward another caged door. He used his key on that and we moved into a darker, more sinister area of the detainment center. We passed through three more locked doors until we came to a long aisle of nine-by-nine-by-nine cages designed to hold men for days, weeks, months, and sometimes for years; these prisoners were black men and brown ones, some Asians, and a sprinkling of whites.

These prisoners were silent and for the most part motionless. They had been defeated by a system so vast and unresponsive, so utterly powerful, that only suicide could counter the weight of it. The hall smelled powerfully of stagnant manhood, the longtime suffering of the guilty, the innocent, and those who just did not belong.

I followed behind Jake Plumb, gazing into the metal crevices. Some men stared out at me with red-rimmed brown-veined eyes, not hopefully but just for a momentary diversion in a life of deadly dull monotony. Madness and cancer, bloodletting and revolution grew like fungus in rooms such as these. I could feel the ghost of my father urging those souls to prepare to tear down those cages, that building, the whole city if they had to.

I wondered if Jake Plumb felt any of what I sensed.

"Right through here, Mr. PI," he said.

We'd come to a solid steel door with a fingerprint-activated lock on the side. I couldn't help but imagine the men we'd just passed hacking off Plumb's hand and using it, the blood still warm, to pop that lock in their bid for freedom—or revenge.

HIS WINDOWLESS OFFICE WAS small, and much neater than I'd expected. Even though we were on the seventh floor it felt to me like an OCD bunker in a lull between bombings.

Plumb's face was flat and wide like a bulldog's but his eyes were Chihuahua-like in their relative size and brightness. His smile was almost a frown.

"So," he said.

We were seated across from each other in this sepulchral workspace.

I didn't reply to the ambiguous beginning of the informal interrogation.

"What do you want with Mr. Sharkey?" he asked.

"His lawyer believes in his innocence and does not think he should be here under federal jurisdiction. The car wasn't his, he didn't cross state lines, he didn't have the keys to the trunk on him, and there's no evidence of him ever having been involved in illegal gun sales."

Plumb's glittery little eyes flared for me.

"Terrorism," he said.

"Come on, Agent Plumb. You yourself called Ron a junkie."

"'Ron'?"

"I like to get personal with the people I try to help. There's not the slightest bit of evidence that Ron had anything to do with terrorists or terrorism. You're more of a terrorist than he could ever be."

That last sentence came unbidden from me.

"What?" he said. It was definitely a threat.

"What you got out there, man?" I said. "Haitians and Dominicans, Moroccans, Syrians, and Palestinians? If they're lucky you'll send them home. If they're unlucky you'll send them home in five years. It doesn't matter what they did, but whatever it is, when they leave here they'll hate me because I'm a citizen of a country that treated them like nothing.

"All Ron Sharkey did was take a joyride. You, on the other hand, got your fist shoved up the ass of every man comes through here."

I couldn't believe what I was saying. These were certainly my father's words. I don't even know if I believed them.

Surprisingly, Jake Plumb smiled.

"Kinda sensitive for a PI, ain't you, Leonid?"

"Bad day," I said, manufacturing a wry grin.

"Your lawyer's client had six semiautomatic weapons that had been altered to fully automatic bundled in his trunk," the federal agent told me. "We think that he knows something about it. We're sure that he does. I don't care about him, or you for that matter. All I want is a name. Because with that I can get out of this shithole and have a job in a proper office doing work I can be proud of."

There was a whole chapter squashed down into those few sentences, things about Jake Plumb that I would never know. But that didn't matter. He was giving me an opportunity, and I was intent on taking it.

"I'm here to secure Ron's freedom," I said. "I will do my best to achieve that end. If that means getting a name for you, I will try my utmost."

The bulldog snarled a smile that made me doubt he had ever been happy a day in his life.

36

The small visitors' room was illuminated by six one-hundred-watt bare bulbs, and still darkness clung to the corners. The furnishings consisted of a short wood table hemmed in by two metal chairs, one on either side. I had been occupying one of the seats for eight and a half minutes when two federal marshals escorted a jittery Ron Sharkey into the room.

Dressed in the same clothes as when I'd seen him last, Sharkey was manacled, hand and foot, with a metal band around his lower abdomen. His hand- and ankle-cuffs were attached by thick leather belts to this band.

"Unchain him," I said to the dark-skinned, probably Hispanic, marshal.

He looked at his white partner, received a nod, and then began to undo the four locks that restrained the wan prisoner.

"Twenty minutes," the white officer said.

The marshals then left us.

"Mr.—" Ron began to say, but I pressed a finger to my lips, silencing him.

I stood up, moved the table against a wall, then brought the chairs together so that, seated, we would be side by side but facing opposite walls.

I sat down and gestured for him to join me. Then I leaned over and whispered, "The room is definitely bugged, so we are going to have to whisper."

His BO didn't bother me so much—mostly because his breath smelled like a line of garbage cans behind the greasiest diner on the block.

"I don't understand, Mr. Tunes. They told me that a guy named Macklil was comin' to see me."

"That's just a name I use to keep 'em guessin'," I said.

"Oh. Oh, yeah."

"You're in trouble, Ron. They're gonna keep you in here till your teeth fall out if they don't get an answer."

"They'd kill me if I talked."

"You don't think they will anyway? They know you've been busted. They know you're a user. There's no way they're gonna trust you to stay quiet."

"But they have to believe me," Ron complained. "I haven't said nuthin' to nobody."

One outstanding characteristic of most career criminals is their innate innocence. Their worldview is often simple, founded upon a basic equation of honesty and betrayal. Ron had been faithful to the big dog and expected the same treatment back. The only way to break that logic was to add a new variable.

"I found Irma," I lied in his ear.

He stood straight up and said, "Where is she?"

"Be quiet," I commanded, pulling him by the shirt back into the huddle.

"Where is she?" he whispered.

"I will take you to her, but first you got to get out of here."

"Bring her here to me."

"I don't work for you, Ron. I work for Lewis, and he, for whatever reason, wants you out of here. The only way I can do that is to provide a patsy for the weapons they found in the car you were driving."

"I can't," he whined.

It was my turn to stand up.

It wasn't an empty gesture. I was sick of Ron and his recidivism. I had a job to do, but if the client wasn't willing, then I had to cut my losses. I'd tried to save my victim, but sometimes trying is the best you can do.

Ron grabbed my hand.

"No," he whined.

"I need a name," I said, sitting once more.

"I don't know who the car belonged to," he said. "I got this, this letter."

"In the mail?"

"No. Under the door at Wilma's. Somebody left me an envelope with three hundred dollars and two keys—one for the car door and the other for the ignition. There was a note saying for me to pick up a yellow Chevy that would be parked across the street. I was supposed to drive it to a parking garage in Queens and leave it there."

"Where?"

"I forget where exactly. It was in Astoria . . . Pixie Parking. Yeah, yeah . . . Pixie Parking."

"What else did the note say?"

"That there'd be another letter with another three hundred if I did what they said. I needed to make the delivery because I already owed out the money they gave me. You see?" he said. "I really don't know nuthin'."

"If you don't know anything then what are you afraid to tell the feds?"

Sharkey swayed away from me for a moment there. I reached over and pulled him back.

"I asked Wilma if she saw who put the letter there and she looked worried," he said. "I know when she gets that look, so I pressed her. She said that she saw Joe Fleming out on the street walking away right after she found the letter."

"Who's Joe Fleming?"

"He's like a private bank in the neighborhood."

"Does he deal in guns?"

"I never heard about it."

"Does he know that you owed three hundred?"

"I always owe somebody somethin'. Joe stopped lending to me a year ago . . . right after he broke my arm."

I considered the information Ron had given me. It was a crazy story. In my experience crazy stories were too often true.

"When can I see Irma?" he asked.

"Soon."

"How soon?"

"As soon as I can find a way to get you out of here without getting you killed."

I could hear, and smell, Ron's ragged breath.

"How long can you hold out?" I asked him.

"I'm okay."

"When are you going to need the pipe again?"

"I'm off the crack, man," Ron Sharkey said.

"Bullshit."

"No. I started usin' H 'bout seven months ago. I used that to ease off the speed. And then I slowed up on the H. I'm just, I'm just chippin' now. I can go three days and not hardly even sweat."

The best and worst lies are when we lie to ourselves. My father told me that three days before he was gone for good.

"Hold on, Ron," I said. "I'll be back in under forty-eight hours."

"WHAT WAS THAT SHIT?" Jake Plumb asked me outside the visitors' room.

"What?"

"You weren't supposed to be neckin' in there."

"I don't like microphones."

"Oh no? How do you feel about prison cells? I could throw you in one right now," the agent said. "I could lock you in a room where even a runt like you couldn't stand up straight. I got a dozen judges on my speed-dial wouldn't even blink before signin' the warrant."

It was all true. The government my father railed against had those powers, had been honing them for nearly a century. I was nothing more than a stalk of wheat against Plumb's scythe of justice.

"Make up your mind, then," I said, while sending up a small prayer to the not-God of my father's pantheon. "Because I got places to be—or not."

37

Agent Plumb took no more than a minute to decide to let me go, but it felt like hours. It was stubbornness and not courage that kept me from falling to my knees, begging him not to imprison me.

I was shivering by the time I'd made it back to the waiting room of that human warehouse. Plumb and Galsworthy ran what an adman might call an "instant prison." At any moment almost any American (barring movie stars, publicly acknowledged billionaires, and sitting members of Congress) could be whisked away to that nameless building, en route to one of our satellite Siberias, and kept there until a botched water torture or the shrug of some judge sent them home.

In the waiting room I went straight for the exit, and then stopped.

Any chance you get to risk your life for the cause is as close to a blessing as a modern man can come. My father's words had no political meaning to me, but their truth outshone their intent.

"Excuse me, ma'am," I said to the Arab woman slumped in the chair.

She looked up at me but didn't say anything. Her children—an older girl and two toddler boys—also stared.

"Your husband has been moved to the Federal Detention Center in Miami. You'd probably do well to call down there."

ON THE STREET I went over the talk I'd had with Ron. I always do that—replay the words and gestures of an interrogation. Usually I find something that I'd overlooked; often that something has nothing to do with the information I was after.

In this situation I remembered comparing the innocence of criminals to an algebraic equation. That reminded me of the famous x, the unknown factor.

In the case of Angie Lear the unknown factor was the black man with no labels in his clothes. The metaphor worked, as far as an intellectual concept was concerned, but it changed drastically when I tried to make it a concrete action in the material world.

The killer was a dangerous man, possibly a hired assassin in league with others of his kind. Delving deeply enough to uncover his name might also set in motion those who would like the questioner silenced.

But time was passing, and someone, maybe even Alphonse Rinaldo, was stalking my client. So I took the A train to the High Street stop and walked over to Montague Street in Brooklyn Heights.

IT WAS ALMOST SIX o'clock by the time I got there, but I was pretty sure that he'd be in.

Randolph Peel's office was just above a bakery and across the street from a bank that was both new and (according to *The New York Times*) failing. I walked up the stairs and knocked on his door, enjoying the smells of bread baking and sugared delights.

A buzzer sounded and I pushed my way into the ex-cop's lair.

It was an odd room; taller than it was deep or wide, it gave the impression of having been turned on its side by an earthquake, or maybe some kind of explosion. The shelving was askew, layered with papers and books that communicated no sense of order. There were manila folders and magazines piled on their sides, books leaning one way and then the other, and appliances, like an old-fashioned iron, various staplers, an espresso machine, and even a .38 pistol thrown haphazardly into the mix.

Peel's oak desk was also out of the Apocalypse. It wasn't even on a level plane. There were newspapers, empty beer bottles, a half-eaten sandwich on a paper plate, and piles of papers that seemed to have been thrown there just for serendipity's sake.

The buildings across the street did not right the room. Looking out of the murky panes you might have thought that the whole world had been turned on its side in order to fit the office of the private investigator Randolph Proteus Peel.

"LT," THE SLOPPY EX-COP said. "How's it goin' down in the gutter?"

Randy was big, with equal parts pink and gray skin making up his porcine face. Needing a shave, he was leaning back in an office chair, diddling around with a pencil in his left hand.

The slob, I knew, was ambidextrous.

"Just chippin' at it nowadays," I said in deference to Ron Sharkey.

"That's what they been tellin' me," he said. "Somethin' like you're reformed or somethin'."

"Something like that," I said.

I took a seat on the worn red velvet hassock he used for a visitor's chair. A night bird whizzed past his window. A car honked in the street.

"I see you've cleaned the place up," I said.

"Fuck you."

"I thought that was your mother's job."

He sat up straight.

"What the fuck do you want, McGill?"

Many people liked Randy in spite of his slovenly ways and dis-honorable discharge. Most white cops still included him in their picnics and at their kids' Communions. With a little help from these friends he'd wrangled himself a PI's license and started to deal in intelligence.

If you wanted to short-circuit the system and get information outside of official channels, you went to Randy. Given enough time, he could get a copy of a handwritten memo page off the desk of the chief of police.

I put a fold of seven hundred dollars down between the harden-ing sandwich and a calendar called *Beaver Shot of the Week*. Randy picked up the money and thumbed through the wad.

"A young woman named Wanda Soa was shot dead in her apartment a few days ago," I said before he finished counting. "Her probable assailant was found next to her, also dead. I'd like to get the coroner's photo of his face."

"Come back tomorrow and I'll have it."

"I'll add eight hundred to that if you do it in the next fifteen minutes."

One thing I knew for sure about Randy was that he didn't like to be rushed. Luckily for me, more often than not, he needed cash more than he hated work. He picked up his black phone and entered a number.

"Hey," he said in a husky, almost sexy, voice. "It's me."

Another interesting aspect to the disgraced cop was that women loved him. You'd think that such a disheveled ne'er-do-well would chase any modern girl away. But they flocked around him, agreed to do shocking things for him on desktops, park benches, and in their own marital beds.

He asked for the photo and made an assignation for later in

the week. They were talking about a problem with somebody, her husband or boyfriend, when the fax machine started up.

"It's comin' through, babe," he said. "I'll call you back in ten minutes."

I stood up, went around to the fax machine, and tore off the image of the dead man I had seen on Wanda Soa's floor.

I reached into another pocket and pulled out the next payment.

When I turned around Randy was pointing a 9mm pistol at my forehead.

"I could kill you right here and now, Leonid McGill."

I dropped the bundle on his desk.

"But you won't," I said.

"Why not?"

"Because you're a lazy fuck. Because I weigh one hundred eighty-seven pounds, and even if you had a silencer you'd have to get rid of the body or explain it to the cops. Either way you'd miss your evening cartoons."

Randy searched my eyes for fear but found none. I'd given up worrying about my mortality a long time before. The first good body shot I took in the ring cured me of that fear.

Anyway, I knew somebody would shoot me down one day. Why not Randy Peel in Brooklyn Heights?

Peel let out a false laugh and lowered his gun.

"I always wanted to see you flinch, LT," he said behind that empty grin. "I guess you're as tough as they say."

38

It was a long ride but all I had to do was catch the 4 train at Borough Hall and take it all the way to the 149th Street stop in the Bronx.

It was a pleasant ride that gave me time to think. . . .

There's a four-story building a block and a half off the shabbiest part of the Grand Concourse. Whatever paint it once had is gone and most of the floors are unoccupied. Now and again a squatter comes in to inhabit one room or another, but a guy named Johnny Nightly finds them soon enough, batters them about the head and shoulders, and then offers them twenty dollars for the promise that they will never come back.

They never do.

The basement of the dilapidated building is a very modern, unregistered pool hall run and tenanted by my comrade Luke Nye. That was the man I was going to see.

I followed a lighted path around the back of the building and approached a cast-iron cage that was painted grass green. There was no button or brass knocker to announce visitors. All you had to do was stand there. Within a minute a buzzer sounded or it didn't.

That evening it did.

I pushed the gate open, walked through the weather-beaten door, and clambered down the dank wooden stairs into darkness.

When I reached the bottom a door swung open before me. The world revealed was all yellow light and green relief.

Johnny Nightly was standing to the right, holding the door open.

Johnny was tall and slender, black as the darkness I had just come from, and able, it was rumored, to kill without question or remorse.

"Good afternoon, Mr. McGill," Johnny said. He was a very courteous man, pleasant, and a good conversationalist when he had to be.

"Hey, Johnny. What's up?"

"Everything is nice and peaceful," he said from within an aura of seemingly unshakable calm.

"LT!" Luke called from the third table in a line of three. "Come on over here."

The floor-through room was uninhabited except for the hustler and his bodyguard. The ceiling was high enough to hang three large dark-blue crystal chandeliers that were formed in an abstract symmetry like spiders' webs beaded with blue dew. The walls were shiny green with the sheen of lacquered metal.

Luke was of medium height with a face that resembled a water-going snake. His eyes were slits and his nose so wide that it didn't seem to stand out from his face. His brown skin had a greenish tinge and his head was shaved bald.

Luke Nye was an animator's dream of an alternate evolution of humanity.

"Hey, Luke," I said.

We shook hands and slapped shoulders.

"Must be somethin' important to have you come all the way out to the Bronx," he said.

I handed him the fax from Randolph Peel's machine.

Luke took the flimsy, grayish sheet, glanced at the image, and handed it back to me.

That was all the time he needed.

Crime revealed itself in different manifestations throughout the various terrain of New York and, probably, the rest of the world. Many groups had very organized systems of criminals: The Russians and Italians, Irish and Chinese had their mafias, gangs, and tongs. These were what you might call highly developed organisms like tigers or flies. There were such groups in the African-American community, gangs and blood brotherhoods that paid allegiance to some central figure or ideal. But the black community also had an impressive number of wildcards and jacks-of-all-trades. Luke Nye was one of these.

He was a born leader who also had a gift with the pool cue. He was tough, smart, and independent-minded. He didn't take orders and didn't expect people to bow before him. He'd been in and out of prison, had killed a man or two, dabbled in the sex trade, gambling, armed robbery, and even counterfeiting—all this before he settled down to high-stakes pool and the dissemination of information.

For a thousand dollars Luke might answer any question you had. He was friendly with bad men from up in his neighborhood all the way down to Wall Street. Information rose like chalk dust from the people who played in his little parlor, and sometimes he'd sell what he knew.

"You sure you want this, LT?" he asked.

"The only way I can answer that is for you to tell me his name."

"It's not in a name," he said with a smile. "It's what that name does and who he does it for."

"That mean I have to pay three thousand dollars?"

"Naw, man. I'll give you it all if you want it."

I nodded.

"The name he's been going by on Flatbush is Sam Bennett,"

Luke said. "But his given name is Adolph Pressman. He was born in Jamaica to a black Jamaican mother and a white German father. Still a citizen of the island there, I hear.

"He's what your friend Hush might call a mid-level hit man. I met him once when he was doing bodyguard work for a man named Pinky."

"Where can I find this Pinky?"

"He's been dead for three years. At least, nobody's seen 'im in that long."

"This Pressman's freelance?"

"No. He works for some group. I never knew who. But just 'cause I can't name 'em don't mean they can't nail you."

I took two thousand of Alphonse Rinaldo's dollars from my pocket and laid them on Luke's table. One for Pressman and the other for our previous conversation about the pimp Gustav.

"There's another thing," I said.

Luke's amphibian eyes glimmered a bit.

"Loan shark named Joe Fleming."

"What about him?"

"I'm wondering if he'd deal in automatic weapons."

"Maybe if the Russians invaded the East Coast and the Secretary of State asked him personally. Maybe then. But, you know, ole Joe is strictly small time. He's jittery as a baby deer, and, you know, guns are likely to go off."

I placed another wad of money on the table, wondering if I should bear the load myself or allow Rinaldo to treat me.

I WAITED UNTIL I was back in my office to make any calls.

It was just after nine and the sun had been down for hours. Gazing out of my window at the Statue of Liberty's torch burning in the dark of the Hudson, I entered a number.

"Hello, Mr. McGill," the young man said in my ear.

"Tiny."

"How can I help you?" he asked.

This greeting was strange. Tiny "Bug" Bateman was at best monotone and at worst taciturn when I called him. The only reason he worked for me at all was because I had done his father a serious favor, and the one true connection the young whiz kid had to the outside world was his old man.

"There's a woman," I said. "Angelique Tara Lear . . ." I gave him her address, date of birth, place of employment, and school history. "What I'd like is any trace information you might be able to dig up. I'll pay you for this. It's for a client, and there are no favors involved."

"I don't want your money, Mr. McGill."

"Since when?"

"Um . . ."

Hesitation?

"You remember that girl you had call me last month on that burglary thing?" he asked.

Someone had stolen a client's grandmother's jewelry. There was some sentimental value attached. I had Zephyra Ximenez call Tiny to pass on my needs, as I was preoccupied with another case.

Zephyra might have been a working woman with a title and a business plan, but she was also beautiful enough to be a runway model in Europe.

"Yeah?" I said.

"I found my discussions with her, um, exhilarating."

"And?"

"I'd like a personal introduction."

"You live on the Internet," I said. "So does she. You know how to get in touch. What more can I do?"

Bug considered himself part of a historically based infrastructural movement that he called *techno-Anarchism*. The members of this (largely unconscious) movement he designated as *monadic particulates*. I could see why the young brown man might be attracted to Zephyra's mind—as well as the rest of her. Of course they hadn't met face-to-face, but I was sure that Bug had found a picture of her online.

"I just want you to put in a good word for me," the computer genius said.

"Listen, Tiny," I said. "You live in a cocoon in a basement in the West Village. She spends most of her time in a house in Queens. What's a word going to do?"

If there existed an Oxford Pictionary, its entry for "butterball" would have been Bug Bateman. He'd work up a good sweat walking a city block on a chilly autumnal afternoon. Even his hands were moist and pudgy. At twenty-nine, he sat in a chair surrounded by computers all day every day, and probably all night every night.

"You're refusing me?" There was actual pain in his voice.

"No. I'm just saying that I need you to work for a client of mine. I will pay your going rate on that and I'll do what I can for you about Zephyra—I'm just sayin' that you can't predict what a woman's gonna do."

"You'll talk to her?"

"Sure. Why not?"

While Tiny pondered the two-word question, I suspected that I'd just revealed to him a major flaw in his isolationist techno-philosophy.

"Um," he said. "I'll look up information on this woman."

My cell phone made the sound of the clang of a single bell. I had another question to ask Tiny but the incoming call was more important.

"I'll talk to Zephyra in the near future. Bye."

I hung up the office phone and answered the cell just as it was calling for the next round.

"Hey, Gordo," I said. "I was wondering if maybe you retired and moved down to Saint Lucia to live."

"Or die," he said in a voice that was even more strained and raspy than usual.

In the taxi ride downtown I drifted into a reverie about my parents: Tolstoy, the self-styled union organizer and radical Communist revolutionary, and Lena, the pious Harlemite who loved her man as much as any jazz lyricist could imagine. He went off to join a Cuban brigade down in South America soon after my twelfth birthday, leaving me fatherless, and virtually motherless, because Lena took to her bed and died soon after. She was the only proof I ever needed that a person could die from a broken heart.

That began my long and uneasy relationship with the various branches of New York City government—including the NYPD. I was continually running away from foster homes, getting into fights, and doing odd jobs for petty criminals. I was in and out of youth facilities. The foster parents I had weren't bad people. Many of them, I think, truly cared about me. But my father had trained me and my younger brother, Nikita, as revolutionaries from the time we could toddle. I hated Tolstoy, but at the same time he was my hero, and so there was little I had in common with the petit bourgeois churchgoers who tried to set me on the right path.

Then one day I stumbled into Gordo's Gym. He was only in his early forties then but he already looked old, craggy. He strapped some gloves on me and put me in the ring with an older, more experienced boy. I lost the round but never stopped coming forward, and so Gordo trained me, for seven years.

Maybe if I had paid closer attention to Gordo, if I would have let his hand guide me, I wouldn't have taken my homegrown revolutionary training and turned it into piecework for the mob. But I couldn't stay on boxing's bicycle—because there was no road, or even a path, that led to my destination.

THEY HAD HIM IN a southwest corner room with three other men on the eighth floor of St. Vincent's Hospital. He looked even smaller than usual in the big mechanical bed. His eyes were closed when I pulled up the chair.

Gordo's brown skin was tinged red from decades of blood rising to the surface as he exhorted his boys to give more. He was the color of rage, the man in your corner, win or lose.

"Leonid," he whispered.

"G."

He sat up a bit by shifting his knobby shoulders one way and then the other.

"Why you look so glum, boy?" he said. "I'm the one down for the count here."

I laughed, feeling a pang of guilt that my sick friend was comforting me.

"What they got you in here for, man?"

"First it was pre-ulcers, then it was plain ulcers, that went into bleedin' ulcers, and now they say I got cancer. An' I believe it, too, 'cause it hurt like a mothahfuckah."

"Stomach cancer?"

"A hole in one, boy. You could go up against Tiger Woods, with the right caddy."

"They gonna operate?"

"Not at first. They wanna nuke it an' then poison it and then if me an' it is still alive they might get the cut man."

"That's a bitch," I said.

"Body shot like you wouldn't believe." Gordo's wry smile turned sour.

"What do you need?"

"What's that lawyer's name you got?"

"Breland Lewis."

"I want you to get him to fill out some papers for me."

"Like what?"

"Augustine."

"Your nephew?"

"He's a good man but he don't have the sense of a termite. I wanna leave him the gym, it's all I got, but you know he'd mess it up in a week. Rack up some kinda fool debt, or maybe just sell the whole buildin' an' blow the money on his good-for-nuthin' kids or that money-hungry fourth wife'a his."

"You own the building?"

"What other landlord than me gonna let a sweaty ole gym don't make a nickel a day stay up there?"

I was astonished. It was a dilapidated old building but it was in the West Thirties, not three blocks from Penn Station. It had to be worth millions upon millions, even in the current real estate slump.

"So what do you want from Breland?" I asked.

"I want him to work out some kinda scheme to leave the place to you and then for you to take care of Augustine. You know, you get a li'l bit and then pass the rest off to him in parcels."

"Why you gonna trust me, G? You know my track record is not a good one."

"Shit. You think I don't know it? Man, if I could find somebody better they'd be sittin' here right now. But you know, boy, even though you about as crooked as one'a them curly bamboo plants, I figure even they grow toward the sun."

I laughed instead of tearing up and we changed the subject to De La Hoya and Pacquiao.

"Oscar should hang up them damn gloves," Gordo said.

"Why?" I asked.

"Because there comes a time when you just don't win anymore."

"But there's always a chance at a comeback," I said with emphasis.

Gordo considered my words for a few moments and then said, "True that."

"THEY'RE GOING TO GIVE him radiation and then chemotherapy," the head nurse at the front station told me. "He's going to be very weak and will probably have to be sent to a nursing home."

"No," I said.

"No?"

"Gordo's my stepfather. When you release him, me and my wife will take him in."

The woman, her name was Naomi Watkins, gave me the papers I needed to have signed and ratified. I gave her my card and got my name put at the top of his list of relatives.

WHEN I GOT HOME I told Katrina about my decision. Maybe I should have asked her before making plans. Maybe I would have asked her if she hadn't run off with that banker for nearly a year.

"That's as it should be," she said, surprising me with her calm. "But we may have to get a nurse to be here for those hours that we're both out."

Before going off to bed, Katrina added, "Dimitri called."

"What'd he say?"

"That he's in love and off with his girl and that they're in Montreal. I wanted to be mad at him, but I was just so happy to hear his voice."

"Did he say when he was coming home?"

"A few days."

"You see?" I said. "I told you that everything was going to be fine."

At least one of us should believe in happy endings.

40

I spent the latter part of the evening rearranging my den for the time when we took Gordo in. I brought in sheets and put my weapons in the safe, straightened up the desk, and even vacuumed.

After all that, I set up my laptop and got online.

The best detectives in the world are the arbiters of spam. They find you wherever you are, like water seeking its level, like blood-hungry mosquitoes in the wild. I had sixteen unwanted communications for various legal and illegal services, offers coming in from Nairobi to Lima, Hong Kong to West Hollywood. I don't think this was what modern economists had in mind when they began constructing their definition of "globalization."

Bug must have been serious about Zephyra because I received a long document from him, giving me all kinds of hitherto unrevealed information about Angie. She'd participated in a few long-distance runs of ten kilometers or more and worked for the Hillary campaign during the primaries. She played Go over the Internet and was pretty good at it, earning an emerald rating in a California club.

There were a lot of other loose details and one salient set of facts: John Prince's phone number and address—he lived in Chelsea, between Sixth and Seventh. There was even a photograph of the handsome young man. This, as I suspected, was the boyfriend on her bedroom wall.

It was just after three in the morning, time for a man in the private-investigating profession to get to work. But I was tired, exhausted by the welter of details coming at me like the furious punches of a flyweight working a speed bag.

I sat down on the daybed, and the next thing I knew I was on my back, witnessing the miracle of sunlight as it filled the window.

I awoke, hoping that Angie had not died in the night while I wasted time sleeping. I wished I had a number for Dimitri, and an answer for Ron Sharkey.

But all I had was a headache pulsating through my consciousness.

I forced down a serving of muesli and cream, drained two cups of press-pot French roast coffee, and made my way to the street, hoping that today would bring the break I needed to get a leg up on the world.

I CALLED JOHN PRINCE from my office at 8:32.

Hello. This is JP speaking. I'm not here right now and so if you'd like to leave a message I'll get back to you as soon as I possibly can.

I hung up, realizing that I hadn't thought about Aura at all that morning. This evidence of healing did not ease my mind. I didn't want to be cured from the only real love I had known in my adult life.

"Mr. McGill?" came Mardi's soft voice over the intercom. She'd come in early.

"Yes?"

"George Toller is out here."

Did he somehow know that I was thinking about his woman?

"Send him in."

HE CAME INTO MY office without knocking this time. He wore a disgusting lime suit crosshatched with a generous amount of dark-green and black thread. In his arms he carried three thick manila folders. There was something dramatic in the way he carried himself, as if he bore tidings of great portent. He stood before my desk and dropped the heavy pile of paper, making a loud slamming noise.

His eyes sought mine as a sneer crossed the lips I hated.

"Take-out menus?" I asked.

"Do you have a minute?" he replied, sitting without being invited.

The question was not polite or considerate, it wasn't even accurate. George Toller believed he'd caught me like a winking Irishman trapping a leprechaun, and his "minute" was meant to be the rest of my natural-born life.

I didn't answer, and so he pressed on.

"Terry Swain," he said.

I blinked innocently.

"Are you telling me that you don't know Swain?"

"This is your show, Mr. Toller. I'm not telling you anything."

"You cosigned for Mr. Swain's hot dog concession, did you not?"

I performed a noncommittal shrug to keep a toe in the realm of good manners.

"Mr. Swain was the building manager before Aura Ullman. He was suspected by the new owners of having defrauded the corporation. They were assembling a good case against him until a lawyer named Breland Lewis stopped criminal proceedings by throwing suspicion on a previous employee who had, conveniently, died."

"Peter Cooly," I said. "He died of a heart attack months before I ever even heard of Terry."

"Breland Lewis is your lawyer."

"This is America, Mr. Toller. Breland is his own man, as I am mine."

"The relationship between the lawyer, the embezzler, and you," he said, "along with the ridiculously low fifteen-year lease you procured is evidence of fraud, at the very least."

Something about Toller's tone reminded me of the posturing of the teenagers at the now-and-again middle schools of my so-called youth. He was playing a role but didn't know it, pretending that he was somehow wounded by actions taken before he was ever involved. He was talking, and I was hearing him, but I wasn't listening—at least not all that closely.

". . . you were arrested for tampering with police evidence in nineteen eighty-nine . . ." he said.

I was thinking that I had to take the next step in uncovering the reason that the assassin was in Soa's apartment.

". . . nineteen ninety-two you were arrested along with Gonzalez family members on an organized-crime charge . . ."

I was thinking about Dimitri, the brooding, bulky young man, kissing some beautiful Russian girl, filling his heart with love. I was also thinking that love never seems to last—except where there's blood involved.

". . . in nineteen ninety-six you were arrested on charges of battery . . ."

With love and blood bound together in my thoughts, the wildflowers on the old stereo box came to mind. Something about their delicate beauty seemed out of place in my life.

A bubble of something like regret formed in my chest.

Toller was reciting a new litany in an angry tone.

I looked up and saw that he was actually reading from his accumulated indictment.

"What does all that shit tell you, Mr. Toller?" I asked, cutting off his rant.

"Excuse me?"

I stood up.

"What does all that shit in your files tell you?"

"I will thank you to keep a civil tongue when addressing me, Mr. McGill."

"All right," I said. "How about this? In exactly ten seconds I'm going to walk around this desk. If you are still in the room I'm going to beat you to death with your own motherfucking files. One . . ."

Toller leaped to his feet, grabbed his papers, and hurried from the room.

I finished the count and went after him.

There were a few loose sheets that had fallen in the hallway.

When I got to the antechamber of my office, Mardi was sitting at her desk. She wore a champagne-colored dress with puffy sleeves.

"Mr. Toller left," she said.

I blinked and wondered if I was actually that close to murder. I decided that I was, and that maybe I needed professional help. So I walked back to my office and called the deadliest man I have ever known.

41

Hush likes his steaks rare to bloody, and so I made a reservation at a steak house at the upscale mall on the southwestern arc of Columbus Circle. The young hostess walked me to a booth in a dark corner of the airy restaurant. The ex–hit man was there before me, lounging thoughtfully behind a glass of tap water, no ice.

"LT," he said in greeting.

I shoved in opposite the most excellent assassin in New York history. He was a plain-looking white man of average height and build with medium brown hair and darker brown eyes. He didn't make much of an impression except for his deep voice. But that wasn't much of a distinction because he rarely spoke.

I was always a little uncomfortable around Hush—maybe more than a little. He knew a thousand ways to kill a man and dozens of techniques to make the body disappear. He was the classic cold-blooded killer who seemed to the world to have no heart or conscience.

Outside of his wife, I was the only person to know both his true name and his professional history.

"Hush," I said.

"You look tired, LT."

"Work's aplenty."

"I ordered you a Wild Turkey and a rib eye," he said. "They're coming."

"Thanks for meeting me on such short notice."

"All I had was a simple day of airport runs," he said.

After retiring from the killing trade Hush became a limo driver for an elite company that sometimes needed bodyguarding along with a driver's license. I really don't know why he even had the job. Hush didn't need the money.

I took the faxed photograph of the dead man and pushed it across the table. Hush laid a hand down on the face as a woman's voice said, "Wild Turkey neat."

She was a young blonde with a severe hairdo that would have been right at home in the conservative part of the sixties. Her makeup was perfect, and even though she was plain you could see that she would make an impact wherever she went.

"Thank you," I said.

As she left, Hush lifted his hand and looked at the picture. Then, with a single digit, he pushed it back across to me.

"I've been informed that he's in your old profession," I said.

"Adolph Pressman. A hack. Okay for a bullet in the back of the head, but no good at all for something that requires finesse. Looks dead."

"Somebody blindsided him while he was killing a girl."

"Sloppy."

We paused on that word for a few moments and the severe blonde came back with our orders.

That finished, I asked, "Well?"

"Adolph, he's kind of like, what do you call it? A spoke in a wheel, if the wheel is a society of killers. Well . . . not a society really because none of them know each other. The only really dangerous part is the hub—a man named Patrick."

"Patrick what?"

Hush shook his head and stuck out his lower lip.

"All I can tell you is that going after Patrick is not for the faint of heart."

"I have never fainted in my life."

Hush smiled and sipped his water.

"Tamara wants to move back up to New York," he said.

I had all the information I needed. If Hush had known where I could find Patrick he would have told me. I could have left right then, but it just wouldn't be friendly to use somebody like that. Besides, I was hungry.

Tamara was Hush's wife. She's a black woman, young and plain-looking but with a spirit that could fill the sails of a three-master. She and their son, Thackery, had been moved to an island off the South Carolina coast after their lives were threatened by Hush's enemies.

"Tired of the country life?"

He gave me a queer glance and then nodded.

"Yeah," he said. "Thackery's got himself a little southern drawl and she hates it."

I was thinking many things. First among these was that Tamara would probably be safe. Hush was out of the business and the only man who had ever threatened her was long dead.

"When are they coming back?" I asked.

It was then that our chopped salads arrived.

By the time we'd grazed our way through the roughage, our rib eyes were served. While eating we talked mostly about sports. Hush liked the team sports, but I was a one-on-one man. We could still converse, though.

It wasn't until we were in the middle of our coffees that he said, "What makes you think that she's coming back?"

"The simple fact that you said she wanted to," I answered.

"That, and I know she and Thackery are the foghorns to your lost humanity."

A man can get used to anything. If one day he found himself coming awake in a lion's den, any sane man would be petrified. Absolute fear would govern his mind for many minutes—possibly for hours. But if the lion didn't attack him, and enough time passed, normalcy, or its near cousin, would return. If days were to pass and some kind of truce were evident, the man might learn to communicate with the king feline. Given time, his fear might abate completely.

But he'd still be in close proximity to a murderous carnivore.

"You think you know me?" Hush asked. There was no friendliness in his tone.

I remembered the first time I'd heard a lion in the zoo roaring at feeding time. The fear I felt was something preverbal, older even than the human breast in which it resided.

"What do you want me to say, Hush?"

His ageless brow creased.

"What?" he asked.

"I assume that Tamara will come back if she wants to," I said, possibly hiding the primal fear I felt. "She's your wife, but she can make up her own mind. That's all I meant."

For a long, hard minute the killer, alongside the man, stared at me. It was like watching war.

Finally he cleared his throat.

"Sorry, LT," he said. "You know, sometimes I fall into an old rut. It's how I was trained."

Me on my tightrope and him in his turret. That line from a poem I'd never write flitted through my mind.

"She's comin' back next week," he said. "I got a place for her on Fifth Avenue, down around Ninth. She told me that she wants your number."

I was the one who saved her when she and Thackery had been kidnapped.

"She can call me anytime," I said. I was born in the lion's den, a fool in spite of my sensible fears.

"Maybe we can all get together some night," he suggested.

"That sounds real good."

42

I went to a bookstore to collect myself after the encounter with my friend—Death.

It was a superstore on the second floor of the mall.

I glanced through the bestsellers but nothing caught my fancy. I searched around until coming across a section that had the new books that were less known, less popular. Among these I came across a book about a thief, a second-story man, who had broken his leg in a botched attempt to break into an old woman's house. He tried to get away but fainted on the street. Many people passed the guy by, mistaking him for some homeless vagabond napping on the sidewalk.

Finally the old woman got home and found him. She had a neighborhood handyman bring him into the house, where she could attend to his broken bone.

It was one of those silly stories that get to you—at least it got to me. I was worried about the man's salvation, and the old woman's life savings, about the witness across the street who had seen the attempted break-in, and the old woman's grandniece, who slowly begins to have feelings for the burglar.

Somebody knocked over a display stand near to the chair where I was reading. The crash threw me out of the story and I couldn't read my way back in. So I got up, went down to the number 1 train, and rode in a car full to brimming over with commuters going from the jobs that they didn't want back to the lives they hadn't bargained for.

THESE DAYLIGHT HOURS WEREN'T wasted. The meeting with Hush, no matter how unsettling, helped me to decide what avenue to take to get to Angie. But there was nothing I could do while the sun still shone, so I headed home, intent on climbing into another cold shower; after that I'd be ready to find my client and inform her of our hitherto unrevealed relationship.

THE LOBBY TO MY apartment building was a small suite of rooms, a throwback to a more genteel era of New York living. I stood upon the threadbare carpet, considered a moment, then decided on the elevator instead of the stairs. I needed to save my strength for the job ahead.

"Mr. McGill?" she said.

There was the trill of Eastern Europe in the English, and a mild vibration to the youthful feminine voice.

She came from the alcove to the right. It was a small sitting room that a few of the older residents used in the daytime when they needed a breather after coming back from shopping or while waiting for their laundry in the basement to finish a washing or drying cycle.

"Yes?" I said, thinking that if she were one of Adolph Pressman's associates I'd already be dead.

"I am Tatyana Baranovich, a friend of your son Dimitri."

She was twenty, svelte, dressed suggestively but only just. Her makeup was minimal and totally unnecessary. All in all, she gave that aura of sexy conservatism that Scandinavian professionals revel in.

"I've been looking forward to meeting you," I said.

As we shook hands she stared into my eyes, not so much to see something but to exhibit how serious her visit was.

"Let's go back into the alcove," I said. "D's mother wouldn't add much to this talk."

Following her into the little half-room, I could see what my son was besotted by. Hell, I could see why a hardened pimp like Gustav didn't want to let her go.

We sat across from each other in stiff padded chairs that were somewhat reminiscent of the crammed-in seats on an overcrowded charter flight.

Tatyana adjusted her position so that I could witness her discomfort. This uneasiness was complemented by the anxiety in her eyes.

"Let me call Katrina first," I said.

"Who is that?"

"D's mother."

"Oh."

"HELLO?" SHE SAID, ANSWERING the second ring.

"Hey."

"Leonid. Where are you?"

"I was on my way home but I got waylaid. I might not be back for an hour or so. I hope that doesn't mess up your plans."

"Shelly is studying till late," she said. "And the boys are still gone. I'll keep something warm for you. But you better let me go so nothing burns."

"Okay. Bye."

I wanted to make sure that Katrina was home and not planning to leave. I didn't want her to see me and Tatyana together. One thing about my wife—she could tell what another woman was up to, and Tatyana was a veritable beacon of intention.

"Why are you here?" I asked her.

"Twill said I must talk to you. He gave me key to the front door."

"You could have gone to my office."

"I called but you were gone. Twill said I could wait here and that you would come. He said I would know you, as I know Dimitri."

Even with my years of experience, something about her made me want to trust the girl.

"So," I said. "Tell me about Gustav."

After a moment's hesitation she said, "He is pimp," in crisp, matter-of-fact language.

"And?"

"My brother is sick," she said. "My younger sister was too young to help. My mother was alone, and a man came to me and said that I could come to America and do . . . what I do for three years and then, after I made his partners a million dollars, I will be free. I send money home and sleep with old fat men."

The buzzer to the front door sounded and my son's school friend Bertrand Arnold rushed in. He pressed the elevator button and concentrated on the door as if to hurry the car along. His being there could have been for any reason. After all, he was my son's friend; he had come to the house before looking for Dimitri.

He could have had any number of reasons for being in my building.

But the choices became somewhat limited by the bouquet of wildflowers nestled in the crook of his right arm. He was probably waiting around the corner. Maybe he and Katrina were to meet somewhere nearby but now that I would be late they might get a few kisses in before I came home.

"He lied to me," Tatyana was saying. She was facing away from the elevator door.

If Bertrand glanced to his right he would have seen me sitting there, staring at him. But the young suitor's attention was somewhere else.

When the door slid open he rushed in, all hormones, fear, and maybe love.

". . . when I told him that I wanted him to do what he promised, he had a man named Vassily beat me and rape me."

"Tatyana," I said.

"Yes?"

"That's a beautiful name."

"Thank you," she said, wondering.

"How did Dimitri get mixed up in all this? I mean, my son has a good heart, but if I were in your position he'd be the last person I'd turn to for help."

She lowered her eyelids and smiled. This young woman and I were equals, at least in her estimation. She might have been right.

"I was very worried. You could see it on my face. He asked me what was wrong and I was so upset that I told him. I had to talk to someone. Dimitri said that he knew someone who might know a place for me to hide until we could do something. I was scared and I didn't know anyone but professors and students . . . and Gustav's whores. Dimitri introduced me to your younger son. At first I thought he was just a boy, but then Twilliam brought me to a house in the Bronx and then out to a beach house on Long Island. He told me that if I was his brother's friend that he would help me. He said that if I left New York with Dimitri he could go to you and that you would know what to do."

I was thinking about my wife and her younger boyfriend, about Dimitri and this tiger he had by the tail. Aura's boyfriend was trying to demolish my whole life, and Ron Sharkey wanted to apologize to the woman who had destroyed his everything.

"How are you and Dimitri living?" I asked.

"I had money hidden in a gym locker at school."

"Where is D right now?"

The beautiful child from Minsk inhaled and held the breath.

"If you don't lie to me," I said, "about anything . . . I will help you."

"He doesn't want me to tell you," she said. "He told me not to come here. Right now he thinks I am getting clothes from a girlfriend of mine."

"Where is he?"

"Please," she said. "I promised I would not tell you."

"Why would he think that you would tell me anything if you're at a girlfriend's house?"

"Twilliam told him that men came here after him. He said that you figured it out. I told him that I would call you."

"Why didn't you?"

"Because Twilliam told me to meet you . . . not on the phone."

"Twill's a teenager."

"He is man." She knew the right diction, I was sure, but this Russian phrasing brought her point home.

I smiled. I had to. Twill was slight of build but he left a footprint like *Tyrannosaurus rex*.

"You won't tell me?" I asked.

She didn't reply.

Her green dress was made from raw silk, her cream-colored jacket might have been merino. Tatyana wore no hose, and her dark-brown shoes were sensible, designed for walking—or running.

She was the right girl in a long life of wrong days; the kind of woman that made you wish everything was different—somehow.

Twill was right. Tatyana's intentions toward my son were meaningless compared to what he would learn from her.

"How many girls does Gustav have?"

"Always less than twenty. Sometimes as little as twelve."

"Is there a place where he keeps them?"

"They work out of a building in the East Village, but they live above the pool hall," she said. "On the fourth and fifth floors. He is protected. There is a policeman who comes there."

"What's his name?"

"Saul Thinnes. He's a captain."

I liked straight talk with the Russian. It felt rare, like plain truth in advertising, a contract with no fine print, or honesty in politics.

I nodded. She understood that I had a plan. She also knew enough not to ask me what that plan was.

"What do you want from me?" she asked.

I shook my head slightly. This caused her brow to furrow, reminding me of Hush.

"It's for Dimitri," I explained.

"Do you want something for him?"

"No."

Again she scrutinized my face, this time looking for danger.

"Sometimes," I said, "things just don't make sense. They happen and we are left to deal with the results. You are one of those things. I am, too."

This explanation seemed to quiet Tatyana's unspoken trepidations. She smiled.

I squelched the urge to kiss her.

"Take D down to Philly for a few days," I said. "No more than three. Things will be fixed when you get back."

She nodded and stood but I remained seated.

"Aren't you going upstairs?" she asked.

"I'm gonna sit here and think for a while."

The conversation with Tatyana had lasted all of a dozen minutes. I intended to leave right after she did. There was nothing I really needed from the apartment. And unless I wanted a very uncomfortable situation I couldn't go there, anyway.

But it was cold outside and my mind was preoccupied with the minefield I'd wandered into over the past few days.

Almost reflexively I took out my cell phone and entered the letters A-U-R. Then I hit the green button.

"Hello?" she said.

"Hey."

"Leonid," Aura Ullman breathed. "I'm surprised."

"Bad time?"

"You can always call me," she said, and for the briefest of moments the weight of my life was lifted. I noticed that my headache was gone.

"Thank you."

"Why are you calling?"

"Just wanted to say hi, I guess."

"No."

"What? I can't call to say hey?"

"You never do. What's going on with you?"

"Too many jobs at once. Trying to make your boss's rent is a bitch."

"Do you need to talk?"

"Yeah, but I don't have anything to say."

That bought me a brief span of silence.

After a bit she spoke up again.

"Tell me one thing," she said.

"What?"

"Anything."

"Okay. Dimitri's fallen in love and run off with a high-end call girl and her pimp wants her back. D's gone and his mother wants *him* back. Twill's got all the plates spinning and I have to catch them one by one before they crash. And that's the least of my troubles."

"Can I help?"

"You already have."

That was what I had been looking for, the turn in the road. It wasn't some clue or confession, threat by the police or flash of intuition about what exactly the crime or who the culprit was. It wasn't even a revelation about my feelings for Aura. I already knew that I loved her. My problem was the crack that had been opened when she told me about Toller. The pain I felt there was what was throwing me off.

It was a deep ache and it wasn't going away, but that didn't matter because now I knew what I was dealing with and I could negotiate a path toward my revival.

I exhaled loudly.

"What?" Aura asked.

"How's Theda?"

"She's fine. Going out for JV basketball. The coach says she has talent."

"I have to go, Aura."

"I know," she said.

SIXTEEN MINUTES LATER BERTRAND ARNOLD came out of the elevator, rushing for the door.

I laughed silently seeing the top of his head out of the window as he went past. I waited for a while more and then made my way up the stairs, the strength in my legs and lungs returning along with my confidence.

I found Katrina in the kitchen wearing a peacock-blue dress under a tan apron, worrying over something in a red enameled pot.

"Hey, babe," I said.

She turned to look at me, trying to hide the desperate sex that was still thrumming in her blood. Her eyes had that startled look of new love. Her lipstick was dulled from the pressure of a dozen hello and goodbye kisses.

"Leonid. I didn't hear you come in."

"I'm sorry," I said, "but I have to run. There's a case and I just had a breakthrough. No time to eat. I probably won't be home tonight."

"All night?"

"Yeah. I've had this case that I haven't been taking seriously but now I've got to get down to business."

"Have you heard from Dimitri?"

"He'll be home in three days like he told you already."

"Is he all right?"

"Is love a disease?"

I left her to ponder that question.

IN MY DEN I put on a long-sleeved black shirt and a pair of dark trousers that were designed to keep me warm in near freezing temperatures.

I had gloves and a roll of burglar tools, a .38 and a knife that had a handle that could also be used as brass knuckles.

I topped it all off with a black beret to take some of the edge off the intentions of my clothes.

She was waiting in the hall outside the den.

"If you're out all night I might go see a movie," she said. She had reapplied her lipstick.

"Yeah. Sure."

"Is there anything wrong, Leonid?"

"You mean other than my oldest friend dying of cancer, my sons missing in action, my lawyer calling me every day, and clients who just don't seem to know how to act?"

Katrina put her hand on my neck. It was warm. Usually her hands were cold.

"Can I help you?" she asked.

"I don't see how."

"Do want me to stay home?"

"How would that help anything?"

"I could be here if you needed to call. If you needed help."

"Thanks anyway, babe. No. You go out and have a good time. And don't worry about me. I just got a little behind, that's all."

Katrina smiled and kissed my cheek.

"You take care of yourself," she said.

"You too, honey."

NOT LONG AFTER THAT I was in a cab going across Twenty-seventh Street. That's where John Prince's apartment was. It was a seedy block with many first-floor businesses and a parking lot, a few apartment buildings and a scattering of cars parked for the night.

I pretended to have made a mistake about the address and had the driver go around the block. After the second pass my plans were set.

Carrying my burglar's briefcase and wearing a black trench coat, I walked with certainty to an eight-story apartment building that didn't seem to have any kind of high-tech security system. I pressed all the buttons, except for the top floor, declaring "UPS!" for anyone who answered.

The buzzer for the outer and inner doors sounded and I rushed in.

This time I waited for the elevator because someone I hoodwinked might be waiting at their door for their hand-delivered package.

Getting off on floor eight, I made my way to the door to the roof. I was happy to see that it was padlocked with a chain. I used a fold-out metal cutter to unlock the door and made my way onto the tarpaper roof. I put a wedge under the door so I wouldn't be disturbed, then walked softly on rubber-soled shoes so as not to disturb the residents below.

There was a ledge and a slanted roof where the building looked down on Twenty-seventh. I nestled there with my nighttime binoculars (which also housed a high-speed digital camera) and cell phone. As long as I remained pretty still, my dark skin and black hat were camouflage enough to keep the casual glance from noticing me.

The street was quiet. Cars passed at an ever lessening rate, and pedestrians came in and out of view, usually alone. Most were going somewhere else, but a few entered buildings like the one I sat astride. A pudgy man wearing a windbreaker and tan khakis went into a bodega next to the parking lot. A woman wearing a fur-collared jacket walked a three-pound dog. Two young lovers stopped for a while, leaning against each other and a stucco wall.

She was a chubby black woman and he a skinny light-skinned guy.

You couldn't pay for the kind of kisses she was giving him.

The night got darker and the traffic waned but never stopped.

At nine I called John Prince's number.

"Hello?"

"John Prince?" I asked, throwing a slight accent into the words.

The ensuing silence fairly wavered. "Yes? Who is this?"

"My name is Henri Ouré. My niece is, was, Wanda Soa. I am just arriving to visit my niece and the police are telling me that she is dead. I once met her friend in Salvador. A young woman named Angelique. This is the number I 'ave for her."

The accent was terrible, but so are all accents in the end. The big chance I was taking was assuming that Angie and John were close when she was down in South America.

"I'm sorry about your niece, sir," John said.

"Do you know what happens? The police won't tell me anything."

"I don't really know, sir. Angie told me about it but she, she didn't know anything a-about it."

Like hell.

"Do you know how I can speak to Angelique?"

"I'm supposed to see her tomorrow," he said. "If you tell me where you are I could ask her to call."

"I am in Queens, at the Miller Hotel," I said.

The Miller was an electronic fabrication presenting a series of recordings designed to make the caller believe that they're connected to a hotel with an automatic phone system that guides its callers through an arcane pathway ending up with them frustrated and having to leave a message.

I gave him the phone for the hotel and my fictitious room number.

While talking to John I kept my magnified eyes on the front door of his building. If Angie was staying with him there was a good chance that, upon hearing someone call for her, she'd bolt.

"I'll have her call you as soon as I speak to her, Mr. Ouré," John was saying.

At the same time a man was walking past the front door of the Prince residence. This man wore a brown windbreaker and tan khaki pants.

"Thank you so much," I said.

"No problem, sir."

The man walked maybe fifty feet up the street and turned. I saw the face in my infrared viewer and snapped the digital camera four times. Then I followed the man back to a dark-colored American-made car parked down toward the other end of the block. I connected the binoculars to my cell phone via a built-in cord, downloaded the pictures, and then sent them to Hush's phone.

I sat there on the roof, wondering what the pudgy little white man meant. He could have been anyone doing anything. Just because he was sitting in a car on Twenty-seventh Street didn't mean that he was looking for Angelique.

My phone vibrated.

Where are you? the text line asked.

I keyed in the answer.

Meet me at Bundy's.

44

Bundy's Barbeque made the hottest sauce in town, and it was only a few blocks away from John Prince's place.

As long as I was waiting for Hush I ordered a big plate of baby back ribs with collard greens and corn bread. They served olive oil with the bread—to cut down on the glut of trans fats, I guess.

I was feeling emotional, like an army reserve corporal who is playing badminton in the backyard with his daughters one day and in the field in Afghanistan the next.

"You sure know how to get into trouble, don't you, LT?" an unmistakable deep voice rumbled.

He was sliding into the opposite side of the booth.

Hush always wore a dark suit and a monochrome tie. There was a spark of excitement in his usually expressionless eyes.

"What?" I asked.

He held out his phone screen with the picture of the dumpy little man on it.

"You remember I told you about a guy named Patrick?"

Hush liked Bundy's because the booth we preferred to sit in was removed from the rest. It was in the back, near the toilet, and was usually the last place anyone wanted to sit.

"This little guy?" I said.

"He's a stone killer, LT. Either walk away or ice him now."

I pretended to think about his words for a few beats, and then said, "You want some ribs?"

Hush let his spine slap against the navy-blue backrest of his bench. A smile, like a jittery mosquito, flitted across his face.

"I know you try to stay away from me, LT," he said. "I know you want a different kind of life. But once you've seen the battlefield you can't pretend that it doesn't exist."

"I'm not tryin' to hide from anything, man. I got a job to do and killing some guy I never met is not in the description."

"I could take a walk down that street," he offered.

"I need him alive."

"Like a cobra needs a mongoose."

"Like the Scarecrow needs a brain."

Again Hush's smile flittered. He slid to his right and stood in an unbroken motion.

"Call me if you have to, Leonid. If Patrick's involved, I can tell you that this is too deep for you alone."

"I got your number."

I'D BROKEN THE LOCK on my lookout building's front door to allow easy access. That night spent on the slanted roof was peaceful. The November chill was bracing and the threat of the man below was like a promise. He, too, felt that Angie was near.

I was the stalker stalking the stalker stalking, like a lone hyena fixed on the spoor of a lion.

At three in the morning I entered a number.

"Hello," he said in a low, guarded tone. You could hardly discern the Spanish accent.

"Diego."

"Brother man."

"Where are you?"

"Down where Indian blood runs pure and often."

DIEGO WAS A CITIZEN of the Third World. I'd met him when a New York crime boss wanted me to do some divorce work for a movie-star friend of his out in Los Angeles. The target, a minor actress, was half Mexican, from L.A.'s barrio. I was teamed up with Diego to make sure the woman would have more trouble than it was worth in a court. She had a brother who was wild. His name was Valentín. Diego and I made sure that Valentín was caught with evidence linking him to the drug trade and very possibly to a string of killings. There was evidence to clear him, but only we had it.

We paved the way for Tony "the Suit" to offer his aid.

That was back when I was working the dark side of the street.

Diego was a phantom no one knew and few remembered. He had done some import-export work for my employer but we became friends over the job.

"I am what they didn't see when they used to look at your people," Diego had once told me.

"I see you just fine," was my reply.

"WHAT CAN I DO for you, LT?" Diego asked over the phone. I heard the loud screech of a bird in the background.

"I'm told by someone I trust that I might need some serious help," I said.

"What kind of help?"

"I need a face that no one here knows."

"What time is it where you are, amigo?"

"Three oh three in the morning."

"I can be to you by midnight. How long?"

"Three days, tops."

"Okay."

"I got five thousand."

"I'll need seven."

"See you then."

NOT FOR THE FIRST time, I wondered about my commitment to leave the criminal life behind. I worked among killers and thieves, made my livelihood from the fact of their existence. I breathed their air and shared their stench. How could I ever stay on the straight and narrow with a length of chain behind me that would put Dickens's Marley to shame?

Diego and Hush (who was retired but not reformed), and Alphonse Rinaldo, for that matter, were all part of the dark matter that was the glue holding together the known, and unsuspecting, world. I was a free-floating radical that sometimes tended the connection between the lightness and this dark.

AT FIVE-THIRTY IN THE morning I clambered downstairs and took a cab to my office.

I'm no Sherlock Holmes. I can't read cigarette ash or pretend to have the most important and up-to-date forensic science stored in my lobes. Neither am I a master of disguises or dialects.

But I do own a ski hat and an old dark-green trench coat that smells strongly of sour sweat—and other human scents. I have a pair of worn-out boots and tattered cotton gloves. And the past few days had produced the grizzled salt-and-pepper beginnings of a beard.

Add to these a pair of plain-glass, thick-rimmed spectacles, and even a Superman like me can be transformed into a down-at-heels black Clark Kent.

"HEY, YOU!" A MAN shouted in the first-floor entrance hall of the Tesla Building. "What are you doing here?"

"Hey, Warren," I said to the building's security guard. "It's me."

"Mr. McGill? What's, what's wrong, sir?"

"It's that damn economic downturn," I said. "Cutting expenses left and right."

The handsome black and Chinese Jamaican stared at me, trying to make sense of the presentation. I smiled at him and shambled out the revolving door.

My heart was fluttering and the morning was just shedding night.

45

Twenty-seventh Street between Sixth and Seventh was my fief-dom that day.

I found a small cardboard box and a shattered ink pen. On a scrap of stiff white paper I scrawled the word *Homeless* and squat-ted down next to a small alleyway between Patrick's car and John Prince's front door.

Whenever somebody passed I muttered "Sir, please," or "Please help, ma'am." My voice warbled and my outstretched hand shook.

After half an hour I was nearly lost to the role. Every fifth or sixth person, it seemed, dropped something into my box. It was cold that day and so the shiver came naturally to my voice. The pain I felt from losing Aura informed my pleas. Even the money added to my fabricated despair. That was the water that the Hard-Hearted Hannah of song poured on a drowning man.

The hours went by and I brayed like an abandoned baby don-key left alone in the world by the harsh circumstances of life. Until . . .

"Who the fuck you think you is, mothahfuckah?"

It was a white guy backed up by a black man, both in clothes the same vintage as my own. They were quite a bit younger than they looked and still they looked younger than I was.

The white one was speaking and I didn't need any deductive skills to uncover his motives. I had cleared upward of eighty-five dollars in the few hours that I'd been begging, and that piece of real estate was obviously their territory.

My knees hurt as I stood up. You could hear the joints cracking.

The men were tall for mendicants, around six foot each. I looked at them, knowing that I should have just given up their piece of my action to keep things running smoothly.

But if I had ever in my life been able to make sensible choices like that I wouldn't have been on that street, in my marriage, under the scrutiny of New York's finest, or in any other way known to evil.

"Y'all two mothahfuckahs better step the hell back," the man I was playing said.

The white guy (who had Mediterranean blue eyes) took half a step forward before seeing the knife with the brass-knuckled handle in my right fist. No one but those two could see it thanks to the barrier of my stinking coat.

Oh shit, said the faces of both men.

"You best to step back or die right here," I said. "I'ma be around for a day or two and then I'll be movin' on. I can leave you bleedin' or I can leave you whole."

The white man took a step back, bumping into his friend. They knew better than to make some parting threat. I was obviously deranged and their luck was not yet a certainty.

A shiver went through my body and I sat back down, realizing, or maybe re-realizing, that I was my own worst enemy. The rage in me couldn't be tamped down for long.

AT ABOUT TWO IN the afternoon I put a Bluetooth bud in my right ear and diddled the cell phone in my pocket. After negotiating an invisible obstacle course of codes I arrived at a single message at the nonexistent Miller Hotel.

"Mr. Ouré?" a young woman's pleasant but sad voice asked. "Hi. I think this is your room. This is Angelique Lear. I don't remember you but I know, I knew, your niece. If you call the same number you called yesterday after eight tonight I'll tell you what I can."

It was the first time I'd heard my client's voice. She chose her words carefully but it was obvious that she wanted to offer some kind of closure to her friend's kin.

I was liking her all the more, which was good, because my street role was difficult. The air was cold and my joints were rusty.

FOR THE NEXT FIVE hours I bleated and begged, stood up to stamp my feet now and again, and kept an eye on the two street entrepreneurs that I had humiliated.

They passed by every hour or so, keeping their distance but studying me still and all. I had made a mistake alienating them but that water had passed under the bridge and flowed out to sea hours before.

I wasn't worried about my newfound antagonists. The trouble I had was in the nature of any through street: Angie could come from either direction. If she came from the west, I was between her and Patrick. If she came from the east, she had to pass him before she passed me. My little piece of turf, I decided, was too far away from Patrick's car—and so I started talking to myself.

"Goddamn mothahfuckahs!" I shouted, leaping up from the wall as if it were alive and my enemy. I kicked my box, scattering change and dollar bills over my little piece of turf. I kicked it again and followed it.

"Oh no," I promised. "You two ain't gonna get me. Shit. I will break y'all necks."

I hunkered down against a wall not seven feet from Patrick's car. The driver's seat was by the curb, so I had my hat pulled down, my coat collar pulled up, and kept my head bowed as I called out curses to imagined foes.

This was the test.

If Patrick was just on a fact-finding mission he would ignore me. But if he was there to kill my soft-spoken client, then my presence would prove unacceptable.

"People sittin' in they mothahfuckin' cars spyin' on us," I said to two passing teenagers, pointing at Patrick. "They got spies all ovah the city tryin' to bring us down."

I was hoping that by calling attention to him, I would force Patrick to retreat and reconsider his plan. The last thing he wanted was people looking at his car—or his face.

The boys laughed at me and passed on.

Patrick looked into the driver's-side mirror. There he must have seen the slender young woman bopping along, grooving on the invisible music of life.

"Miss," I said when she was within earshot. "Miss, let me ask you something."

"What's that, father?" the brown-skinned girl asked. She wore brightly striped hose that shot up under a brown leather skirt. Her sweater was Afghan and the voluminous multicolored hat I thought was probably the repository for long dreadlocks.

"What you think a white man be doin' just sittin' in his car lookin' at a man like me?"

I pointed at Patrick and the child turned to look.

He did a masterful job of turning his head just enough not to seem obvious but at the same time obscuring his features.

"Do you need something, father?" the girl asked.

Her eyes were an unsettling golden brown. I felt their scrutiny and was suddenly ashamed for pulling her into my deadly game.

"I'm all right," I said in my normal voice. "You just go on and I'll make my way to shelter."

She leaned over and touched the foul-smelling homeless man's cheek, reminding me exactly why I was trying to find the off-ramp to redemption from the dark highway I was on.

When the flower child was fifty feet away I saw Patrick checking his rearview mirror again. There was no one at that moment coming down our side of the block.

When I heard the *snick* of his car door I knew one thing for sure—that Angie was very important to Patrick and that he meant to kill her as soon as she came within range.

This one possibility was why I had contacted Diego.

This fact also meant that my life was soon to be threatened by a man that even Hush had respect for.

I raised my left hand to the ski-mask hat that I was wearing. I had gotten the hat from Twill when he was planning to use it for cover when assassinating Mardi's father. I foiled that attempt, but liked the hat. Now it was my good-luck charm.

I pulled the mask over my face and rose to my feet at the same time. I was almost to his door when dumpy little Patrick surged from behind the steering wheel with disheartening speed.

There was something in his right hand.

I had something in my right, too.

He came up fast. My boxer's training made my body sway to the right. As I swung the brass knuckles of my killing knife I felt the searing hot pain of his blade in my left triceps. He made ready to attack again but my first blow had slowed him. The second chopping punch knocked him back into the open door of his Dodge.

His head was on the passenger's seat and his feet were tangled on the driver's side. I could feel warm blood trickling down the baby finger of my left hand, but before I saw to my own health I leaned in and hit Patrick one more time.

That pudgy little guy had come closer to killing me than

anyone ever had. Four inches and he would have had my heart on a skewer.

I shoved him into the car, jumped in behind, closed the door, and secured his wrists behind him and his ankles together with police-grade plastic ties that I always carry on serious cases.

It was only after putting electrical tape over his mouth and shoving his unconscious body into the backseat that I pulled off my coat, sweater, and shirt to check out the wound.

Another thing I carry around when I'm doing fieldwork is a first-aid kit.

The cut was deep but the bleeding was only moderate. I slapped two broad cloth bandages over the wound. Patrick had left the keys in the ignition. I drove to a comparatively desolate block near the West Side Highway, a few blocks north of the Convention Center. There I stopped to put pressure on the wound until the bleeding stopped—or at least slowed. That took about twenty minutes.

I slumped down then, exhausted from the survival mode I'd been in.

When the head popped up in the backseat, I sat up, too. Without thinking I threw a deadly straight right hand, knocking Patrick at least into unconsciousness.

After four more minutes had passed I used my newfound energy to drive some blocks to the north, where I knew there was street parking and a few pay phones.

46

There's a man I know named Barry Holcombe. Barry's business is subletting various specialty properties around New York. People often need rooms for assignations, secret meetings, and other activities that have to be held off the grid. Sometimes these rooms need to be soundproofed and partitioned, with see-through, one-way glass between one space and the next.

I only ever call Barry from a pay phone.

"Hello," he answered on the first ring.

"It's Leonid. I need a place to interview a potential employee."

"I might have something. You want to see the property?"

"No time."

"Rent's gone up five hundred."

"That's not a concern."

"It's a pleasure doing business with you."

I DROVE DOWN TO Eighteenth Street near the West Side Highway, opened the trunk of Patrick's car, and was pleasantly surprised to find a large swath of burlap deposited back there. Then I went to the backseat and trussed the unconscious Patrick up, making him seem somewhat less than human. Then I waited seventeen long minutes—until no car or pedestrian was coming.

I hefted the little man, moving as quickly as I could, and installed him in the trunk. I used two more ties to secure his feet and hands to a hook under the latch. This greatly lessened his chances of noisily beating against the trunk lid.

There was an envelope waiting for me at the front desk of the Tesla. Barry Holcombe is an efficient and speedy landlord.

THE ADDRESS I WAS given was near the Brooklyn Naval Yards. The directions led me down an alley on a street of abandoned warehouses. I drove down the narrow lane, used the first of three keys on an outer door and the second one on a two-man elevator. I dragged Patrick's body into the lift and traveled three floors down to a hallway that ended at a maroon metal door. This led to two concrete rooms that were connected by a door and by a jury-rigged monitor and camera that allowed a man in one room to watch what happened in the other. The second of these rooms had an aluminum chair that was bolted to the floor replete with manacles and leg irons, also bolted down, for the prisoner's hands and feet.

Just when I'd finished chaining Patrick my cell phone sounded.

I went into the watcher's room, closing the door behind me, and answered the phone.

"Hello?"

"It's me," Diego said. "Baggage of American Airlines, international."

"Twenty-five minutes."

STANDING STRAIGHT, AN OLIVE duffel bag on the floor next to him, Diego was an image of something not of this world. His collarless jacket was black, as were his shapeless trousers. His shoes were of woven red-brown leather, and the straw hat he wore was an ancient ancestor of the Guatemalan-made Panama variety.

Diego's skin was the dusky color of dark-red brick that they made factories from when children still worked fourteen hours a day. His face was wide and filled with empathy for something long gone—or maybe just hidden.

"Hey, man," I said, approaching him. No names in public.

He was my height, with only a slightly smaller bone structure. There was a vitality to the South American that made me appear sleepy by comparison. His hands seemed powerful enough to crush single walnuts.

He held out a paw and we tested our strength with the show of friendship.

"Come on," I said.

"THERE'S ONLY ONE THING I need to know from this guy," I was saying as we rode toward the temporary hideout. "Who hired him to kill Angelique Lear?"

"That's all?"

"That's everything."

"How's Twill?" he asked then.

Twill and I had gone fishing with Diego up near Lake Tahoe a few years before. Dimitri refused to come along, and Shelly didn't like doing anything where she couldn't wear a dress.

"In trouble."

Diego grinned.

"He's a good boy," my very foreign friend said. "He will always be there for you like you are for him."

My emotional state at that time made the timbre of my voice untrustworthy, so I nodded and drove on.

WHEN WE GOT TO Barry Holcombe's rooms, Patrick was awake. We could see his eyes via the monitor. They were boring into the camera lens.

After looking at him for a quarter of an hour Diego picked up a three-legged wooden stool from a corner and walked into the room. I watched him as he set the stool in front of Patrick and squatted down.

A kind of jolt went through Patrick's body, giving the impression that the prisoner had something to say. He didn't speak, however, and neither did Diego.

For at least twenty minutes the men stared at each other. Finally Diego stood and moved closer to the prisoner. The left side of Patrick's jaw was swollen from the blows he'd received in our brief contest. When Diego reached over to touch that side, Patrick tried to bite him. But my friend was quicker. He pulled the fingers away and delivered a vicious slap with his other hand.

Again he tried to touch the swelling. Again Patrick snapped, and was slapped. Again . . .

Somewhere around the thirteenth or fourteenth attempt, Patrick allowed Diego to touch the swollen left side of his face. By this time the right side was puffed up, too. His mouth was bloody and his right eye almost closed.

Diego sat there, staring, for six or seven minutes more. Then he picked up the stool and exited the room.

He didn't talk to me at first, instead moving close to the CCTV to watch his unwilling penitent.

IT'S NOT EASY TO explain my relationship with Diego. We rarely talked, and yet a certain sympathy had formed between us on that job in L.A.

One day when we were following the actress's brother, mapping out his routine, we were sitting in a car near a big house. There was a team of men in the front yard hacking away at a broad and hunched-over old oak. The tree was gnarled with age. It took a lot of work to bring that old monster down.

"You see them?" Diego had said out of the silence of the ages.

"Uh-huh."

"Not one of them men is over thirty. That tree is two hundred years old, maybe three. It's been there since before their grandparents were born, but they still come at it with their axes and saws. Somebody said it's in the way. Somebody paid somebody, and life is torn from the ground."

That's the reason I called on Diego. Hush was like those axmen. He lived by a logic that was completely of the modern world. Hush had the sensibility of a long history of conquerors. His laws were man-made, while Diego's came from a deeper place.

"CAN I KILL HIM?" he asked me.

"No."

"You can see in his eyes that he's a killer. He might come after you."

"He doesn't know who I am. And I doubt if he could ever figure out who you are."

"You don't know who hired him, but you will before the sun rises."

"Do we have a problem?" I asked.

"No. I'm not afraid of him."

Diego looked into my eyes, seeking my response. Then he grinned. The light in his face spoke of innocence and strength, something that maybe I knew at one time, before the roots of New York had gotten tangled in my soul.

WHEN DIEGO ENTERED THE room again he was carrying my brutal knife. Without a word he began cutting off Patrick's clothes. First he followed the seams of his windbreaker, going from the left wrist up over the shoulders and down the right side. He pulled off the segmented jacket and then did the same with the dark-blue woolen shirt. After that he started in on the khaki pants.

Like some kind of mad tailor, working in reverse, Diego cut off all of Patrick's clothes, leaving him wearing only his socks, shoes, and chains.

It was cold in that room, very cold.

Patrick's skin grew pale. He shivered slightly but otherwise bore up under the divestment rather well.

Diego settled down and stared at his victim for over an hour.

Suddenly, without warning, Diego stood up, took Patrick's left wrist, and cut into it with the point of the knife. Then he calmly returned to his stool, and we both watched the blood trickle down onto Patrick's knee, flowing from there around his calf, past the ankle, to pool on the cold concrete around his feet.

The wait continued.

Half an hour later, Patrick could no longer control his shivering.

"What the fuck do you want?" the killer asked the human embodiment of twilight that sat before him.

Diego did not answer.

Something about the preceding silence kept me from any emotional attachment to the extreme interrogation. It didn't seem like torture, so long as the men were equals in silence. But hearing the pleading tone in Patrick's voice tore at me.

The sound brought me to my feet.

Ten minutes went by. In that time I began to have second

thoughts about my actions. There was no question but that I needed to know why Patrick was on that street—and who had sent him—but I felt ashamed hiding in another room while Diego asked the questions. And, beyond shame, I felt guilty. There was no excuse for me putting the South American on Patrick. I was culpable, and I knew I would have to pay for it.

"Tell me!" Patrick screamed.

"I will only ask you once," Diego warned.

"Just ask me."

"And if you hesitate or if you lie, then I will leave you here to bleed. And believe me, my friend, no one will find you down here."

I was too close to an answer to break the trance.

"What?" Patrick barked.

"Who hired you to kill Angelique Lear?"

The question was an ominous hum on the quiet subterranean air. For a few beats the audio feed from the interrogation room was silent.

Patrick studied the face of his death and wondered . . . but not for long.

"Terry Lord," he said, shivering. "Terry Lord, from down in D.C."

47

cGill?" Alphonse Rinaldo said, answering his special cell phone at 3:17 in the morning. I must've disturbed his sleep, but his voice sounded clear and awake.

"Yeah."

"Go back to sleep, honey," he said to someone in the room with him. "It's just something I have to take care of about work."

I had never expected to be so close to the Important Man's family life. Even at that intense moment I was impressed by how low the great could come.

"I got a name here that I want to put past you."

"Go on."

"I'm told that a person named Terry Lord ordered a hit on the woman you call Tara Lear."

Silence.

Diego came back into the observation room while I waited.

"We have to meet," Rinaldo said.

"Fine," I said. "But can you tell me if that claim makes sense. We have the operator here."

"I don't understand it, but it could very well make sense," Alphonse said. "And no one in his right mind would give you Terry's name as a ruse."

"I'll meet you at six at Grimaldi's Diner, at Fifty-sixth and

First," I said. "And do you have some connection with law enforcement without using Christian?"

"Of course. What do you need?"

I gave him some coordinates near Columbus Circle.

"Have your police search a dark-green Dodge that will be parked there in an hour. Tell them to arrest and hold the man they find for as long as they can."

He repeated the position and said it would be done.

I gave Diego a syringe loaded with a sedative.

"Only give him half," I said. "Considering all the blood he's lost, the whole thing might kill him."

AT 5:00 A. M. I was seeing Diego off on an airport bus shuttle across the street from Grand Central. We'd bandaged the assassin's wound and left him unconscious in the backseat of his Dodge, under the coarse burlap, on a side street in Midtown.

"How'd you know he'd talk?" I asked my comrade.

"He knew too much about killing. He knew where I would go if he didn't bend."

I shuddered, visibly. Diego stared at this with his innocent, ruthless gaze.

"You should have killed him," he said. "Alive, he will try to find you."

"Yeah," I said. "Maybe so. See you, my friend."

We clasped hands and Diego smiled, his broad face expressing friendship combined with something like pity.

I WAS FIFTEEN MINUTES early to Grimaldi's but Alphonse still beat me. It wasn't the first time that he reminded me of Twill . . . and Hush.

The suit he wore was Italian, in a price range that was akin to middle-class family vacations. It was dark, dark red, with a white shirt that hinted at a scarlet blush. His hands were manicured. The bluish silk tie he wore simulated snakeskin perfectly. His presence transformed the booth into a kind of portable papal chamber you might find in some corner in a vast room of the Vatican.

I suppressed the urge to make a sarcastic bow and moved in across from him.

We stared at each other for a few moments and I was reminded of Diego and Patrick. The feeling was unsettling.

I expected the Big Man to get right down to the matter at hand. That's how he had always conducted business before. But the last week had been full of revelations.

"I want to thank you for this, Leonid," he said. "I know I haven't given you much support."

Before I could respond, another voice said, "What can I get you, bud?"

It was a nut-brown white man dressed all in cook's white. He was small, wiry, and pretty much emotionless at his job.

"Black coffee, scrambled eggs, and ham," I said.

"Hash browns?"

"No thanks."

The cook/waiter turned away.

"Terry Lord is called 'the Impresario' in his field," Alphonse said. "He's a freelancer of the highest caliber, an entrepreneur who, how shall I say, leverages events."

"What kind of events?"

"Like you used to do," Alphonse said, "but on a much larger scale."

There was subtlety to Rinaldo's description. I was surprised that he remembered how my life had shifted from being a crook to trying to make amends in some way. My life seemed like such a small thing compared to the world in which he traveled. For my circumstances to fall under his purview seemed . . . improbable—like a mountain claiming to feel the passage of a caterpillar.

"So you think Lord might be, um, leveraging Tara?"

Rinaldo sucked in his lips and then tried to cover the faux pas with his left hand.

"I don't know," he said. "It makes sense that if he was going after me he might approach her. I suppose he could decide to kill her, but I can't think why. At any rate, it's nothing personal. He's working for someone else. I need to find out who that is."

"I take it that you can't do something so delicate through Strange or Latour," I speculated.

"No."

"What about Tara?"

"What about her?"

"What does she have to do with you?"

Alphonse Rinaldo winced, if only slightly. He shuddered and looked away. In those few gestures he conveyed to me that this subject, the central purpose of our business, was off limits.

"Then tell me what you know about Lord," I said.

"There was once a congressman," Rinaldo began, on confident footing.

"Here's yer eggs and ham," the nut-brown cook said. He set down the food and coffee and left.

"There was once a congressman . . ." I said, to restart the story.

". . . who was looking into the pricing practices of the oil companies. He was a brash midwesterner who didn't understand the protocols necessary in taking such an action. The process of bringing to light these practices . . . was protracted. Terry Lord was hired to follow it from inside a shadow.

"Her name was Alana Ash, and she was everything a happily married man could want in a prostitute. The arrangement went on for eleven months. Just before the congressman was to bring the case of the oil companies to his fellows, Alana moved to Virginia, not far from downtown D.C. One day the congressman sent his car for her. The FBI had him in custody for interstate sex trafficking before the sweat had dried."

It was a simple scenario, one that I might have arranged myself, on a slightly smaller scale.

"So he's got a lot of clout, huh?" I said.

"He could crush you without a second thought, Leonid."

A smile I could not suppress slid across my mouth and I said, "No one is safe from anyone else in this world."

"Is there anything else you need from me?" he asked.

"What do you know about an ADA named Broderick Tinely?"

"I know the name. Why?"

"He's pressing the investigation of Soa's murder, going above and beyond."

"I'll look into it."

"There's a guy named Grant. He was looking into Angie's whereabouts when Wanda Soa was murdered."

"Forget him. He was working for me through Sam Strange."

"What about Lamont Jennings? He represented Soa at one time."

"Same thing. Anything else?"

"No, not that I can think of."

"Will you continue the investigation?" Rinaldo asked.

"Right after I eat these eggs."

48

The Big Man paid the bill in cash, then left me to my protein and caffeine.

My phone made the sound of mission bells. It was Aura calling me. I feared that if I spoke with her I might be thrown off my game again and trampled by one of the many enemies I was accruing.

I decided to let her leave a message.

The eggs were crumbly and the tough ham was shot through with the harsh taste of preservatives. The coffee was strong enough, but the hour was too early.

After scarfing down this breakfast, I took a cab to Wilma Spyres's apartment building.

SHE ANSWERED THE DOOR quickly, didn't even ask who it was. Her tattered robe was partly open. Upon seeing me she closed the fabric gap and produced a perfect sneer with her small mouth.

"What do you want?" she asked

"What all men want," I said.

This statement sparked interest in the former beauty's muddled eyes. Then a wave of suspicion washed away the momentary vulnerability.

"What's that?" she asked.

"Truth."

"I don't have time for this," she said.

"Unless you want to be doing time you better find a few minutes for me."

"Fuck you."

She stepped back and moved to close the door.

"You shut me out and I go right to Joe Fleming," I said.

That stayed her slam hand.

"What are you talking about?"

"Let me in or I go to Joe."

"Ron's not here," she said. I didn't know what she meant by it. Maybe it was a stab at old-fashioned respectability—you couldn't enter a man's domicile with his woman if he was not present.

"I know that."

"Come on, then," she said, turning her back, leaving me to close the door behind us.

Wilma sat on the dark-blue sofa and I returned to the relative safety of the folding chair.

"What?" she asked. Even the potential for beauty disappeared behind her wall of anger, this buttressed by a lifetime of fear.

"I have a very simple job, Ms. Spyres," I said. "I have to keep Ron out of trouble. I don't care about you, your habits, or your friends. Tomorrow they could crown you queen of England or lay you in your grave—it's all the same to me."

These words sobered her rampant emotions a bit.

"What do you want?"

"The truth."

"What truth?"

"Tell me something," I said. "If I were to have put a sealed envelope with Ron's name on it under your door instead of knocking, would you just put it down there next to that bong and wait for him to come home?"

I took no pleasure in seeing the fear that flooded the junkie's girlfriend's eyes.

"It was Joe Fleming," she said, stammering over every other word.

"No."

"It was Joe set Ronnie up," she pleaded.

"No."

Wilma jumped to her feet.

"Sit down," I said, with no particular emphasis to my voice.

She obeyed and muttered something that I didn't understand.

"What?"

She looked away, biting back the tears.

"What did you say?" I asked.

"He made me do it," she said loudly and clearly, her tone somehow underscoring the clichéd phrase.

"Who?"

"He . . ." she stopped after the syllable and took a breath. "He told me that we could, could get together. All I had to do was make the deal with Ron. Once the car was picked up, me and him would go away to Atlantic City to this time-share he got down there. It used to belong to his auntie, but she died and left it to him."

"His name."

"But the cops busted Ron and now it's all shit. You know, if I could just get away from the losers around here for just a mont' I know I could get straight." With one hand Wilma scratched her face and with the other she pulled at her hair. "I was gonna leave Ron with this place. He could'a stayed here until the rent ran out. I didn't mean for him to go to jail. Now what am I gonna do?"

"His name," I said.

"What am I gonna do?" she asked again.

"Who gave you the money?"

"Cary Bottoms. They call him 'Scary' a lot, but he can be real sweet."

"What does this, uh, Cary do?"

Wilma looked at me, bringing her hands away from her face.

"He's killed people before," she said. "But that's just because he doesn't know how to get away from here, either. If we, if we could'a got that money from them guns we could'a moved out to Atlantic City."

"Have you seen Bottoms since Ron was arrested?"

She shook her head, looking away again.

"Do you know how to get in touch with him?"

"Maybe. I got a number but he told me never, never to call it."

Again I was reminded of the innocence of most career criminals.

"I want you to listen to me, Wilma. Ron is in jail and I have to tell him what you did."

"Why?"

"Because I'm working for his lawyer. But that doesn't matter. You want to get away and make a life for yourself, right?"

She nodded, trying her damnedest to understand.

"I know a man named Plumb. He works for the government, and he needs a big case to get from where he is to where he wants to be—just like you. I believe that he'd be willing to make a deal with you."

"Money?" she said.

I nodded. "All we have to do is get you in touch with Ron's lawyer for him to make the deal. And you don't have to worry about Scary. He's not a big enough fish. Plumb will want the people he's buying from and selling to. Maybe in the end you'll both get to go to Atlantic City."

Wilma smiled at that scenario. I felt like a real dog. But this was the best of all possible worlds.

"There's one thing, though, Wilma."

"What?"

"Scary's a killer and he knows that you can send him to jail."

"He would never hurt me."

I didn't even have to speak, just to look in her face was enough to crush her adolescent hope for love from the misunderstood gun dealer.

"Oh no," she said.

She stood up and glanced around the room, determining with alacrity what she should and should not take with her.

"I can go with you in a taxi to Ron's lawyer's office," I said. "He has a room where you can wait until he's made the deal with Plumb."

"How much?" Wilma asked.

"A few thousand," I said. "Maybe a little more."

She nodded and action took the place of words, deceptions, and self-deception.

While Wilma put her important belongings into a brown paper bag I called Breland's cell phone. He was already on his way to work. We made a plan that we hoped would produce a small fee and immunity for Wilma, and immediate release for Ron.

I rode with her in the cab and together we walked into Breland's seventh-floor office on Madison, just below Forty-second. After the two shook hands we sat at the round teakwood table in a room off from the reception area of Breland's office.

Shirley, his female jack-of-all-trades, was not in yet and so we had the place to ourselves for a while.

"So," Breland said after an hour of serious interrogation, "are you willing to identify Mr. Bottoms as the source of the money, car, and weapons?"

"Yes," Wilma whispered.

"You'll have to speak up, Ms. Spyres."

"Yes."

"And are you willing to name the people you suspect that

he's doing business with?" Breland asked, sounding more like a hard-nosed prosecutor than a defense attorney.

"Lazar," she said. "His name is Richard Lazar. Cary's been movin' guns for him for years."

"COME AGAIN?" JAKE PLUMB said to me over one of Breland's eight lines.

It was only eight-thirty, but he was at work and I was in a hurry to get to my next disaster.

"I can give you the name of the guy who owned the car and the guns," I said, "testimony that my client didn't have knowledge of the contents of the trunk, and the name of the man that the weapons were being moved for."

"How the hell did you get all that?"

"I need ten thousand and immunity for the information my client can provide," was my reply, "and you drop all charges against Sharkey. Also, I want you to get one of your Rolodex judges to enroll him in a three-month detox program, courtesy of the Fed."

"Why not just wait until he's begging for the H?" I could imagine Plumb's evil smile.

"He doesn't know the truth, and the one who does is fidgety . . . ready to fly."

"You got some record, McGill," Plumb told me. "I had a New York cop tell me to hold you on one'a my special writs. He promised me he'd come up with charges that would stick."

"Yeah. I could make a castle out of a single grain of sand."

"This stuff is straight?"

"I'll put Sharkey's lawyer on the line."

49

At 9:47 I parked my classic green-and-white 1957 Pontiac down the street from John Prince's door. I had with me a new MP3 player that was specially made by Bug Bateman and loaded with thousands of songs that I had listened to while living out my childhood, such as it was, on the streets of New York.

I had modern music, too. The first song that cued up through the shuffle function was "Helpless," written by Neil Young and sung by k.d. lang. It was a good cover—a lot better than my fancy-ass car.

But I wasn't trying to hide that morning. Nobody was looking for me yet. Patrick was locked away, I was sure of that. Rinaldo might have been limited by his distrust of his minions, but he was still the most powerful man in New York City.

Sitting there, I wondered if Patrick's and my blood was still on the street. Nobody paid much attention to small patches of street blood. That was just a now-and-then occurrence in a city with so many people living and dying in such a small space—you had to bleed somewhere.

My plan was to break into Prince's apartment once I was sure that he and Angie were out. I could bug the phone, search her things, and plant mikes in various rooms. I would call later, but first I needed to rest. I'd phone Prince at a decent hour—10:30. Before the appointed time I could sit, peacefully listening to music and enjoying my life—while it lasted.

Katrina called me at a little after ten.

"Where are you?" she asked after the one-word pleasantries were done.

"In my car on Twenty-seventh, staking out a young couple."

"What have they done?"

"Nothing that I know of."

"Have you heard from Dimitri or Twill?"

"I thought D called you?"

"I mean since then."

"No, but I spoke to D's girlfriend. She passed through town and we had a little sit-down."

I wanted to go from there to where I had met with Tatyana and from there to who I had seen bringing Katrina the flowers that she set in a bowl before me as if to mark the spot where the cuckold supped. But for some reason the words stuck in my throat.

"What was she like?" Katrina asked.

"Serious."

"Pretty?"

"No," I said, thinking that it was true. Tatyana was beautiful.

"Is Dimitri all right?"

"Twill has done an excellent job looking out for his brother. He'll be home when he told you he would."

Again I tried to mention Bertrand, but a feeling of exhaustion took the place of my words.

"I'm glad Dimitri has found love in his life," Katrina said. "Everybody needs love."

At that moment John Prince, accompanied by Angelique Tara Lear, emerged from his apartment building door.

"They just showed up, Katrina. I'll call you later."

I disconnected the cell phone and climbed out of the car.

I recognized her waif's body and even her careless gait, though I had only seen hints of it in stills. Her loose tan dress was half covered by a dark-brown suede jacket and her shoes were flat and tan. Her pocketbook was bright red and her hair combed but still, somehow, unruly. I would have recognized her out of the corner of my eye.

John Prince wasn't quite six foot. Apart from that, his slender physique was well proportioned. His wool slacks were gray and his shirt cream. The faux army jacket probably set him back five hundred dollars, but he still wore sneakers.

They turned in the opposite direction from where I stood. This pointed them toward Seventh Avenue. She had an olive backpack hanging from her shoulders and he was carrying a medium-sized pink suitcase.

I followed at a safe distance. If they both got into a cab I knew that I'd have at least thirty minutes to toss the apartment. The problem was that both bags were probably hers and so there wouldn't be much to search.

A block north on Seventh they went into a fancy chain coffee shop. For a moment I considered waiting outside. The less chance they had of seeing my face, the better. But I was remembering something that Mr. Nichols of Plenty Realty had told me—that Angie had argued over the rent rate he offered even though it was well below the market price. And so I blundered in after the couple, stopping at the doorway to scope out the seating arrangement at the coffee house.

The small tables were mostly occupied, and the line for espressos and cappuccinos was long. There were two small tables in a far corner that were empty; one, which had yet to be bussed, still had a paper coffee cup on it.

I settled at the messy table, moving my chair so that it seemed that I was taking up both spaces. I lifted the paper cup, pretended to drink, and waited.

"Is this table taken?" a young man asked. There was another man behind him. They were both mustachioed, wearing suits and ties.

While asking, he moved forward as if he were going to sit.

"Yes it is," I told him.

"I don't see anybody."

John and Angie were talking. She took the suitcase from him.

I pulled the vacant table next to me and stared into the young white-collar worker's eyes—my meaning as plain as a guard dog's sneer.

As the young men moved away, Angie waded into the pond of busy tables, holding the suitcase with both hands.

I took a sip of the leftover coffee. It was cold, both sweet and bitter—a perfect brew for New York.

"Is this table taken?" she asked me.

Sometimes things work out.

"No," I said. "My two friends just left."

We smiled at each other and I pushed the table toward her. She shrugged off the backpack and pushed the suitcase up against the glass wall.

"That looks heavy," I said.

"My whole life," she told me, thumping the backpack with her small white fist.

I smiled at her words and pulled out my souped-up MP3 player. I set the device down on the table and inserted the earbuds. Then I pulled out a book, *The Chrysalids* by John Wyndham, and turned to a dog-eared page.

Bug's little device, which looked very much like an iPod, was what Twill would call "way cool." It worked as a regular player unless I pressed a button on the side. Once activated, the device itself gave off, from one side, the mild sounds of whatever song was playing while the left side worked as a directional microphone. All I had to do was point the thing at Angie's table and turn my back with my nose in the book. The sound emanating from the device would seem to be coming from the earpieces, and so she and Prince would be lulled into a sense of privacy.

And that's just how it worked. John came with their coffees and the two moved close together and whispered.

"I wish you'd let me come with you," he said.

"What would Michele Lee say about that?" she replied, sounding bravely playful.

"This isn't funny," he said. "We should go to the police."

"How could I explain it to them? They'd throw me in jail for the rest of my life."

"That's better than being killed."

"No it isn't," she said.

They'd been quiet for a long while when he said, "At least get in touch with me so that I know you're okay."

"I'll have to wait for a while," she whispered.

"How long?"

There was silence and then the subtle rustling of clothes. I imagined that they were kissing.

"I love you," he whispered.

"Go on to work, John."

"I'll go with you to the train station."

"No."

"Why not? These bags are heavy."

"I'm going to have to get used to carrying them on my own and, and I don't want you to know anything about where I am. This way you won't know if I left by train or bus . . ."

Or plane, I thought.

"I can't just leave you here," he said.

"Yes you can. Go on now."

That loop in the conversation went on for ten minutes or so. Finally she got him on his feet and shuffling toward the door. Their parting was melodramatic but there was real feeling behind it.

When he was gone I took off the headphones and turned so that I could look upon my unsuspecting client.

SHE SIPPED HER COFFEE and stared ahead. I did the same. I wasn't worried about disease from the used cup. One thing I was certain about— at least most of the time—my death would sneak up on me, a master thief that I'd never see coming.

Seemingly staring off into space, I wondered. One thing I knew for sure about Alphonse Rinaldo was that he expected his instructions to be followed without question or variation. I was not supposed to talk to Angie. Breaking this rule would at the very least sour my relationship with the Big Man.

Yes . . . definitely . . . I would be a massive idiot even to entertain such an idea.

"Excuse me, ma'am," I said.

"Yes?" Her smile was immediate and natural.

"Um . . ." I hesitated, or at least pretended to. "Let me show you my card."

I took out my antediluvian red-brown wallet and produced a card printed with my real name, occupation, address, and office and cell-phone numbers.

She read the information and handed the card back.

"Yes?" she said again.

"I just stopped by here to get some coffee," I said. "I've been working a couple of cases at the same time and needed the stimulus. But it seemed to me that you and your friend were very upset."

Her eyes said that I was right but that she couldn't talk about it.

There was an intimacy to this communication that I had expected from the girl.

"I understand," I said. "Here I am, a stranger. But you've read my card. We're both here, living completely different lives . . .

"I solve people's problems for a living. Before you finish that coffee, you could ask me a question, without giving any details, and I could give you my opinion on the situation."

I could see it in her expression, the unguarded belief that anything could happen. That was why she wasn't suspicious when her rent turned out to be one-third the going rate in Manhattan. In Angie's life good things, like me, just happened.

50

On the surface it really was a good offer. I had seen the distress in her conversation with John Prince but I couldn't have overheard them. And even if I had, they hadn't said anything that would identify her or her specific problem.

Staring at me, Angie saw a chubby, bald black man in an off-the-rack dark-blue utility suit. I could have been an MTA manager or a door-to-door vacuum cleaner salesman in the old Midwest. I certainly was not a criminal mastermind or anybody who had anything to do with her life up until that moment.

"What if a client came into your office and told you that they had been associated with a crime but they were innocent?"

"I'd ask why they'd come to me rather than go to the police."

This, I could see by her breathing, was the right answer.

"And if they told you that they had done . . . something, and the circumstances might make her look guilty?"

"I'd say that the police are really very good at their job and that they can usually sort out the innocent from the culpable."

Angie sat back and smiled. It was a real smile, hinting at mirth.

"You don't seem to want to get hired by this woman," she said.

"This is a perfect situation," I replied. "If some rich woman with an emerald necklace and a little lapdog walked into my office I might be more persuasive. But this is just a busman's holiday."

She liked the collegiate language.

"What if I told you the woman in question had been threatened by a man already and when she went to the police they told her to call again if he did something else?"

I sighed and shrugged.

"Yeah," I said. "I'd believe that."

"And then if she told them that men had tried to kidnap her in front of her house but still the police did nothing?"

"Nothing?"

"They came to her place and went through the motions. They said that they'd look into it but never called back. I . . . she called them, but they never even returned the call."

I sipped my secondhand coffee and wondered. The direction I had imagined for the morning had done a U-turn. I had to choose my words very carefully.

"The main job of the private detective is an emotional one," I said.

"What does that mean?"

"There's an insecurity in the client's life and it's my job to advise them on how to alleviate the anxiety. A cheating spouse or an embezzling employee, it doesn't matter. I have to shed light on the uncertainty. Sometimes the cause is money, and other times it's love."

"There's no love in this situation," Angelique Lear said.

"I can see that."

"So what advice would you give your client?" she asked a stranger.

"That depends on the nature of the criminal situation that this hypothetical client has been drawn into," I said. "If it's a physical crime I'd ask if there was any way that the evidence can point at the client. Could there be any witnesses? Someone who might have seen her, even in passing? Did she touch anything or leave any physical evidence like hair, handwriting, or maybe a bill from some purchase? Like I said, the NYPD can be very efficient. And a serious crime will have a bright light shone on it.

"It might take years, but the wheels of justice do turn and often they catch onto some scrap that the client has left behind."

Angie had to swallow before asking, "And, and if it's not a physical crime?"

"I don't think that's a question in this case."

"Why not?"

"The hypothetical client has been threatened with violence twice. And, if there's no love involved, the crime would almost have to be a physical one."

I waited patiently, wondering where I'd be taken from there while Angie assessed her life along the lines that I had presented.

"So, Mr. McGill," she said at last, "how would you advise your client in this situation?"

"I'd tell her that running was an option but not an easy one. She'd have to change her name and get a new Social Security number. I could give some suggestions along those lines. But I would have to tell her that she'd have to abandon any hope of reconnecting with her former life while living among strangers. And even in this new life she would remain a stranger. She could never tell the truth about her history or upbringing or education. And that young man who just left would never see her again.

"That's what I'd say about long-distance running. But, regardless, she'd have to run for a little while. If I took her on as a client I'd tell her to go to ground for a week or so while I investigated the threats and attempted kidnapping. I wouldn't want to hear about any supposed crime that she might be implicated in. That way I could keep my nose clean if the cops got involved."

"But what good would it do if you couldn't prove that she's innocent of the crime?"

"If the threats and the attack are the cause of the crime, I should be able to prove it—blind, as it were, to the circumstances."

"That seems kind of self-defeating," Angie Lear said.

"Yes, it does," I agreed. "But it protects the client from admitting any involvement with a crime and it shields the detective from prosecution. Later on, if it comes to an interrogation room, or a courtroom, the detective can say that he was simply trying to help a young woman where the authorities had failed. And if the crimes are connected, it will serve to add weight to the client's innocence."

Of course I didn't mean what I was saying. I already knew her crime. I just wanted Angie to feel comfortable talking to me about her problems.

"How much?" she asked.

"Tell me about the threats and the attack and I'll give you a number."

Just the topic, even though she was the one who raised it, brought suspicion into my client's face.

"Can I see your card again?"

I handed it over.

She studied the information for a full minute and then got out her cell phone.

"What's your receptionist's name?" she asked.

"Mardi."

"Marty?"

"Replace the '*t*' with a '*d*' and you've got it."

She entered the number, stood up, and walked away from our little tables. I watched her talking but couldn't hear what she was saying. That didn't matter, though.

Later on, Mardi told me that Angie identified herself by name and then waited to see if it was recognized. When Mardi had no particular reaction, Angie left the message that she called.

She came back to the table and sat down. There was decisiveness in her movements now.

"Four weeks ago a man named Shell called me at my office," she said. "He told me that he was a headhunter and that he had a job for me. It was the perfect job at a start-up ad agency in San Francisco. The salary was great. They'd agree to move me and all my things, and help to find me an apartment. I'd, I'd just broken up with my boyfriend and wanted to make a new start. It was everything I wanted."

"Sounds too good to be true."

"It was, but in my life I've had a great deal of good luck. Scholarships, good jobs, even my apartment was a lucky deal. I got into college because a counselor from Hunter came into a diner where I worked one day and we had a talk about how much I wanted to go to school."

"So you went to see this Mr. Shell?"

"Yes. At first it was all pretty straightforward. He knew about my education and my work for Laughton and Price . . . that's where I worked. But then he knew other things that had nothing to do with the job. He asked me about a man I never heard of."

"What man?"

"Rinaldo."

"Rinaldo what?"

"I forget. That might have been his last name."

"And you never heard of this Rinaldo?"

"No. I had no idea who he was. That's what I told Mr. Shell, and he started listing things—like grants and scholarships, even my job—things that he said I'd gotten over the years because of this Rinaldo. But I told him that I never heard of the man."

"And what did he say to that?"

"Up until then he was very professional, nice. I mean if he wasn't I would have left. But then he said that he hoped I was lying. I asked him why and he said because if I did know this Rinaldo he could do a lot for me, but if I didn't that still wouldn't get me off the hook."

"What'd he mean by that?"

"I don't know. I tried to explain to him that I had no idea what he was talking about, but he didn't listen. He told me that he'd wait a few days but that if I didn't get back to him by then there'd be consequences. He also told me that if I spoke to this Rinaldo about our talk that I'd end up being collateral damage."

"And you really don't know this guy?"

"I never heard of him."

I didn't think that she was lying. If she wanted to cover her relationship with Rinaldo she'd never have mentioned his name.

"What did this Shell look like?" I asked.

"White guy," she said. "Kinda tall."

"Fat? Skinny?"

"Just normal. You got the feeling he was pretty strong. His hair was dark but I don't think that was his natural color. Here's the card he gave me," she said, handing it over.

There was just a name, Oscar Shell, and a phone number with a 917 area code. I tried the number right then but the automatic operator told me that the line had been disconnected.

"Where was it that you met him?" I asked.

"The Leontine Building, on Park and Thirty-first."

After that she told me about the attack in front of her building. I pretended to listen as if this were all new information. I even asked a few questions about the men. But none of that mattered.

Three-quarters of an hour had gone by when we had finished with her stories.

"Three thousand dollars," I said, "plus expenses. You can pay me when I prove that you are innocent on all counts."

"But you don't even know what you're saying you'll prove me innocent of."

"Doesn't matter. I'm sure that this Shell is dirty. All I have to do is show him to the cops and they'll do the legwork."

"And if you don't prove it?"

"You save three thousand dollars and you can still run away."

"I never told you that I was going anywhere."

"Your bags did that."

"And so I should just stay here until I hear from you?" she asked rather hopefully.

"No," I said. "I don't think so. You need to go where nobody knows you. You need a new name and identity."

I fished a Visa credit card out of my wallet. It was in my daughter's name. This I handed over to Miss Lear.

"Michelle Constance McGill," Angie read. "Is this your daughter?"

"Yeah."

"Won't she mind?"

"She doesn't even know the card exists. It has a fifteen-hundred-dollar limit. But remember—every cent you spend will go for expenses. Go find a cheap hotel someplace and call me at my office every day at four-thirty. If I'm out, Mardi will put you through to me wherever I am."

"Why are you doing all this?" she asked.

"You look like a good kid," I said easily. "If it works out, I make my weekly nut and see that justice is done—for a change."

51

It only took a minute for Tiny "Bug" Bateman to disengage the lock on the shamrock-green, reinforced metal door to his underground apartment/workshop. This door was eight feet below street level on Charles, near Hudson.

The electronics lab that had once been a living space was now a series of rooms lined with worktables containing every sort of gadget that a spy-store devotee could imagine. Listening devices, hidden lenses, specialized walkie-talkie telephones, motion sensors, and a lot of things I couldn't even begin to explain.

I was walking down the hall toward the one-time master bedroom that was now filled with a dozen or more linked CPUs that combined to make one of the fastest civilian computers in the world.

Bug met me in the hall.

I had never seen Tiny outside of the hole cut into the round table that dominated his control room. There he always sat, surrounded by more than a dozen screens, swiveling this way and that between keyboards and other, more exotic, devices.

I had never seen his fat, café au lait feet before. As usual, he was wearing blue-jean overalls with no shirt and the red-and-blue iridescent glasses used to track the otherwise invisible spectrums that appeared on some of his more bizarre screens. He was four inches taller than I, close to three hundred pounds, and very, very soft. His curly hair was longish and unruly.

"Tiny?"

He lifted his hinged ultraviolet lenses, so that they flipped up over his forehead, and gave a rare smile.

"Did you talk to her?" he asked.

"What?"

"Zephyra," he said as if he were the pope and I a priest who had somehow forgotten the Latinate Lord's Prayer.

"No, man," I said. "I've been on a case. I've been working."

"You couldn't make a call?"

"Zephyra Ximenez is not a *call* girl," I said. "Not when it comes to something like this, anyway. I was thinking that if I survived the next few days I'd meet with her at the Naked Ear and we'd talk. But now that I see you got feet that actually work, maybe all three of us could meet there."

The look on the brooding young man's face was classic. He went from monadic particulate to an eight-year-old boy in no time.

"Um . . ." he said.

"I'll take that as a yes. Now can we get down to some business?"

EVEN ONCE HE WAS back in his hole, Tiny was still a little off at first. I kept having to repeat myself when explaining about the Leontine Building and the man named Shell.

In order to prime him for more challenging work, I had him look up the license-plate number I got from Lonnie, the redheaded ex-con, but that was just a rental to a guy named Bob Brown.

"And you want to know where this Shell is?" Tiny asked once we were back into the meat of my visit.

"If that'll help me find out who he's working for," I said. "I need to know who's behind all this."

After some time Tiny settled down to his usual brilliance and brought his bug-eyes to bear on the subject of Oscar Shell.

Problems showed up immediately when it became clear that no one by that name worked for any company situated in the Leontine Building. No Oscar Shell had ever rented space there. As a matter of fact, there wasn't an Oscar Shell that fit Angie's description anywhere in the tristate area.

"This isn't gonna work," Tiny said after an hour on the bully's trail. "How about we take another route?"

"The building?" I asked.

From there the fat genius went into overdrive.

T. D. Donnie and Sons were listed as the owners of the Leontine but they actually owned less than one percent of the building, making their money as absentee property managers. The corporation they answered to was Graski Incorporated, which was located in Chicago. Graski had gone out of business in 1955, however, though the corporate name was owned by a woman named Hedda Martins of Miami. Hedda had died three years earlier, and a Florida lawyer's report had informed her heirs that Hedda was a small partner in a company in San Francisco called Real Innovations. RI had listed among its properties the Leontine.

The trail might have ended there, except for one of Hedda's pesky heirs—a man named Thom Soams. Soams filed suits in New York, Illinois, Florida, and California in an attempt to receive payment for what he felt was the heirs' rightful due. After two and half years of wrangling with a new firm, Mallory Investments, Soams collected the sum of $22,307.31 in settlement.

Mallory Investments was a subsidiary of Regents Bank of New York, a private institution owned lock, stock, and barrel by a sometime socialite oddly named Sandra Sanderson III.

It wasn't exactly a smoking gun, but at least I had a business, and maybe even a name.

The articles we pulled up on Sanderson painted her as a hands-on tyrant in her multibillion-dollar business. She fought long and hard against anyone who stood in her way. The New York skyline owed a lot to Regents Bank, which collected its interest with a stopwatch and a stable of lawyers.

Her son, Desmond, had died of a rare heart disease at the beginning of 2008, and Sandra had gone into seclusion, which was peculiar, because mother and son had been on the outs for years.

The structure of this story put me in a rather literary frame of mind.

If Desmond was Grendel, and Sandra Grendel's mama, then maybe Alphonse was Beowulf and this was all a reenactment of a classic masterpiece.

I smiled to myself, leaning on Tiny's round white table as I read the articles he'd produced for me.

"Uh-oh," the genius said.

"What?"

"Somebody's trying to track me down."

"Regents?"

"Not by the signature, but you can bet whoever it is, they work for them."

"How close are they?"

"I've laid down four thousand ninety-six false trails," he said, unrattled. "They might could get through them all, but I doubt it."

"What if they do?"

"If they pushed hard enough they might break the shield on my place."

"That's a lot of work, isn't it?"

"I hacked their database," he said blandly. "They're worth billions. But don't worry, I have a lot of traps set. It's very unlikely that they'd make it all the way here."

"'Unlikely' is not a word I swear by," I said. "Maybe we should get you out of here for a couple of days."

"No."

"No?"

"No one drives me from my home. My life's work is here in this room. I'll die before I let anyone take it from me or me from it."

"You don't really mean that," I said.

"This bunker could withstand a nuclear blast," he told me. I believed him. "It would take a crew of construction engineers just to take down my front door. Being underground, I don't have any assailable walls, and the apartment overhead is mine, with a reinforced floor. There's booby traps all down the hallway and even in the toilet and I have plastic explosives embedded in all four walls of this room. If they ever got this far—they'd never get out."

I didn't doubt a word that Tiny had said. I did, however, wonder if he had considered how vulnerable someone like Zephyra would make him. She wouldn't agree to live in a hole, or to a suicide pact, in order to protect data.

"You got a pencil?" I asked him.

He reached under the table, coming out with a cheap retractable pen and a violet notepad. I scribbled down a phone number and pushed the tiny binder back at him.

"What's this?"

"That's a special number that every important person in the city has. It connects to a solitary 911 operator who has at her beck and call an elite SWAT unit, one in each borough. All you have to do is call that number and the police will be here in force in under five minutes—no questions asked."

In my years moving among gangsters and bent businessmen I'd accumulated a whole treasure trove of information. The special emergency number came from Alphonse Rinaldo himself.

"Wow." It was a rare thing to impress Bug.

"Yeah," I said. "Before you level the block, you might just use that."

52

Regents Bank's main office was on Sixth, at Fifty-third. They owned the entire building. The ground floor brought to mind a futuristic grand ballroom with forty-foot ceilings and crystal walls. The floor was a huge mosaic, a copy of an Australian Aboriginal rock painting depicting their god, the Great Lizard, passing over the Land of Man.

Most of the floor was empty of furniture or partitions. Small groups stood here and there, discussing who knows what. There was a large semicircular desk toward the far end of the vast room where three young women waited to grant or disallow entrance to the higher levels of Regents.

The desk was made from plastic, or maybe glass, with an emerald tint. The young women were Asian, African-American, and Hispanic—all young and, to one degree or another, lovely.

"Yes? Can I help you?" the smiling Asian child asked.

"Leonid Trotter McGill," I said. "For Mr. Oscar Shell."

"What department?"

"He's a special operative in the employ of Sandra Sanderson the Third."

Something like fear entered the young woman's eyes. However, the smile managed to keep a place hold on the lower half of her face.

She turned to her girlfriends and huddled.

A guard with an earphone entered from stage right. I gazed wistfully at the red-and-ochre mosaic tiles at my feet.

All three of the women stood and approached me.

"What is your business?" the black woman asked me.

"Is Mr. Shell here?"

"That's not what I asked you."

"The only thing you need to know is that my business with you is getting to Mr. Shell."

No one there liked me.

"I'm sorry, we, we don't have anybody by that name here," the Hispanic woman said.

"Then I'll leave."

The suited guard took a step toward me.

Evoking my beloved, and favorite, son, I did a single shoulder shrug and made to turn away.

"Excuse me," the Asian woman said.

I noticed then that all three were the same height.

"Yes?"

"Does this business have to do with Regents?"

"No," I said. "I'm pretty sure not. At least I hope not."

"What does that mean?"

Another guard appeared—stage left.

"A woman may have been threatened by Mr. Shell. And we believe that he is known to Ms. Sanderson. I came here to investigate along that line of inquiry."

"'We'?"

"I represent a consortium that reports to a central body interested in the welfare of this woman and the actions of those connected with said Mr. Shell."

Highbrow language usually gets under the skin of the underlings of power.

One of the guards spoke into his left cuff. I wondered if their earphones were somehow connected to a transmitter at the clear green reception desk.

"But you say that there is no Mr. Shell here?" I said.

"No," the first receptionist I spoke to said.

"Then we've been misinformed." I turned to go.

"Sir?" the black receptionist said. She was holding a small green wireless phone against the left side of her face.

"Yes?"

"Take the elevator through the door behind our desk."

I glanced at the portal and wondered.

"To what floor?" I asked.

"It only goes to one floor."

"Will Oscar Shell be there?"

"I can only tell you what I've been told."

I hesitated a moment more. I hadn't actually expected admission to Regents' inner sanctum. I only wanted to shake things up a bit. But there I was, flanked by two mortal descendants of Cerberus and faced with three modern-day sirens.

Knowing the mythology, I should have walked out.

"Okay," I said.

The Latina raised a section of the round desk as the Asian used an electronic card to open the door.

I walked through into a small cylindrical room that was colored dark red from ceiling to floor. Before me stood an onyx elevator door that slid open, seemingly at my approach.

The black car had two buttons: a green disc over a cream-colored one. I pressed the upper button, and, after a moment, the car began a speedy ascent.

Maybe eighty seconds later, the car came to a stop and the door opened onto a large space that was more like a living room than an office. The floors were white marble and the distant windows looked eastward, toward Long Island. There was a rainstorm passing in the distance.

"Forgive me, sir," a well-built white man in an olive-green suit said.

"For what?"

"I'm going to search you."

He was tall enough, in his forties, I guessed, and bald. Probably pretty strong.

"No," I said.

Mild surprise rippled across his handsome features.

"I'm afraid I'll have to insist."

"You should be—afraid, that is. Because I'm mad as a mothah-fuckah and I don't believe you can take me. At the very least you have to prove it before you can see what's in my pockets."

The bodyguard's face had a tan complexion. His intelligent eyes gave the impression of education—both formal and from the street. He had seen a lot of struggle in his life but did not expect it in this rarefied atmosphere.

I noticed a jet in the distant sky, taking off from Kennedy, no doubt.

The bodyguard took a step in my direction.

I smiled invitingly.

"Mr. Corman," a deep feminine voice intoned.

From somewhere to the left a tall and slender woman approached.

"Yes, ma'am?"

"Let's forgo the routine this time. I'm sure that Mr. McGill isn't here to make trouble."

"But Ms. Sanderson—"

"Stand aside," she said. She had a voice that was used to being obeyed.

Mr. Corman backed away as the woman strode forward.

At first I couldn't make out her features because of the light from behind. But then, suddenly, the light of the entryway revealed her face.

It was the mask of a forty-year-old woman perfectly molded to a skull that sat atop a fit seventy-year-old body. She had done her Pilates and eaten acres of broccoli but that hadn't stopped the clock, not completely.

"You'll have to forgive Mr. Corman," she said. "He's a new employee and hasn't yet mastered the subtleties of his position."

"Is another one of your employees an Oscar Shell?" I asked.

"Thousands of people work for me. You can't expect that I would know them all by name."

Twelve feet behind her sat two black sofas on a bright pine floor.

"What do you want with this Mr. Shell?" she asked.

Her steel-gray pants suit and lilac blouse were designed for the forty-year-old she was impersonating. But the backs of her hands were discolored and wrinkled.

I glanced to the left to see what Corman was up to. He watched me with the same purpose.

"Mr. McGill?" Sandra Sanderson III prodded.

"I wanted to ask him a question."

"What's that?"

"Who hired him to frighten and harass my client?"

"You're a lawyer?"

"A dick."

"I see. And who is your client?"

"My business."

"And how much is this client paying?"

"She's paying the going rate. The only rate I ever charge."

"I see."

"You don't know him?"

"No."

"Then why am I here?" I asked.

"I wanted to get a look at you." Her words accomplished their sinister intent.

"May I ask you something?"

"If you wish."

"I never heard of a woman, outside of royalty and cruise ships, called 'the Third.' Did your mother go by 'Junior'?"

"I come from a long line of strong women, Mr. McGill. I believe you will discover that fact at some point in your misguided investigation."

"Are you telling me that you don't own the Leontine Building over on Park?" I said.

That did something to the old woman's eyes.

"Come sit with me for a moment, Mr. McGill," she commanded.

We strode into the block-long living room—Sandra in the lead, me in close pursuit, and Corman bringing up the rear.

She gestured toward one of the black sofas and I sat at the end nearest me. Sandra perched in the middle of her ebony divan and brought her hands together, as if in symbolic, passionless prayer.

"Do you have children, Mr. McGill?"

"I have friends with guns," I said in answer to a perceived threat.

"I have wealth beyond the everyday citizen's ability to comprehend," she said, "and still I could not save my son's life."

"I read about that. I'm sorry."

"I would do anything to make my son's memory a part of the fabric of this city that he loved."

"New York's like a boiling cauldron," I said, only dimly understanding why. "We are all consumed therein."

"That's down in the street you're talking about," Sanderson told me with a dismissive wave of her liver-spotted hand. "Up here it's different. Up here we can make a difference."

I stared out the window, wondering at the nature of the combination of folly and wealth.

"Do you know a man named . . . Alphonse Rinaldo?" she asked.

"No. Who is he?"

Despite my usual sangfroid, sweat sprouted on my head.

"I could make you a rich man," she offered.

"I'm sure."

"Where can I find Angelique Lear?"

There were no planes in the sky, no rain.

"I don't know."

"Are you a fool, Mr. McGill?"

"That I am."

"I will have my memorial or that child will die, as my son died."

"Not while I'm here."

"You are nothing," she said.

There was a finality to her sentence. I felt as if a high court had just pronounced judgment on my soul.

"Grant," she said then, speaking to Mr. Corman. "See our guest out."

"I can push the button myself," I said.

I stood up on boxer's pins. I might have been wobbled, but I was going to end that round on my feet.

53

I had made it past the green desk and more than half the way across Regents Bank's broad entrance hall.

"Excuse me, sir," one of the burly business-suited guards from earlier said.

I kept walking.

"Excuse me."

Moving at a pretty good clip, I was less than fifteen feet from the revolving door when one of the men got in front of me. His partner was there at my side a moment later.

One was black, the other white, but for the most part they were interchangeable minions of the Corporation. Their suits were both dark blue, their heights indistinguishably tall.

"Yes?"

"Come with us, please," the white one said. "We have some questions."

"No thanks."

"We have to insist."

"You will swallow all your front teeth before I go anywhere with either one of you."

"What?" the black corporate cop said. He put a hand on my shoulder.

For a man in his mid-fifties I'm pretty fast. I crouched down and hooked a good left into the black man's midsection. I felt the wound inflicted by Patrick tear a bit, but it was worth it. I could tell by the guard's deep exhalation that he would need a few moments to recover. I stood up behind a right uppercut that the white guard had no defense for. He sprawled out on his back and I started walking toward the doors again.

People shouted behind me, but my point had been made effectively. No one else tried to block my egress. I exited the building feeling right with the world for the first time in many days.

"HOLD IT RIGHT THERE," a voice commanded on Forty-ninth between Fifth and Sixth.

I stopped and turned. Four uniforms were approaching.

"Yes, officers?" I asked, smiling sincerely.

"Don't move."

"Is there a problem?"

I liked the makeup of the modern NYPD even if they had no use for me. The small group consisted of a black woman, a black man, one Asian gentleman, and a strawberry-blond white rookie who somehow brought to my mind the phrase *one-hit wonder.*

The black man was the one addressing me. He was solidly built, not a hair over five eight.

"Where you coming from?" he asked.

"Just out for a walk, officer."

"From where?"

"I don't know. Walkin' around is all."

"Let me see your knuckles."

"Why?"

"Show me your hands."

"Give me a reason," I said. I hadn't meant for it to sound like a threat but I could see a jolt go through the assembled constabulary.

THE ARREST TOOK A long time.

When taking a suspect into custody on the streets of Midtown Manhattan the police dot all *i*'s and cross their *t*'s and *f*'s. They ask you questions and, if you're me, you give them indecipherable answers.

I wasn't worried about assault charges. The fight was on tape, no doubt. Two men had assaulted me in the bank. They didn't have badges or uniforms. I hadn't said a word in provocation—not really.

After a while the police got around to binding my hands behind my back. Maybe forty minutes later I was hustled into the back of a police cruiser driven by the Asian and attended by Blondie.

Half the way to the midtown precinct the white kid's cell phone rang.

After twenty seconds of conversation he looked at his partner and said, "They want us to bring him over to the Port Authority, Park."

"Why?"

"Didn't say."

"Who was it?"

"The sergeant."

WITH MY HANDS STILL bound behind me I was taken through a series of doors and down innumerable hallways to a Port Authority Police office somewhere in the bowels of the building.

"Hello, McGill," Bethann Bonilla said.

"Are you Lieutenant Bonilla, ma'am?" the white kid asked.

"Release him and leave us," she replied.

The young cops did as they were told. They asked no questions . . . this told me something.

The room was small and stale. The beat-up oak desk had stood there as long as the Port Authority itself and the floor had been battered by ten thousand feet. Many a purse snatcher and pickpocket had been detained here before their deportation to the Tombs, or maybe straight to their arraignment. It was a sad stopover for pimps, prostitutes, and the mentally deranged.

I felt right at home.

"To what do I owe my freedom?" I asked, taking a seat across from the cop.

"The bank sent down notice to drop charges," she said. "But I had already been notified. I decided to have them bring you here because NYPD won't be able to yank you out too quickly."

She smiled.

"Who are you worried about yanking me?"

"Kitteridge, Charbon," she said. "There's a DA named Tinely who seems to want his pound of flesh."

"And what do you want, Lieutenant?"

The wisp-thin, steel-hard lady cop placed her maroon elbows on the old-time desk. She laced her fingers, pressed the pads of her thumbs together, and considered me.

"That depends on what you have," she answered.

"You want to make a trade?"

"What do you need from me?"

"There's a pimp named Gustav on East Houston who's paying off a Lieutenant Saul Thinnes. One of the girls is a friend. I need Gustav busted—busted bad."

"And what do I get out of that?"

"Have you got a name for the dead man in Wanda Soa's apartment?"

Her eyes couldn't conceal the excitement.

I gave her Pressman's name and his alias. I told her that he was a hit man on staff with a killer known only as Patrick.

"Why would somebody want this Soa dead?" she asked.

"Maybe her drug connections. Can you drop a hammer on Gustav?"

"Oh yeah."

"You aren't worried about Thinnes?"

"If he's crooked he better be worried about me."

THERE WAS YET ANOTHER bartender at the Naked Ear when I got there at 7:06; a thirty-something white guy with slim shoulders and a little belly. I perched down at the far end of the bar and ordered my three cognacs. The bartender was named Ely. He knew everything about sports and so we had a long talk, between orders, about Henry Armstrong, the only boxer who ever held three title belts in three different weight classes at the same time. In the space of twelve months, he successfully campaigned in nineteen defenses of those belts.

"I think he was superior to Sugar Ray Robinson," Ely said. "Pound for pound."

"Yeah," I said, "but it's not like math."

"What do you mean?"

"In weight lifting the man who lifts the heaviest weight wins. But in boxing, after a certain point, it's all heart."

"Hi," a woman said.

I turned and there was Lucy.

Ely slapped me on the forearm and moved on down the bar.

"He called me," she said. "I asked all the bartenders to call me if you came in."

"What happened the other night?" I asked. "I was here."

"I wanted to see if you'd come twice."

"I'M OUT OF CONDOMS," Lucy apologized at one in the morning. "I only bought a box of three. I mean, I guess I could do something else."

I pulled the blankets off her and kissed her navel. She giggled and rolled away. She went too far and tumbled off the side of the bed. We both laughed and I pulled her back on.

We'd been in that bed for four hours. If I'd been taking an erectile-dysfunction drug I'd've had to go to the emergency room.

"I think it's all the tension in my life," I said. "That and the fact that both my wife and my girlfriend have boyfriends now."

"What's bad for the boy-goose is good for the girl-goose bartender," she said.

I kissed her.

There must have been some kind of hesitation in the kiss or my body language because she said, "Don't worry. I'm not asking for any more than I already got. I really am married. Jeff's a painter. He's at an art colony in New Hampshire. He's the kind of guy can't go three days without sex, so I know he's with someone."

"So I'm your revenge?"

"My solace," she said, and we held each other a while.

I GOT OUT OF the taxi, drunk on more than liquor. I was still high from the brief fight with the Regents security team and the passion that Lucy the bartender drew from me. I took a deep breath at the front door of my building. A man touched my left triceps. It hurt my wound. Turning toward him, I swiveled my torso at the hip when the blow came from behind.

There was only a moment of consciousness left to me, a sliver of fading light that I squandered wondering if I had been shot in the back of the head.

54

The smells of wood ash and pine needles were the first signs of returning consciousness. I was in a seated position. My fingers were numb from the tight bonds around my wrists, which were tied to the arm of the heavy chair. My feet weren't going anywhere, seeing that they were lashed to the front legs of the chair.

It took a moment for me to identify the speeding fire engine, its horns blaring. It was the headache brought on by the blow to my skull.

There were lights here and there in the room but the pulsating pain made them seem like stars—points in the darkness that illuminated nothing but themselves.

"He's awake," a gruff voice said.

There was motion in the room.

Two large shapes moved in my direction. Men in suits. One was large and brutal. The other looked like a professional manager of a large, glass-walled office.

"Mr. McGill," the manager said.

"Who is that?" I had to squint to see past the pain.

"My name is Shell," he said. "I hear that you've been looking for me."

Something about the connectivity between the ideas cleared up my vision. I was in a cabin, probably in the woods, judging by the smells. The larger man was quite hairy and wore a woolly gray suit. Silently I dubbed him Mammoth. Shell's suit was a muted silver-gray color and he wore expensive Italian shoes cut from red-brown leather.

"You coulda just called me," I said.

I had the urge to vomit but squelched it. Neither Mammoth or Shell looked like they'd have cleaned me up afterwards.

"There's a time for all things," Shell intoned. "This, my friend, is not the moment for bravery."

"Oh no? Why's that?"

The blow Shell delivered was hard—very hard. The heaviness of the chair anchored me, which only added to the power of the clout. I'm used to getting hit. I've sparred and fought real fights for nearly forty years. But Shell's blow was something real, a second fire engine crashing headlong into the first.

The next thing I knew there was cold water in my ears and running down my neck. That chill was the first time I was reminded of Patrick and Diego—but not the last.

"You can get seriously damaged if you don't answer my questions," Shell said.

I blinked twice. There was blood coming down the left side of my forehead. The upper part of the back of my left arm burned.

I remember thinking that my investigation was a success, that everything was falling into place—on top of me.

Shell hit me again but I maintained consciousness.

"Where's Angelique?" he asked.

"I don't know."

"You don't know what?"

"Where Angelique is."

He struck again, doused me with water again.

I was getting colder. The iciness kept Patrick in my mind.

"You have to know her," Shell said. "You knew about me."

"I met her," I told him, "in a coffee shop. She told me her problem and I agreed to look into it."

He hit me twice.

"I followed the line of ownership for the Leontine Building . . ."

He hit me.

". . . and found out that Regents Bank owned it. I figured that Shell, you, worked for Regents."

He hit me again.

I've been in boxing gyms regularly since the age of fourteen. I've been hit two hundred times in an evening by light heavyweights and heavyweights who know how to hit. I might've looked like shit, but you can't judge a book by its cover, or a boxer by his cuts.

"Where is she?" Shell asked.

I realized that my mind had been wandering, sent on its circuitous route by Shell's power shots.

"I don't know where she is."

"Then how did you know to come to Regents?"

"She told me about you, at least somebody with your name, about meeting this man at his office in the Leontine. I'm a detective. I followed it down from there."

Mammoth came over and hit me then. That threw the chair over and me into dreamland.

When I awoke I was sitting up again. Mammoth had moved back toward the fake-log wall, and the fireplace was blazing but throwing off very little heat.

"Where is she?" Shell asked from somewhere off to the left.

I turned to him.

"Don't let that guy hit me again," I said. That was the beginning of my plan. It wasn't much of a strategy but it was mine and I was sticking to it.

"Then tell me where she is."

"She had money on her," I said. "Three thousand dollars. She was going to take a bus out west. I told her to hang around, to go to a hotel and call my office after five days. She gave me five hundred and went to ground."

I thought my nose was broken after his next punch. It wasn't, but it sure felt like it.

"Where is she?"

THE BEATING WENT ON for a quite a while. It got harder and faster when they realized that I was going to hang tough. Unluckily for me these guys weren't sadomasochists. I say unluckily because if they had pulled out a knife, or even just a burning cigarette, I could have put my plan into action. But all they were doing was hitting me. I didn't want to make it too easy on them so I took the punishment until I figured they'd hit me enough to have broken someone not trained in the fistic arts.

I once studied the Method under a wonderful thespian named Anja Klieger. I had no intention of going onstage, but I figured that my profession demanded believable emotional pretense from time to time.

Anja had taught me to remember a time when I had the feeling that the character I was portraying felt.

I thought about my father walking out the door with his army-surplus duffel bag. I remembered his last hug and then the months of my mother's decline. At last I thought about a boy entering puberty, alone in the world for no reason that made sense.

I wasn't in a cabin in the woods. I wasn't being beaten by hard men. I was a child bereft of the only love he'd known. The tears began to flow and I cried for the first time in over a decade.

"I'll tell you," I said. "Just stop it. Stop it."

"Where's the girl?" Shell asked. He was a little winded from the exertions of beating me. I'm sure his knuckles were sore.

"I don't know where she is but I know who has her."

"Who?"

"A guy named Brennan. I told him that I'd call when it was safe."

"What's the number?"

I gave it to him. "But if anybody but me calls he'll hang up and run."

Shell brought out a gun and pointed it at my forehead.

"Untie his hands, Leo," Shell said.

Mammoth did so.

"Hand our friend the phone," the cruel manager added.

I tried to take the landline receiver but it fell from my numb fingers.

"What the fuck?" Leo said.

"It's my hands," I said hastily. "They're numb from being tied for so long."

"Take your time," Shell said generously.

After a few minutes I entered a number. As soon as the phone started ringing Shell picked up an extension line.

The phone rang seven times before Hush answered.

"Hello?" he said.

"You got the girl, Brennan?"

"You know I do," he said easily.

"I need to see her."

"Sure."

"Where do you have her?"

"You know that private cemetery in Hicksville?"

"Yeah."

"Show up at the gate after the sun rises and I'll buzz you in."

He hung up and I took a deep breath.

I looked up into Shell's eyes. He was wondering, and I was, too, if he should kill me right then and there. That might have been much easier. It would have certainly been safer.

But he didn't know anything about the cemetery except that the gates were locked.

"Where's this place?" he asked.

I shook my head.

"I want out of this," I said.

"Who you working for?"

"The girl."

"You told the people at Regents that you were part of a group."

"Just me and Brennan, man. Just me and him."

55

It was daylight by the time we made it to Hicksville.

We went in a dark-green Lexus. Leo the Mammoth was driving, with Shell riding shotgun. I was on the floor in the back, bound hand and foot and happy to be so misused.

Happy because the only alternative to my discomfort was death.

"Okay," Shell said. "We're at North Broadway. Where to now?"

"Go four more blocks to Lathrop and turn right. Follow the street past the houses and keep on going until you get to a big stone wall that has a gateway."

The number I had called was *the number*. I got the idea when Alphonse Rinaldo had given me that special 911 number for the elite NYPD SWAT team. I thought that I should have my own personal emergency number.

I got special phones for me and Hush dedicated to this purpose. We had come up with passwords, like little boys initiating a clubhouse. Mine were Tolstoy, Nikita, Dimitri, and John-John. Anything else meant, "Get me out of here!"

This was taking a big chance. I didn't want to be involved with killing, if at all possible. Hush knew this, but he was also a psychopathic killer, by nature and by trade—even if he was retired. We were friends and he respected me but still the urge to kill was a natural place for him to go and I had called that number for the first time.

The car came to a stop.

For two minutes there were no words spoken.

"I don't like this," Leo grumbled.

"Who is this Brennan guy?" Shell asked me.

"He does bodyguarding for me sometimes. His cousin manages this cemetery."

Actually the place was managed by a man who, after sizing him up for a week, Hush decided to let live. It was a long and convoluted story that had to do with a dog and a little girl. The man paid Hush a fortune and the assassin helped him to create a new identity.

"Do you trust him with your life?" Shell asked. "Because we're going to have guns on you."

"He'll have a gun too," I said. "But he'll talk before shooting."

These words paved the way to a few more minutes of silence.

I used that time to make my peace with what was going to happen to Mammoth and Shell. I wasn't angry with them. They tortured me, but I'd done the same to Patrick.

And I'd done worse.

Once, many years before, I'd destroyed the life of a young girl who grew up into a woman self-named Karma. Karma kept coming back, from a restless grave, to give me as I had given.

But this wasn't about me. It was about Angie and her persecution. Shell was a part of that, and he'd have to meet his own fate. I'd save him and his woolly friend if possible, but what could I do with my hands and feet bound?

"Get back there and cut him loose, Leo," Shell said.

The big man cut the heavy tape that bound me. Then he showed me a long-barreled six-shooter, an anachronism in a caveman's hand.

"You fuck up, buddy," he said, "and I will give you all'a these here caps."

I nodded, did a sit-up, and pressed myself from the floor in the back of the car.

THERE WAS AN INTERCOM system at the gate of the old Quaker Cemetery. The last body had been interred nearly a century before. Visitors rarely came and the few who did made appointments.

I pressed a button.

"LT?" Hush said through a haze of static.

"Hey, Bren," I said. "I got a couple'a guys wit' me might help the girl."

"Come on in," the electric voice crackled.

The car-wide gate rolled open.

In the backseat again, Shell sat next to me with a gun muzzle pressed against my side. The tension in the car was palpable. I was afraid that they'd off me before we got to Hush; that he'd slaughter them before my eyes if I made it that far. They were afraid of the unknown that lay ahead of them. Working for Sanderson, no doubt, Shell had already messed up with Angie three times. The thug had fallen short in his attempt to intimidate her. The men in front of her apartment, obviously his, had failed to grab her. Later, his hired assassins had also missed the mark.

The car rolled down a cobblestone lane between silent pines until it got to the stone chapel at the end. We got out of the car. Leo took the lead, with Shell at the back, his gun nudging my spine.

Some kind of bird made a strangled cry off in the woods as we stood in the secluded circular driveway in front of the silent yellow-and-white stone building.

Half a minute passed.

"Call him," Shell hissed.

"Hey you!" someone screamed from my right.

The pressure left my vertebrae and I heard a loud *thunk*.

Shell groaned and fell to the ground.

"What?" Leo grunted as he turned his old-fashioned gun to the right.

Another *thunk* and the big woolly man was on his knees, something like a small white pillow bouncing away from him. He was hit in the diaphragm by another pillowy round and joined Shell in painful semiconsciousness.

"Hey, LT," Hush said, coming from the blind of trees. He was holding a canister gun, like a miniature bazooka. "Crowd-control device they use in Taiwan. Knocks a normal man out with just one shot."

He went to the fallen men and secured their hands and feet with flex-cuffs. We dragged them into the chapel and carried them down into the basement, where we secured them behind a heavy oaken door.

Leo weighed two fifty at least, but I'm a light heavyweight in training and Hush is much, much stronger than he looks.

HUSH LED ME TO the study on the second floor of the old building. There was plenty of sunlight coming in through clear and stained-glass windows. My savior gave me a first-aid kit and a snifter of brandy.

After dressing my face and downing the liquor I told Hush what I knew.

"You should'a killed Patrick," was his first observation.

"He never saw my face clearly."

"But Rinaldo left a trail by having him arrested. He might find a way back to you. You know, this isn't a game, LT. It's not like you can take a piece off the board and he stays in the box. These are killers, flawed men who go out after money and revenge."

"How long can we keep 'em down there?" I asked, to change the subject.

"Ike's closed the cemetery for a few days," Hush said. "He's going to have to change jobs unless you want to use an empty crypt in the north corner."

"I thought you gave up killing."

"I haven't killed anybody, have I?"

That bought him a wry grin.

"But let me ask you something," he said.

"What?"

"How deep do you plan to dig this hole before you gonna let 'em bury you in it?"

56

"Leonid?" my wife of twenty-three years said.

She was standing at the door of my den, soon to be Gordo's sanatorium. I was sitting on the daybed, staring at the floor.

"Yeah, babe?"

"What happened to your face?"

"Nothing."

She crossed the threshold dressed in a plush purple nightgown. I gestured and she sat down next to me.

"Does it have to do with Dimitri?"

"No. He's fine. I got an e-mail from Twill. They're both down in Philly for a day or two more. Don't worry. He'll be home when I said."

My voice was thick. Night had come and my plans were made—for better or for worse.

Angelique had called at four-thirty, as planned. Mardi patched the call through to me and I told my client that I had found Shell and planned to meet with him the next day. That seemed to satisfy her for the moment.

"What's wrong?" Katrina asked.

"I wish that there was some kind of guy I could hire. Some detective who I could just give a list of all my problems—Gordo and Twill, a misspent life and . . . and everything else."

"You can talk to me." She even put a hand on mine.

I looked at her, wondering if I would mention her young lover, if she could read the knowledge in my eyes.

"Thanks for letting me bring Gordo here," I said.

"The children love him."

I looked down again.

"Come to bed, Leonid."

"You go on, Katrina. I have to think. I got a big day tomorrow and everything has to go just right."

A moment passed and then another. Katrina stood up and walked away. The wind was whistling outside the windows of my den. The nights were getting longer.

WHERE'S THAT OTHER SUIT? Lucy had asked when she was pulling down the zipper of my pants.

I hate it, I'd said, holding my breath after.

I thought it was kinda cool.

So I donned the ochre suit before leaving the house. I got my car out of the garage and headed for Long Island City at six the next morning.

She was on a lower floor of a Best Western, number sixteen. One of the many benefits of Bug's expertise was my being able to hack into almost any database—including the occupancy floor plans for almost any chain hotel.

I knocked and waited, knocked again. I was just getting nervous when she opened the door. Her dress was a fluid mixture of cranberry and blueberry hues. Her feet were bare.

"Mr. McGill?"

"Hi."

"What happened to your face?"

"It's a special interrogation technique. I beat myself until my prisoner can't take it anymore and has to tell me what I want to know."

I walked in, pushing the door only enough to make room for my bulk.

"How did you know where I was?" she asked.

I sat on the bed heavily. My face and left arm ached, and I hadn't been to sleep in well over twenty-four hours.

"The reason you did well to hire me," I said. "All I had to do was trace the expenditures on the card and I found this place."

"But how did you find my room?"

"Trade secret."

"Do you have news?"

"Yeah."

"What is it?"

"I found a guy who has all the answers. We just have to go see him and everything will be cleared up."

"I don't know if I should go with you," she said. "I called John last night and he said that you can't just trust somebody that you meet in a coffee shop."

"You shouldn't have called your boyfriend. Call could have been traced. And not just somebody—a private detective, like me, who's good enough to know that your real name is Angelique Tara Lear and that you, against all odds, stabbed and killed an armed assassin in your friend Wanda Soa's apartment."

Angie backed away from me, toward the door.

"Look, kid," I said. "If I wanted to grab you or hurt you I wouldn't be sitting here. I told you that I'd figure out what happened, and I have. But in order to explain it to you, and to get you out of trouble, I have to bring you to an office in lower Manhattan. Come with me and you can go back to your old life."

"I'm afraid."

"Nothing wrong with fear. It keeps the eyes open and your feet ready to run."

For some reason this made her smile.

"WE NEED TO GET a few things straight before we talk to this guy," I said when we were headed east on the BQE.

"What?"

"The man who killed Wanda was named Adolph Pressman."

Angie turned from me and looked out on Brooklyn.

"I know how he found you. I figure that he knocked at Wanda's door with some pretext. You hid and he came in with a gun. Somehow he didn't see you and you went at him with the kitchen knife you were holding for self-defense."

When she turned to me the tears were flowing from her eyes.

"And I murdered my best friend," she cried.

"You have to hear me on this one, Miss Lear," I said in the calmest of deep tones. "That man came to your house with the express intention of killing you. He would have killed Wanda too. You tried to save your life and hers. You did your best. The murderer, the man who killed your friend, is dead."

"But why?" she moaned.

I couldn't help but think that this utterance was the bedrock foundation of all philosophical inquiry.

I gave no answer and she expected none.

"What did you do with the gun?" I asked after the proper interval.

She turned back to the window and fiddled with her hair.

"Come on, now," I said. "If I can figure it out you know the cops can, too."

"I left it at John's. He said that he'd get rid of it the next time he goes out to Long Island."

"Why didn't you toss it into a river?"

"I was afraid that somebody'd see me."

I thought that we should drop by Prince's apartment and pick up the weapon. That was a loose end that needed to be tied. But I was very tired. So much so that any detour seemed beyond comprehension.

WE TOOK THE STAIRS to the seventh floor of the nondescript downtown office building. I walked her down the dowdy green corridor to a door with no signage on it.

"Where are we?" she said.

"The man in this office," I replied, "is a very powerful person who likes his privacy . . . maybe a little bit too much."

I knocked and waited.

The door clicked open on a bare reception room. There, behind a maroon metal desk, sat a slender, posture-perfect, middle-aged black man wearing silver-rimmed glasses and a thin aqua tie. The lapels of his suit jacket were almost nonexistent. His sensual lips had never smiled, would never do so, for me.

This was Christian Latour, the Important Man's first lines of defense and offence.

"You don't have an appointment, Mr. McGill."

"I bet you that tie he'll see us."

"I see that you've brought Miss Lear," Christian said without even looking at Angie.

"Push the button, Chris."

It wasn't a good idea to bait Latour but I was tired and he was a prig. I liked the guy, but sometimes he had too much attitude.

There was a small black box on left side of Christian's desk. The hole in the top suddenly shone a brilliant blue.

"He will see you," the exasperated receptionist said.

A door behind him opened automatically and I ushered my client through.

THE WALLS WERE ROYAL BLUE and the carpet burgundy. An ever-changing gallery of Renaissance masterpieces on loan from the Met hung along the walls on our way to the Big Man's desk.

Rinaldo was standing in front of the desk (something he had never done for me alone) when we got to him.

"Mr. Brown?" Angie said hesitantly. "Is that you?"

"Hi, Tara." There was an unfamiliar smile on his lips.

"What, what are you doing here?"

"This is my office."

"Are those paintings for real?"

"Why don't we all have a seat?" he offered.

ANGIE WAS LOOKING AROUND the office, seated on a seventeenth-century French chair, while I watched her from my favorite perch: a chair of carved lava stone that was once a pre-Columbian sacrificial altar.

"Mr. McGill?" Alphonse Rinaldo said. If you didn't know him you might not have perceived the threat.

"Sandra Sanderson the Third," I replied.

"Oh."

"Who?" Angie asked.

"Mr. McGill has informed me about your situation," Rinaldo said in a soft and very understanding voice. "He's brought the problem to me and I have resolved to straighten it out. You'll have to excuse us for a few minutes if you don't mind, Tara."

"I don't understand, Mr. Brown. What do you have to do with any of this?"

"I'll explain after Mr. McGill and I confer. Can I get you something to drink or eat while you wait?"

"I haven't had breakfast yet."

Rinaldo picked up the phone and waited a beat. Then, "Mr. Latour, the young lady in my office needs breakfast. Come in and get her order. Mr. McGill and I will be in the library.

"Come with me, Mr. McGill."

He stood and so did I. I followed him to a shadowy corner on the north side of the office. There we passed through a door into a good-sized room that was lined with bookshelves and books. There was a round ash table in the center of the room surrounded by four red-velvet padded chairs.

"Have a seat."

I did so. It felt really good to sit down, like I'd been extremely tired and up to that point unaware of the extent of my exhaustion.

"Nice suit," he said.

"Yeah. My wife bought it for me. I hated it at first. But now it's kind of growing on me."

"I specifically instructed you not to speak to Tara."

"Sometimes a good agent has to make decisions on his own."

"You should have called and asked me before taking such action."

"There was no time to call."

"You should not have brought her to me."

"It's the only place I could be sure that she wouldn't be killed."

That caused him to cross his legs, right over left.

For a moment there my future was in question. I had disobeyed. Even in his weakened position he was that caged lion and I a mere mortal on the wrong side of the bars.

"Give it to me," he said at last.

I laid it all out. The assailants, all six of them, and the threats. I told him about Shell and Leo locked in a cellar in Queens and

Sandra Sanderson's obvious involvement. I explained how I decided the only way to approach the problem was to put Angie first as my client.

He listened very closely to my story.

Usually when we spoke he was in some kind of hurry. An ambassador from some foreign nation or an insistent billionaire was in the waiting room in line for a meeting. But that day I could have gone on for hours.

"Your actions have put a strain on our relationship, Leonid," he said when I had finished. "Even if I am pleased with the outcome, I won't be able to put my full trust in you again."

"You mind explaining what it is that we've done here?" I asked. There was no reason to cry over spilt influence.

"You know that I report to City Hall," he said. "Not directly to the mayor but we know each other to speak. A long time ago this, unofficial, position was created in order to keep things running smoothly without bringing attention to the actions necessary. I'm what you might call a chief bureaucrat—with teeth.

"When I first took the position, I was . . . anxious. My decisions are often taken on my own, without counsel or review. I was uncertain . . .

"On Tuesday and Thursday mornings I'd go to a diner not far from here. Angelique was seventeen and a waitress at the time. Her first name was too long for the tag so she used Tara as her name. We used to talk. Those conversations relaxed me. She made me feel normal, and I suppose, I fell in love with her a little."

Rinaldo uncrossed his legs, clasped his hands together, sat up straight.

"Not in a sexual way. More like a man feels toward the daughter of a good friend. We had long talks in between her customers. She saw me in an avuncular way, and I, behind the scenes, tried to help her get on with her life.

"She never had a father in the house, and her mother . . . had problems. So I tapped a college counselor to develop a friendship with her—"

"Iris Lindsay," I said, remembering the gravestone in the photograph.

"Yes. Poor Iris died only a few months ago. She greased the wheels for Tara to get into college, and a few other things. Tara never knew. She didn't even know my real name.

"After she left the diner I had Christian research her background, and Sam Strange's predecessor set up certain monies and benefits for her—with the help of an ever-watchful Ms. Lindsay. Helping Tara made me feel more balanced.

"I've kept up the support, and over time she's developed relationships with certain city employees who answer to this office. I could never tell her what I was doing, but I kept an eye on her. If she filed a complaint about some neighbor or applied for a scholarship or a job, I was usually able to help. I thought I was being discreet, but I guess Sanderson's people found out. They must have kept her report to the police out of the system."

"What would she care about some woman you help out?"

Rinaldo let his hands rise in an uncommon show of helplessness.

"Sandra's life has no partitions," he explained. "Her son died a while ago—a rare heart condition that went undiagnosed until the postmortem. Then she got it in her head to erect a building in memoriam for Desmond. Some monolithic downtown waterfront monstrosity. The city was against it. A dozen interest groups were against it. She came to me to try to work a way around the problem. I might have gone along, but this 'memorial' was also going to make her bank over a billion dollars. It seemed to me that she was more concerned over profit than she was for the memory of her son.

"But, like I said, there are no partitions in her life. I knew she was bitter over my refusal to get involved. I didn't realize that she was also a little insane."

"You think she went after Angie for revenge?"

"Either that or to blackmail me. We'll never know now."

"Is Grant's last name Corman?" I asked then.

"Why?"

"A Grant Corman is bodyguarding Sanderson."

"I see."

"That's a very sloppy mistake, if you don't mind my saying so."

"A man is only as good as those who represent him," Alphonse said. "You disobey . . . and Mr. Strange gets careless."

57

Rinaldo decided to take the afternoon off with Angie. They were going to have lunch at the old diner where they'd met. She was on his office phone, calling all her friends, telling them that she was fine, when he took me aside again.

"I'm not used to having people disobey my directions, Leonid," he said.

"It's a long way from Mr. Brown at the diner, huh?"

Not only did he smile at my little insight, he was surprised at his own humor.

"I have to admit, however," he said, "that you've done a very good job. Still, I can't continue to include you in my, my inner circle, as you've proven yourself to be a wild card. I cannot, this office cannot afford that kind of behavior."

"So you repay me by cutting me off?" I asked.

I was thinking that separation from Rinaldo and his world might be the best thing that ever happened to me.

"Do not come here again," he said. "If I ever need you, I have your number."

"What about Sanderson? Do I have to worry about her?"

"I'll take care of everything connected to me," he said. "That includes Sanderson and her actions."

I wondered at the machinations the Special Assistant planned.

I guess I winced a bit at the possible fates of Grant Corman and Sam Strange.

"Is there something wrong?" Alphonse asked.

"No," I said, almost wistfully. "My arm hurts some and I'm really tired."

"Should I have Christian get you a car?"

"No thanks. I drove here."

"STOP!" SOMEONE SHOUTED.

I was three blocks from Rinaldo's office on lower Broadway. My troubles were over, and so I just kept walking. It wasn't until the uniformed cops had surrounded me that I realized I was, once again, the subject of a major arrest.

"What's this about?" I asked as they grabbed me and chained my arms behind my back.

No one answered my questions. They didn't inform me of my rights or ask anything, just shoved me in the back of a police cruiser and drove me to One Police Plaza.

I was taken to a windowless gray room that was too small even for an interrogation. There they left me to wonder if Rinaldo had lost his juice. Or, maybe, I was a loose end now that the job was done.

I sat on the aluminum chair, my wrists in chains, for a very long time—hours. No one spoke to me, much less offered water or the use of a toilet.

I was growing more and more certain that Sanderson had caused me to be brought here. And if I was identified as one of Rinaldo's operatives, then Patrick was probably free.

I wasn't scared, though. That was the business. Sometimes you lost.

Hush would protect Katrina and the kids. He'd settle any recurring problems with Dimitri and the pimp; and if he didn't, Twill certainly would. Katrina would honor my commitment to Gordo.

There was a lot of unfinished business in my life, but that was okay, too. At times, when faced by Death or imprisonment, I was reminded of when I was a child and President Kennedy had been assassinated. There had been twenty-four-hour coverage of the tragedy on television and radio. And then one afternoon I saw the image of a very tall man standing next to the First Lady—Jacqueline Kennedy.

"Who's that man?" I asked my father.

"That's their president, son."

"No, Dad. The president's dead."

"The minute he died this new one took his place."

"That fast?"

"No one is so important that somebody else can't take his place," he told me.

I never forgot it.

"WAKE UP!" SOMEONE SHOUTED, making me realize that I had fallen asleep.

"What?"

"You're going to have a little talk," the man said.

He was flanked by three uniforms. They took me seriously in police circles. You kill one monster of a man with your bare hands and they never forget.

"You should let me use a urinal before I get there or I'm gonna piss all over your floor."

CAPTAIN JAMES CHARBON'S OFFICE was on a high floor with a great view. I could see the Statue of Liberty through the window over his shoulder.

I was feeling warm, feverish. This played tricks with my vision. But I would have been able to pick out Charbon with my eyes closed. He wore a particular brand of cologne that had very little sweetness to it. His eyes were steel gray. His haircut was military, and his handsome features were offset by an innate cruelty.

"Mr. McGill," he said.

One of the men who had brought me there pushed me into a chair. He didn't have to use much muscle.

There were a lot of people in the good captain's office: my four policemen, a woman taking notes on a court stenographer's machine, and a fleshy, middle-aged man perched on the corner of the big mahogany desk.

"We got you," the captain said.

"No question about that. Can you free my arms?"

"No."

"I see."

We, all eight of us, remained silent for the next span of seconds. I was expected to say something but didn't.

"Do you know what we found in the trunk of your car?" the man sitting on the desk asked.

"Who are you?" I asked.

"Broderick Tinely."

"Oh," I said. "The prosecutor."

He wasn't pleased that I knew him.

"There was a pistol in the trunk of your car. The same gun used to slaughter poor Wanda Soa."

"Oh."

As in a darkened cinema, I imagined faceless men in suits, on a broad screen. They make their way into John Prince's empty apartment, find a pistol in a drawer and take it away.

"Do you have anything to say?" Tinely asked.

"Um . . . no."

"This is murder, McGill," the city prosecutor informed me. "Even if you slither out from under the primary charge, we'll get you as an accomplice after the fact."

"I finally got you, Leonid," Charbon said.

I couldn't think of a word to contradict him.

"WHERE'D YOU GET THE GUN?" Prosecutor Broderick Tinely asked for the hundredth time.

We were back in my cramped little cell. I was surprised that they fit in there with me.

He was flanked by James Charbon, who, I could only suppose, wanted to be there when I finally broke.

I had a full fever by then. My head was pounding and I could barely concentrate on the words spoken.

The interrogation had been going on for hours. I was so weak that I could hardly hold my head up. The pain down my left arm was excruciating.

"Where'd you get the gun?"

One hundred and one.

I looked up into the prosecutor's face. His jowls were fat and his head bald, like mine, only white.

"Sandra Sanderson the Third," I said in a loud and clear voice.

The fear in his eyes made me chortle.

Charbon slapped me, pretty hard.

I knew then that I must have been very sick because I didn't feel even a sting from the blow.

The door behind the two swung open and Carson Kitteridge walked in.

"What's the meaning of this, Lieutenant?" Charbon bellowed.

"Excuse me, Captain," Carson said. "I'm sorry to interrupt your interrogation but I'm here to arrest Mr. Tinely."

"What?"

"For accepting bribes, sir," Kitteridge said, playing it meek and mild.

"Get the hell out of here," Charbon said.

"No, Captain," said another voice. "Lieutenant Kitteridge and I are taking Tinely into custody, and we're also relieving you of this interview."

Nathan Samuels, assistant chief prosecutor for the city, walked into the room. There was a nimbus of light around him. I attributed this to my fever.

"But, Mr. Samuels . . ." Charbon said.

"Leave us, Captain." He didn't have to say it twice.

"And you, Mr. Tinely," the pudgy boss of the DA's office said. "You go with the officers in the hall."

People seemed to be leaving. Along with them flowed my consciousness.

"Come on," Kitteridge said to me. "Stand up."

I managed to get to my feet but couldn't keep the balance. I fell, in what felt like sections, to the floor. The concrete felt cold on my skin, and that was best sensation I'd known in a long time.

58

When I opened my eyes I was on my back, gazing at a white ceiling. The headache was gone, along with most other feelings. I rubbed my fingertips together, felt very little.

"Leonid?"

Aura was sitting there next to me, wearing the black dress and red shawl I'd bought for her when we first got together.

"Am I dying?"

"No," she said. "But you are very sick. The wound on your arm became infected and you were suffering from a serious concussion. The doctors were worried, but I knew you'd pull through.

"When they see that you've regained consciousness the staff will call your family. They were all here until an hour ago. I waited for them to leave before I came to sit with you."

"Where's your boyfriend?"

Aura smiled and took my hand. "You should have told me that George was threatening you."

"Wasn't your business."

"I saw the folders on his desk and he explained them to me. I pointed out that he was trying to prove that you were connected to some of the most dangerous crime families in New York. I asked him what he thought they might do to him if he dragged their friend into court."

"What'd he say?"

"He's just a poor fool. It took twenty-four hours for the gravity of the situation to sink in. But after that he was ready to leave immediately."

"A whole day? Is that how long I've been here?"

"Two."

"So George left his CFO job?"

"He left New York. He wanted me to move down to Florida with him, but I said no."

"I don't like the weather down there myself."

"I didn't want to leave you, Leonid."

She leaned over and kissed me.

"Things'll be different when I get out of here," I promised.

"You just get better."

"I'm sorry about George."

"He served his purpose," she said.

"What's that?"

"He showed me who my real man was."

TWILL BROUGHT ME HOME in the Pontiac the next day.

Gordo was already ensconced in the den. He looked better than I did. The doctor said that it was the next few months that would tell the tale.

Lieutenant Bonilla was true to her word. Gustav's operation closed down a day or so after our talk.

Dimitri rarely came home in those first weeks. He and Tatyana celebrated her freedom night and day.

Hush called me on a Wednesday afternoon and asked me to take a look at page thirteen of the *New York Post*. A fellow named Mallory Davis had been found strangled in his East Side apartment. The photograph of Davis looked an awful lot like Patrick.

As a kind of final favor to me, Rinaldo sent men to free Shell and Mammoth. He said that he'd find work for them.

And Sandra Sanderson III was committed to a mental institution in California; something about a suicidal depression. Her son's children took the reins of Regents Bank and decided to turn it into a publicly traded corporation. A few weeks after that, Sandra took a lethal overdose of sleeping pills.

When I could sit up and see straight I called Breland and told him to tell Ron that if he made it all the way through the program Jake Plumb enrolled him in that I would bring him together with his ex-wife and son.

"HEY, POPS," TWILL SAID the morning after I'd been brought home.

I was in the bed, resting. Katrina was out somewhere—probably with her boyfriend.

"Boy."

"You take workin' hard to a whole new level," my son said.

"Thanks for tryin' to help your brother. But please just call me when you get in trouble again. You shouldn't take so many risks."

"You the one got to take it easy, Pops. You know, somebody out there might could kill you one day."